Praise for *The Watery Part*

"A lush feat of historical speculation … *The Watery Part of the World*—that evocative title comes from *Moby-Dick*—is an emotionally acute tale … Pirates and aristocrats in one century; elderly ladies and their handyman in another … Parker has managed to stir them together in a vivid tale about the tenacity of habit and the odd relationships that form in very small, difficult places."   —*The Washington Post*

"I found *The Watery Part of the World* all but impossible to put down … Through the lives of its characters, this elegantly written tale reflects on the nature of race, love, regret, dependence, fear, sorrow, honor and envy—the eternal challenges of being human. The characters, even the minor ones, are fully formed, the setting is so vividly described that you feel you know it intimately, and Parker's writing is purely wonderful."
—Nancy Pearl, NPR.org

"A touching historical novel."   —*Entertainment Weekly*

"Parker slices open each isolated life with humor and gentleness, and the familiar battles with loss and loneliness he chronicles make even this remotest of locations feel close to home."   —*People,* 4-star review

"I adore the way Michael Parker mixes hurricanes and history in this amazing new novel. *The Watery Part of the World* is ambitious yet down-to-earth, bold yet quiet. Parker's book is filled from stem to stern with the bleak beauty of the tempest-tossed Carolina coast, but also with the internal beauty of those people who inhabit it, hard people, strong people, complicated people. This book stirs up so much about what makes the South such an ornery and necessary place: race, place, family, roots. Michael Parker knows everything about the human heart. He is an astonishing American writer."   —Randall Kenan

"All beautifully told, and so compellingly that it qualifies as adventure."
—*The Seattle Times*

"*The Watery Part of the World* offers a glimpse of what it means to bring the two halves of our story together—the part we tell each other and the part we don't. It might be the only way to cast off from that safe but isolated island known as our self."
—*The Atlanta Journal-Constitution*

"A remarkable story . . . The entire novel has a blue-green, underwater feel, a timeless forgetfulness."
—*Los Angeles Times*

"The island at the center of Michael Parker's *The Watery Part of the World* enchants and haunts to at least as great a degree as any of the humans who populate it . . . There is more than just the powerful, intoxicating nature of the book's setting that lends it strength. Parker has a way with words . . . and he proves immensely talented at creating three-dimensional characters, which often proves a challenge in historical fiction more concerned with nailing down the politics and culture of a given time and place."
—*[TK] Reviews*

"Imaginative . . . Parker's prose . . . is the strongest aspect of this novel . . . *The Watery Part of the World* is expert at conveying a sense of people and place."
—*The New York Times Book Review*

"There's a big-hearted fearlessness in Michael Parker's work that, quite honestly, I envy."
—Colum McCann, winner of the
National Book Award for *Let the Great World Spin*

THE WATERY PART *of the* WORLD

THE
WATERY
PART
of the
WORLD

a novel by

MICHAEL PARKER

ALGONQUIN BOOKS OF CHAPEL HILL
2012

Published by
ALGONQUIN BOOKS OF CHAPEL HILL
Post Office Box 2225
Chapel Hill, North Carolina 27515-2225

a division of
WORKMAN PUBLISHING
225 Varick Street
New York, New York 10014

First paperback edition, Algonquin Books of Chapel Hill, June 2012.
Originally published by Algonquin Books of Chapel Hill in 2011.
Printed in the United States of America.
Published simultaneously in Canada by Thomas Allen & Son Limited.
Design by Anne Winslow.

Portions of this novel were previously published, in a different form, in *Five Points,*
New Stories from the South, and *The Pushcart Prize* anthology.

This is a work of fiction. While, as in all fiction, the literary perceptions and
insights are based on experience, all names, characters, places, and incidents either
are products of the author's imagination or are used fictitiously.

Library of Congress Cataloging-in-Publication Data
Parker, Michael, [date]
The watery part of the world : a novel / by Michael Parker.
p. cm.
ISBN 978-1-56512-682-4 (HC)
1. Young women—Fiction.   2. African Americans—Fiction.
3. Freedmen—Fiction.   4. Outer Banks (N.C.)—Fiction.   5. North
Carolina—History—1775–1865—Fiction.   I. Title.
PS3566.A683W38 2011
813'.54—dc22   2010037684

ISBN 978-1-61620-143-2 (PB)

10 9 8 7 6 5 4 3 2 1
First Paperback Edition

FOR KATHY PORIES

I

THEODOSIA BURR ALSTON
Nag's Head, North Carolina

THE DAY WHALEY CAME for her she had spent among the live oaks, huddling and shivering in the squalls of frigid rain. The low tight trees provided tolerable canopy, yet eventually the driving rain came at her sideways. No protection from its furious winds. The coast brought out the worst in rain. What a few miles inland would have been restorative, replenishing, here seemed unutterably desperate. The hues, or, rather, hue, of the landscape exacerbated the loneliness, for everything turned the dun color of wet sand. Even the dull green of the live-oak leaves. Especially the roiling ocean.

Hours in the wet sand. She knew she needed to rouse herself and stroll the beach, for that was where they would be searching for her, the party her father would have sent to rescue her, but she could not summon the strength to abandon her paltry shelter. Her shivering turned the supplications she repeated into stutter.

But her father heard. Late in the day he came to sit with her. He covered her in blankets, pulled dry wood from a satchel. He made her a cup of tea. Cakes and fresh strawberries. Don't speak, child, he said when she tried to form syllables unbroken by shiver, tried to tell him how she had come to be abandoned on this island: how the ship she'd boarded in Charleston to visit him in New York hit high wind and rough water off the Outer Banks of North Carolina; how she'd left her maidservant retching below deck and made her way topside to find even the captain ashen and unsettled; how, through the wind-slanted rain, Theo had spied a blinking, had pointed to the ship and they'd made for it, only it wasn't a ship but a lantern tied to the head of a nag by thieves luring ships to the shallows; how, when Theo was brought above deck by the men who boarded the ship and presented to their leader, Daniels, she had refused to let go of the portrait she had brought along to present to her father upon his return from exile in Europe; how the woman in the portrait had spoken to her and how she had spoken back to the woman, who was no longer a reasonable likeness of her but her protector and savior; how she had screamed her name, her father's name, what stray phrases entered her head: *I do not love my husband the governor I am the empress of Mexico not a ship at all but the head of a nag;* how Daniels, disturbed by her outburst, had deemed her "touched by God," and spared her life. How this was the moment Theodosia Burr Alston died, and the woman who spent her days scouring the beaches for the glint of a bottle, a sheet of parchment curled within, her father's beautifully slanted hand visible beneath the sea-clouded glass, was less born than unsheathed, for who was she all along but a fraud incapable of the simplest virtues.

She explained none of this to her father because he would not let her speak. Every time she tried he shushed her and drew the blanket tighter around her body. The fire caught and crackled as he fed it. Never before had she been so comforted by such an essential element as fire.

He said, finally: It's a pity, the way the world treats its most vigilant servants. Both of us end up exiled from the things we love. Sent to some purgatory where we are doomed to hide who we really are.

She asked why.

Oh Theo, it's not for me to answer why such hardships occur in the world.

No, why us? Why is this happening to us? What did we do to deserve this? For surely we provoked it?

You speak as if we're such great sinners, he said. The fire was dying down. His voice was as cold and gray as the ocean twisting and crashing in the distance.

Father, she said, but he was gone, as was his fire, the warm mug of cinnamon-spiced tea.

In his place hovered the other island ward. Old Whaley, he was called. On his knees in the wet sand, one hand holding back a branch. She blinked, as if this would make him disappear. But he was even more present when she opened her eyes.

They watched each other. Rain dripped off their noses, their chins. Theo had seen him only a few times, always in the distance: moving over a dune, disappearing into a copse. He lived alone in a lean-to in a wood by the sound. A hermit, he sold his catch or traded it for sugar, coffee, his few store-bought needs. Mostly he survived on what he scavenged. He looked like it—rail thin, skin the ghastly gray-white of a fish belly. His beard was a tangle. Yet nothing could dampen his eyes, which were vivid blue beacons.

"Come with me now, miss," said Whaley. She realized, staring at him, that he was a lot younger than most who called him Old Whaley.

Since he too was a ward, did that mean she had to keep up her pretense around him?

Just in case, she fell back on her failsafe silence.

Whaley shrugged. "You want to stay here? Out in this mess? It's set in now."

He raised his shoulders again, no shrug this time, but a respectful acknowledgment of the heavens—perhaps of the God whose touch damned and saved the both of them. Theo could only acknowledge the irony of God's touch determining her fate. Her faith was Sabbath faith, and her lack of devotion if made known to even one other person or even fully admitted in her heart would have filled her great-grandfather Jonathan Edwards with ire and shame. God was the one thing lacking in her rigorously modern and masculine education, since her father, the son and grandson of preachers, had replaced the Calvinist dogma of his youth with freethinking Greeks and Romans after reading Mary Wollstonecraft and deciding his daughter should be educated as he had been, minus the scripture.

"It'll not likely let up anytime soon," said Old Whaley.

She looked past him at the screen of rain.

"I don't have much but it's dry."

She spoke before she could stop herself. "Do you have a fire?"

He smiled. She saw his brown chiseled teeth and thought of food and of a place to stay for more than a few nights. For months they had moved her around the island, sheltered her in shacks and sound-side cottages. The families who had been ordered to take her in all but ignored her. Mostly she ate what would have been slopped in those households lucky enough to own a few pigs. If she was lucky, she got salt fish, biscuits, tack. Vegetables were dreamed. Fantasies of fresh ears of corn slick with hot butter, salt-studded. What a thing to dream, given all her thousand wants, yet there it was in front of her, slowly spinning, golden with promise as a rising sun.

"Yes. I have a fireplace." He nodded and scooted out backward. Beyond the thin shelter of her live oak, he turned and waited. But she hesitated. She'd been talking to her father and blinked awake to find Old Whaley. Therefore this Whaley was a figment. What awaited her should she follow was surely worse than a few more frigid hours beneath her tree.

"Come on then," he said. "Let's get you next to that fire."

She shook her head no.

"You'll die out here," he said. She watched the wisps his words made. What was language but steam? Better not to speak at all than to waste precious breath in a dissipating cloud.

Old Whaley went away. Her father did not return. Only Theo and the wind, rain-laden, unrelenting, determined to take both her and island apart.

II

WOODROW THORNTON
Yaupon Island, North Carolina

AFTER SO MANY STORMS hit the island the people started to move away. Back pews and balcony of the church thinned so much the preacher asked the couple dozen of them still in attendance to spread out so it would look like he'd drawn a crowd. Weeks later the preacher himself went off island, hymnals he said he needed, and never came back. Woodrow watched those last to arrive leave first, and in time the descendents of families who had been around as long as the wild island ponies, rumored remnants of seventeenth-century Spanish explorers shipwrecked along the Outer Banks, packed it in for Salter Path, Beaufort, Elizabeth City, anyplace not stuck out here on this six square miles of sea oat and hummock afloat off the cocked hip of North Carolina.

Then Wilma blew through, taking with it the power and the light and Woodrow's dear sweet Sarah, love of his days and mother of his eleven children. After Wilma it was only the three of them left: Woodrow Thornton on the sound side of the creek, Miss Whaley and Miss Maggie up what they'd called the hill. Sisters, though night and day different: Maggie with her dirty same old skirt and that T-shirt her boy lover had given her years earlier, her dead daddy's old waders she wore to slosh across the creek nights when she came stumbling down to this place to hide out from her prissy sister, who in all the years Woodrow had been knowing her had always worn a plain brown dress down to her shins almost and hid her hair up in a bobby-pinned bun. Woodrow hated hearing those boots squishing his porch boards, though he could not blame Maggie wanting to get away from Whaley. He did a good amount of hiding out from her himself, stuck mostly to his side of the creek.

Those that Woodrow called the Tape Recorders, down from Raleigh twice a year with their questions and their tape machines, liked to point out to Woodrow what they thought he'd not taken note of: three breathing bodies left on this island and a Colored Town right on until the end. But that was the way it was and the way it was going to be and Woodrow had a sweet spread of close to four acres where he kept his stock and in the season ran an ornery little garden, eggplant, radish, turnips, squash, beans, okra, watermelon, anything what would not mind some sand. He and his people had long since got used to staying off by themselves, though since it was only the three of them left, Woodrow was all the time having to cross the creek up to where his white women lived.

Sisters, but Miss Maggie had got married and then unmarried and hated to be called by Midgette, her ex-husband's name, so she went by her first, not that hardly anybody'd be inclined to call her anything but. She stayed like a child on up into her sixties, dressed so don't-give-a-damn, like she struck out of a morning bone-naked and that ratty skirt and that nearly see-through, stretch-necked T-shirt dropped out of the sky and she scrambled into them only to keep the sun from getting up anywhere it might sting. She did not give a damn about a whole lot, clothes and what people thought she'd look like in or out of them either.

Lord God, her big sister cared. She cared about names, now. She clung to that family name of Whaley like the three of them clung to their island after the storms kept coming, though it was her first name, the one nobody ever called her for years and years— Theodosia—that really puffed her up. She'd tell anybody about her famous ancestor, daughter of some famous white man shot some other famous white man. Sarah used to say, Me, I couldn't go claiming some cold killer, I believe I'd be leaving him out of my tree. That's all she got to claim I reckon, Woodrow'd say, not really defending her, but seeming like it to Sarah, surely. But Whaley, well—she'd been named after the daughter of this famous killer and above everything she cherished a picture of the woman hung over her fireplace.

But Whaley would as soon drag up something happened to her great-great-great-grandmother than to root around in what across the sound had gotten up to 1970. Woodrow only knew this because his oldest boy, Crawl, wrote and said so. Woodrow didn't think in year-of-our-Lords. He thought: wind, tide, moon, blues running,

hog killing, oyster harvesting, when to plant his ornery sand garden.
He didn't have a thing against numbers but now that Sarah was
gone what really was the point of keeping a count? Crawl wanted
him to know, though. He kept reminding him, as if it meant the
same on the island as it did off. One night the three of them were
sitting on the steps of the church listening to Whaley read aloud
the grocery store ads, and Maggie read Woodrow Crawl's letter.
Crawl claimed he'd given up fishing menhaden out of Morehead to
run a club up near Lenoxville. Said in his letter he'd purchased this
spinning ball for the club, had it shipped down from Baltimore,
said the insurance on the ball was more than what Woodrow spent
in a year. Woodrow didn't doubt that. He did not trade in paper or
coin unless he was over to Meherrituck to stock up on store-bought
for him and the sisters. He didn't see what a spinning ball or insurance for it was doing in a letter Crawl wrote to him. Didn't he
have anything else to allow? Or was this what people wrote letters
about, talked about, across the sound in 1970?

Maggie read aloud how Crawl said he'd spent all he'd saved
up fishing menhaden on the inside and outside decor of his club
and it was, if he said so himself, looking mighty fine. Y'all have
to come up and see it, Daddy, all the High Life you can drink on
the house.

Who did Crawl mean, *y'all*? Surely not the white women who
he knew were reading his letter aloud on the church steps to his il-
literate daddy. Woodrow tried to imagine the three of them step-
ping into Crawl's club. Miss Maggie would not even notice all the

black heads switching around to stare her out when she walked up in there—she'd be at the bar about the time it took for Woodrow to get in the door good—but Miss Whaley would rather swear on the grave of her famous ancestor than go in any club, much less a colored one with a spinning ball, insured or not.

Crawl closed like always, telling his daddy he needed to think about leaving the island and moving in with him and his Vanessa and all them kids over in Morehead and Maggie like always left that part out though Woodrow could tell what was not read, he could hear it in her sucked-in breath, could see the unread words tightening her eyes up under those reading glasses.

She did read, this time, about how Crawl claimed he was coming across in a couple weeks, bringing the young'uns. Told Woodrow he better get to work, catch them some croaker to fry. But Crawl liked to claim he was coming over there and then get busy with something else, inside and outside club decor, whatever it was people got busy with across over in 1970.

Then the letter was over but not over because all three of them knew what was left out. They always waited a moment or two in silence after the letter, like they were observing the words not read aloud, which did not make a damn bit of sense to Woodrow since they were the ones leaving it out. This time he could not listen to their silence. He jumped right in after the Your Son, Crawl, said, "Write Crawl tell him send us over one of them balls, we'll put it in the church, hang it up above the old organ, reckon that's what you do with one of them."

Now what made him say such a thing? Why should he be the one acting all embarrassed because they did not want to tell him straight out the words his son had written to him?

Miss Maggie said, "I have no earthly idea what Crawl's talking about!" But Miss Whaley pretended she knew. She acted like she knew all about everything because she read the Norfolk paper. Well, part of it. Really all she liked to read were the ads. Every morning Woodrow poled his skiff out to fish for dinner. Most days, good weather allowing, he stayed out to meet the O'Malley boys out of Meherrituck bringing in the mail off the Pine Island ferry. "Be sure you give me all them flyers," he'd say every time, and the O'Malleys would hand him a bunch of grocery and dime store circulars sent over from the mainland advertising everything. Miss Whaley liked to call out the prices at night. "They got turkey breast twenty-nine cents a pound! Look at these chairs, I wouldn't have one of them in my shed and they're wanting thirty dollars a piece, not a pair, I wouldn't own one myself."

All it took to make Woodrow wonder how come he stayed around after Wilma was to sit around on the church steps long enough to hear Whaley say such things three times a night about a two-week-old manager's special one hundred miles away up in Norfolk.

But most of the time he'd never wonder how come he stayed. He'd never go lusting after some spinning ball, dancing up under it, imagining how such a ball, lit by special bulbs, would glitter diamonds all up and down your partner. He'd never get lost in a vision of him twirling sweet Sarah in a waterspout of diamonds because evenings he'd sit on his porch and stare out across the marsh to where night came rolling blue-black and final over the sound and he'd say no thank you to some ball, we got stars.

Not long after Crawl wrote about his club—couple weeks Woodrow reckoned—he showed up on the island. Had three of his boys with him. Woodrow hadn't seen him in a while. Crawl was wearing his hair springy long and had on wide-legged pants made out of looked like cardboard and zip-up ankle boots. Woodrow picked up the littlest of the grandbabies, knee baby also named Woodrow, had some dried salt around his eyes from where the crossing had beat tears out of him. Woodrow wiped away the salt and some snot with a rag, then took the boy inside and scrubbed at his face, trying to be Sarah and Woodrow all at once, pushing food on the boys, some three-day-old bread with butter which they carried around in their hands like they didn't know what to do with food not bought off a shelf in a store.

Everything was different now with Sarah gone. Nothing was easy.

Crawl sent the boys down to poke around the empty houses waiting on their owners to come back, sitting up on brickbat haunches like a dog will do you when you go off for a while. Woodrow and Crawl sat on the porch and Crawl pulled out a pint of Canadian.

Smooth as liver, he claimed. "Have a drink, Daddy."

Woodrow took a pull though he favored a High Life. Crawl talked on about his club. Night Life was what he was calling it. He had some pictures of it. To Woodrow the club wasn't much from the outside: cinder-block hut, oystershell parking lot, big old ditch out in front for drunks to get their ride stuck in. He showed some pictures of the inside that was dark and red and Woodrow said, "Un-hunh, okay, all right, I see, that's nice." Seemed like he made sounds, not words. He'd look up from the pictures wanting his grandbabies to come back. He wanted to take them down to the inlet and let them jerk crabs out of the sound on a chicken liver tied to a string, but when finally he mentioned going after them Crawl said, "Naw, we got to get back across."

"Y'all can't stay through? Plenty of room for all y'all."

Crawl reached down, tugged at his boot zipper. To Woodrow, boots ought not to come with a zipper, but it was Crawl's feet, he could cover them however he wanted.

Crawl said, "I reckon those boys used to electricity." Then he added, all of a sudden loud, "Besides, we didn't come over here to stay, we came over here to get you to come back with us."

Woodrow couldn't see himself going anywhere with duded-up Crawl. He smiled and asked after Crawl's wife's people who he used to know a little when he lived in Morehead, where if you asked him everybody put too much notion into how long and wide and clean was the car somebody drove around town.

"Everybody's doing fine," said Crawl. "But me and Violet and the boys, we worry about you over here all alone now."

When Woodrow said he wasn't alone, seemed like Crawl'd been hiding in a blind with his gun cocked, waiting on these very words to fly out of Woodrow's mouth.

"You know you don't got to stay here looking after them sisters until they die or you one. Those women don't have no business staying over here anyway. Surely they got some kin somewhere will take them in."

"Them two?" said Woodrow. He didn't know of any kin, or even any friends except little Liz who worked for Dr. Levinson running his tape machine and slapping mosquitoes off his neck and making sure he ate something. Anymore, little Liz was about the only person he knew who even checked in on them. She wrote letters that Whaley claimed were only to her but whenever Maggie snatched them out of her sister's hand and read them aloud they always asked after her and said something too about him, How's Woodrow, Tell Woodrow I'm going to bring him some peaches, even once, Give Woodrow my love, which made Maggie snicker and liked to got away with Whaley.

"All I'm saying is, it's not your job to look after them. Older they get worse it's going to be. Least now they can still walk down to the dock to meet the mail boat."

"We ain't had mail in three years," said Woodrow. "I been catching O'Malley and them out in the channel when they come back from meeting the ferry."

Crawl shook his head at this, as if Woodrow wasn't out on the water most days anyway.

"Come on, Daddy, just pack a bag. You don't need much, I'll carry you back across over here any time you want to go, let's get in the boat."

The boys were back by then, sitting on the steps, listening in. Woodrow got up and hugged little Woodrow so hard the boy went to squirm. When he embraced the older two he felt in their slack muscles the beginnings of that eye-cutting stage. They would not be coming back to the island to see him. Woodrow even wondered if they were not old enough for Crawl to run his daddy down in front of them. Look at your old granddaddy fussing after his white women, what for?

He sat out on the dock, finishing the pint of Canadian that Crawl had left him, watching the sun sink over the water and wondering what he'd be over there, off island, across the sound. Now who would he be over there? This he could not say but it wasn't what they all thought: scared to find out. There were some things he feared—he didn't think you could live and not be scared of something—say the Pamlico Sound, known to go from glassy to six-foot seas in an hour. Other people, their strange and unknowable motives, scared him. The lonely time that come up on him after Sarah died, swooped up close overhead like a vee of geese.

Fear of what they'd be if they left the island might have been what kept the sisters over here, though they had their other reasons, surely. Maggie would do right much what her big sister said when it came right down to it. Else, why was she still here? Why didn't she leave when that Boyd asked her to go away with him? If she would not leave then, she'd not be leaving this island.

Whaley, well: seems like she stayed for when the Tape Recorders come over from Raleigh every spring. Every April, always the fat bearded one with his bird glasses called himself a doctor but would not look at Miss Maggie's bad toes and for the past ten years little Liz, who Woodrow liked.

Whaley lived to get that letter said the Tape Recorders were due to visit. A good month before they arrived she spent setting up the Salter place where they stayed, planning meals, fetching items from Meherrituck, which meant Woodrow was the one running himself ragged to prepare for their arrival, all Whaley's errands on top of his daily chores.

The moment they stepped off the boat Whaley'd switch into her high-tider talk, what the Tape Recorders loved to call an Old English brogue. They claimed Woodrow spoke it too, though how Woodrow could have come out talking like an Old English did not square with the story they liked to tell about how he'd come to be on this island in the first place. Said Woodrow's people were brought over back when the island did big business as a seaport. Seven hundred settlers and one hundred of them slaves. Ships too heavy with goods to cross the bar needed their cargoes transferred to smaller vessels to navigate the shallows. Lightering, they called it, and his people were the ones did the lightering. That was before the war come and the Confederates turned tail and abandoned the fort over on Meherrituck and that time it wasn't a storm forced everybody off island except the slaves and a single white woman named Ophelia Roberts, so fat she could not fit through the front door. Like as not Woodrow's people took care of her until the war was over and only half the population of the island returned from the mainland, according to the Tape Recorders. Then it was a steady dwindling. Ships went north to Hatteras where a storm had opened up a new inlet. Woodrow heard all this from the Tape Recorders and yet he'd heard other stories contradicted their so-called facts. His own father had talked about his ancestor, a man named Hezekiah Thornton his daddy claimed come to the island a free man. Never did a lick of lightering in his days, according to Woodrow's daddy.

He could have come back at the Tape Recorders with all this but Woodrow did not much mess with them. Oh, he'd sit for them but he wouldn't answer the questions like they wanted him to because seemed to Woodrow they had the answers already, that the questions were swole up with the answer, like a snake had swallowed a frog. *Tell us what it has been like for your family living here all these years the only blacks on the island. How have you kept up with your heritage? Do you think the gains of the civil rights movement have reached you here on this island? How have these gains affected your day-to-day existence?*

Woodrow said the only thing affecting his day-to-day existence was where them fish was hiding.

The story of the three of them on this island, to Woodrow's mind, was just that: three people on an island. You could even leave off the island part, though the Tape Recorders, why would they do that? They wanted to turn it into something else again: something they wanted to believe in, something about how lost the three of them were across the water, all cut off from the rest of the world and turned peculiar because of it.

Seemed to Woodrow they weren't all that interested in Maggie's telling her side of the story because she'd up and start in on something inside of her, which the Tape Recorders, excepting that little Liz who tended just to let you talk, weren't interested at all in what somebody felt. Also, Maggie when it came down to it did not give a squat for history. She lived up in the right along through now.

Well, no, Woodrow took that one back. He believed it was Boyd she thought about nearly all the time, not Boyd as he was now, across the sound, but Boyd back when she had him, Boyd when he got off the boat and come asking Woodrow to teach him to fish, young Boyd, green smiley innocent Boyd.

It drove the Tape Recorders crazy how Woodrow would not act the way they needed him to, say the things they wanted him to say. They were all the time trying to get him to act like he hadn't ever been off island at all. He played along even though he'd spent more time off island than either of the white women sisters. Two years at the Coast Guard base up at Bayside, four years in the Norfolk shipyards. There he took up welding and he did decent at it. Now his children reached right up the East Coast to Troy, New York, like stops on a train: Morehead City, Elizabeth City, Norfolk, Baltimore, Philly, Brooklyn, all the way up to Kingston and Troy. He'd even taken that train a few times. Sarah lived to visit her babies, usually in the fall when the heat and bugs still lingered on the island and the storms rolled in sometimes two in the same moon. Woodrow went with her a couple of times. They took the train went up be-hind everything, back of people's houses, back of factories, where you could see the ungussied part of the world—the porches sagging with beat-up furniture and washing machines, the yards chewed up by mean old fenced-in dogs, the piles of rusting engine parts and junk cars behind the warehouses and businesses. He liked this view better than what people put on for a show. But he got so he hated leaving the island. He did it twice, then let her go on ahead. Woodrow hadn't lost anything on that backyard train.

Sarah was all the time talking about moving. Retiring, she called it. But what was it to retire from? He had come home a good welder but what was it to weld on this island? Can't weld conch, kelp, fishbone. Woodrow made a little money selling crabs and flounder, but it won't nothing he could retire from. Wood-row answered Sarah's talk about retiring by not answering, which back then seemed like the decent way to respond. No sense trot-ting out a lot of words. She knew damn well how he was after so many years together. If he did not want to do something she wanted him to do, well, he didn't spend words telling her what she knew already by the way he'd walk out to visit with his pigs.

He ought to have talked to Sarah about all this retiring, though. Stabbing the hardest now, hurting the most was all he did not do for her, things he never got around to giving her.

Too busy waiting on them white women sisters, Crawl and them would claim. Sarah never said as much but she was surely thinking it. She had given up talking to him about Maggie and

Whaley. Woodrow told himself she'd accepted it, the way it had to be if they were going to stay on this island, the price of living right down across the creek where both of them were born. *But why do we have to pay?* he sometimes imagined Sarah saying to him when he was out on the water and there was nothing biting, and he had flat quiet time to himself while he drifted, waiting on the O'Malleys to show with the mail.

Everybody got to pay, he'd of said to Sarah.

To live where they were born and raised up at? To stay right where they belong?

She had that fire in her voice. Every question raised up in time to her eyebrows, the lift of her left shoulder. But at least she was in the boat with him. Good God, woman, come close lay your uppity attitude on my lap let's stretch out across the bottom of this boat.

Everybody pay. He'd say it over as if saying it over made it true.

Let me ask you Woodrow Thornton how Whaley's sour self's paying to live where she was born? She's going to come out here tomorrow meet the mail and catch your supper, let you stay home and nap?

She pays. You would not want that woman's suffering.

If I could suffer up out of this sun, in the shade, I'd surely trade.

Don't go saying you'd take on somebody else's mess you don't even know what it is.

All I'm saying, how hard could it be? She's a selfish, stuck-up, putting-on-airs, all-the-time-bragging-about-her-great-great-great-great-granddaddy-done-killed-somebody-famous mess.

She pays. Her and Maggie both.

I never said Maggie. That girl owes, what it is. All the sinning she done in her life, she'll be paying on into the next one, and in a place going to finally maybe make her appreciate this island she spent years complaining about.

Hey now, said Woodrow. He hated to hear anyone talk bad about Maggie. True that much of her pain was of her own making but she wasn't alone in that. Right then, bringing his Sarah into the flat afternoon quiet, wasn't he making himself miserable? Couldn't he remember the good times, those afternoons when Crawl and the older sisters took care of the younger ones and he and Sarah sneaked off to the summer kitchen for some slow all afternoon loving? And later when it was just them on this island, all their children moved on, and the two of them would sit on the porch in silence for hours of a Sunday afternoon, the wind the only thing stopped by to see them all day and both of them just fine with that, with each other, with only each other?

He ought to have brought *that* Sarah in the boat with him to keep him company. But instead he stirred up all this unfinished business, got her to talking about the things she liked to talk about, give his same old side of it for the hundredth time, tried to tell himself it was final, he had the last word.

Which, talking down to a dead person, the one you loved most in this world, wrapping it up when they didn't have a chance to defend, well—he'd've felt a whole lot of worse about it if it had worked. But it did not do a damn bit of good. Mostly only made him feel worse.

Still, he had these talks with her, every day. Sometimes all day long. Ever since he left her alone that day when Wilma came through.

He'd gone across to Meherrituck on an errand for Whaley. She was wanting him to meet the mailman at the store around four o'clock. She knew he'd been fishing the ditch up behind Blue Harbor, knew it wasn't too far out of his way. She also knew he would not want to kill time in Meherrituck, where people treated him mostly bad, made jokes behind his back on account of the O'Malleys when they met him for the mail sometimes would pass him a Sweet to smoke and a High Life to sip on, get him talking about the sisters, went right back to tell it all over Meherrituck how he was getting something off Miss Maggie and Miss Whaley liked to watch. He'd heard that. It had got back to him. From his house down by the inlet he could see across to Meherrituck and the winking lights of Blue Harbor and the lighthouse tossing its milky beam around but Woodrow hadn't lost anything over there. Neither him nor the sisters crossed over unless one got bad sick. Whaley knew he did not want to go across that day. She knew he would not want to kill time over there, knew that to Woodrow Meherrituck had got just as bad as the mainland with all the ferries unloading the tourists and the natives getting it in their heads they were some rich somebodies.

Oh, he could of said no to Whaley that day. He'd told her no before. He felt the storm coming, saw it in all the telling signs: way his stock behaved, scratching around in the yard all skittery, refusing to eat, squealing and whinnying at the way the wind died then rose, died and rose. He saw it in the shading of the clouds, black and fast and backlit by the last leaking away of any sun that day. When he tried to tell Whaley it was a storm coming and he did not want to leave Sarah, she said to him, Take Sarah with you, do her good to get off island, surely y'all got people over there to visit.

This got away with Woodrow. Seemed like she was wanting him to take Sarah off the island so she and Maggie could have it to themselves, like they was wanting some white-only time on that island where his people had lived going back more than a hundred years, not so long as hers, true, but long enough so with only the four of them left it was by God his and Sarah's island much as it was theirs.

Before he left, he made them promise to check on Sarah should it start to blow (*if* he said, though he knew by then *when* was the word he needed) and he got up early that day as always and loaded up coolers to keep his catch cold while he killed time on ain't-lost-nothing-over-to-Meherrituck. Sarah even came down to the dock to see him off, which she never did, but Woodrow tried to act like it was just another day out on the water. As soon as he was out on the water he felt the storm rising. He had seen seven or eight hours where he could of turned around, gone back. He spent that time wavering. Ain't looking good, I'm going back, he'd think, but then he'd remember Whaley's attempt to get Sarah in the

boat with him, and say, Hell with that woman and her whites-
only-for-a-day island. She needs some color in her world.

He'd been over to Meherrituck for a while when it started to
really blow. Wind and water made up his mind for him—you ain't
going nowhere now, Woodrow Thornton, you had your chance.
He sat up in the community store with O'Malley Senior and his
sons, listening to the island come down around them, all night
long the pop and crash of things picked up by the wind, the curl
and rip of scissored-off strips of tin roofs, the store gone to shadow
in the candlelight, everybody drinking something to take their
mind off the wind, though it just made worse what fear they felt,
the liquor and the wine and the beer.

Woodrow left soon as the seas died down enough to where he
could cross, throttled wide open over there, hull batted wave to
wave. He lost: cooler full of fish, spare gas tank, a net, rod-and-
reel, waders, all of it tossed overboard, a sacrifice, sea can have all
that if she just lets me find my Sarah alive and well.

Someone was waiting for him down at the dock. Wouldn't anyone meet him but his bride, and Woodrow at the sight of the figure
on the dock cussed himself for tearing ass over across the inlet, sac-
rificing his worldly goods for nothing. Then he grew close enough
to spot Maggie. He recognized her before he could make out the
color of her skin; it was the way she stood, which he remembered
from all the times he'd seen her standing similar, waiting on him to
bring Boyd back from a day's fishing. Arms crossed over her chest,
holding her heart, protecting it. He thought at first, well, wind done

knocked out the power and the light, mixed her up. She'd lost her place in time, come down to wait on Boyd, who at that point had been gone a good many years. Woodrow'd seen people take a little vacation from good God-given sense after a particularly big blow.

Then he got a little closer and saw the look on her face and he changed his mind. It's Whaley, he thought. Most people would put their money on Maggie to be the first to go. She'd courted nearly everything you can court to shave some years off—she smoked roll-your-owns for years, drank whenever she could get her hands on some liquor, loved nothing more than lying out stitchless under the noontime sun. But Woodrow always thought it'd be Whaley because in the end, though she lived better, ate better, worked harder than her sister, she cut herself off from people, she didn't know nothing about how to love, she couldn't even listen. Death comes quicker to those who don't know how to listen. He worried about Crawl. His own son didn't know how to hear another man's pain. Get too busy thinking about your own mess, that'll kill you deader than hell. You got nobody to sustain you, you're going to go quick, and it's going to hurt too, knowing you left nobody in your wake. He thought about Whaley lying there on her deathbed knowing after she's gone all that's left is some same-old stories in a book about an island nobody cares to hear about.

Well, least she went easy, quick. Best she didn't linger, because if she did, Woodrow'd have to sit with her, at least help take care of her, and he'd be telling some lies even bringing around food to sustain her one more hour, because he couldn't out-and-out say he would miss her if she was gone. He could say the out-and-out opposite. Better he didn't have to get himself mixed up in a big last lie.

When he cut the engine and nosed the skiff up alongside the dock and got close enough to toss Maggie the line, he saw the blood on her dress and noticed her shivering. Everything froze: line in his hands, coiled, ready to throw. Skiff took its own course, bow nosing around in a half circle. Maggie stared into the shallows but not like she'd lost something down there. She had a little bit of sleeve in her mouth. Her chin was quivering and she was chewing that little bit of sleeve. Woodrow knew then it wasn't Whaley.

Then and there he saw what all had happened. Maggie, well— he could read her easy, just like Sarah could read him. Neither of them were ones could hide what they were feeling.

"Where's she at?"

Maggie said, "In the church." She reached her hand out for the line to tie the skiff to the dock but Woodrow didn't want her help. What good was her help now or ever after if she could not help when he asked her to help? He jumped right out in the water which was chilly that day despite the big-sky brilliance. But he did not even feel the cold. He could feel her fall in behind him and once he heard her talking.

"She would not let me go after her," Maggie said, talking about Whaley. "She would not let me I tried to she said it won't safe, said I'd die going down there to check on her."

Woodrow said, "Hush up now," and she did. She struggled to

keep up with him as he pushed up the hill toward the church passing on the way his house and seeing the roof of the kitchen gone off somewhere and only one wall of that tacked-on kitchen still standing and understanding it was his faulty work maybe what killed her as he'd built that kitchen to help her out. He'd added it on to make it easier on Sarah so she would not have to haul and tote everything from the summer kitchen. He'd built it out of washed-up timber and some he'd traded the O'Malleys for which won't much better grade than what the tide brung up.

He stopped to look. Maggie behind him gave out a wheezy cry.

"Y'all found her back there?"

"In the kitchen."

"Roof fell in on her?"

"Cut her up bad."

"She bled to death?"

Maggie didn't answer this. She couldn't of bled to death in any hour. They must of left her there all night. They left her there all night long on the floor and then the waters rose and had they gone down there and at least moved her up the hill she'd be sitting up head-bandaged but good to go.

Woodrow went on up to the church. Maggie followed as far as Whaley's front yard. He felt her about to say something and then he felt her think better of it. It was that quiet after the storm, on the island and in Woodrow's head. The shock of imagining Sarah's last hours cleared everything out of his head. Nothing much either in his heart. He did not feel anything walking alone now up the hill to the church. He did not notice the debris in the way and he walked over planks and shingles and gill nets and broken glass and chicken wire. He did not see the watermark on the side of the old post office where the surge crested. One of Whaley's sheep lay drowned in the front yard of the Salter place and he did not see or smell it. He could not feel his shoes sucking into the mud. Somehow breath came in and out of him.

She was laid out on the altar three steps above the crust of mud and swollen hymnbooks and trash left behind when the sea said enough and took its leave. Appeared to Woodrow the sea itself and not one of his white women sisters had laid her out, then went right back to wherever it came from or wherever it was off to next. He'd rather this than anyone touching her, especially those who let her die.

Same clothes on as when he left her, though her hair had been hiding behind a kerchief and the kerchief was gone.

"Where is your kerchief?" he said, standing above her, looking down on her. One of her arms, tucked up tight alongside her, had fallen off onto a lower step. "Where?" he said. "What did they do with it?"

The silence following the slight echo of his stupid question in the high-ceilinged sanctuary brought Woodrow to his knees. Prayer was what he tried to make come out of his mouth next. Prayer had never really took with Woodrow. He'd wandered off from thanking or apologizing into a list of things he needed to do to get across the water for his boat. He felt so bad that he couldn't even manage to give thirty seconds to God Almighty that he left off the entire endeavor. Here he was trying it again and aloud but what he heard in that high sanctuary was not anything even God could understand, unless it was true he understood everything and if that was so why even talk? So Woodrow just went to bawling, kneeling, rocking, spit streaming out of his mouth, so lost he was letting it drip all over, Dear Sarah Dear God I am sorry I ought never to have left you. Ought never to have trusted them. But it's not their fault. Mine for not letting you leave.

Late that night moonlight came striping the middle pews through the stained glass and that the only light they had now: moon, sun, lantern, candle. The power and the light were gone for good then. What use was there in turning it back on for only three people? No one figured on anyone staying on that island with no power and no light. Woodrow himself didn't think whether he'd stay or not at first. He sat up in the dark with Sarah. Sometime in the night Maggie brought him food and blankets. She said Whaley had taken sick after the storm.

"Sick," said Woodrow in a way that made Maggie kneel and moan.

She sat with him for a good hour not speaking. He could hear her sniffling. Sometimes she said something but words did not work or count in this space or else their meaning was lost to Woodrow. He knew she would stay until he told her to go so he told her he wanted to be alone with Sarah. Before she left she told him how Sarah was holding a pair of scissors in her hand whenever she found her.

"Found her?" said Woodrow, but he lacked even the energy to punish Maggie, even as he pictured Sarah lying up under the debris in what once was his kitchen, the piece of tin that had sliced her neck still atop of her, her head wedged whichways upside the cook stove.

Woodrow looked up at her. "Say what?"

She said, "A pair of scissors."

Woodrow nodded, went back to not looking at her, hoping she'd go away and when she did he got up and covered Sarah in a clean blanket Maggie'd brought for him and went down to his house. He found his lanterns and lit them and by their light he scoured the wreckage of the kitchen until he discovered beneath the crimped tin a pair of bloody scissors.

What in the world? What was she fixing to cut in the middle of a storm? The thought of those scissors from the moment Maggie mentioned them until he flung them into the inlet liked to drove Woodrow crazy. He wanted to know everything about his wife in her last hour and he had his story down tight. In his story there never were any scissors.

The next day Whaley showed up in the church just as he and Maggie were getting Sarah ready to take across the water to bury. He just had to load her up in the boat. She'd asked him long ago not to bury her on this island. They'd fought about it. He kept after her on this in a way he never would have about anything else because he had already staked out a plot for the both of them up behind the church. He wasn't about to let her leave him in death. Might as well leave him now, he told her. But she wouldn't budge. And Woodrow had never once figured on her dying before him. She was fifteen years younger, for one, and two, women just lived longer. He could count on three fingers the husbands had outlived wives on this island which was hard on everybody but hardest on the men who worked the sea.

Whaley said to him, "I'm so sorry, Woodrow." She stood back from him a good ways, though it might well have been the smell that stopped her rather than respect for the dead or his grieving.

"Sorry's about the word I'd use," Woodrow said. He had not spoken since he'd told Maggie to leave him alone. His words came out a slurry whisper.

If she heard him she didn't allow it. She said, "It wasn't anything I could do. We'd of lost another one, going down there to get her."

"I know, Miss Whaley," Woodrow said. "Wind wants you, can't do nothing to stop it."

He looked up at her. She was staring at the floorboards. He saw her bottom lip tighten.

"Least y'all could of done is get her out of the way of the water," he said.

"We all will meet our time," said Whaley.

Woodrow said, "Ain't no sense helping the time come."

"It was not like that, Woodrow Thornton."

Woodrow started to tell her he knew his name, she didn't need to be using it in full, but instead he said he needed to be burying his wife, not standing around chitchatting, she and Maggie'd have to make do for a few days.

"Of course," said Whaley. "You take as long as you want over there, we've got plenty to do around here." Then she launched into a list of chores and kept right on listing until Woodrow turned around left them there alone in that church once so white and clean with its steeple pointing everyone who came to the island toward Lord God in heaven who Woodrow could not talk to either.

He took Sarah to Morehead, buried her there. The preacher preached himself sweaty and the choir lifted the curtains in soaring take-me-home-Jesus song and someone had to douse the trash burner from the kettle steaming atop it, so hot did it get up in that church. Woodrow stayed for as short a time as he could get away with, told Crawl he had to get back across the water.

Crawl started in with his You-don't-got-to-look-after-them-no-more-Daddy, especially-not-now. Woodrow just loaded up his boat, hugged his grandbabies, the ones who'd let him get his arms around them, allowed Crawl's wife to wrap him up some leftovers, took off across the sound.

III

Theodosia Burr Alston
Nag's Head, North Carolina

IT WASN'T THE SUN that awakened her from her shivering slumber but the cries of proggers. Moments after a storm receded the beach would fill with natives. Progging, they called it, and ingenious were they at discovering functions for objects the intended purpose of which, on this strip of sea oat and hummock and dune, was rendered useless soon as it washed ashore. An island of second chances. She'd come not to judge those who made their way pillaging the losses of others but to admire them, for of the eight trunks she'd watched her husband's slaves load into the hold of the ship when she'd left Charleston, seven and three-quarters held frill.

Progging she was allowed to participate in. At least no one stopped her. To Theo this ritual seemed the most important social occasion here, more important than church or school, though what she knew of this island was akin, she realized, to what a field hand knew of South Carolina society.

Somehow she managed to rouse herself and join the throngs on the beach. A whale had washed up and a line of boys were put to work sawing off blubber with double-handled band saws. Nearby a fire raged, a cauldron set up on a tripod to boil the blubber down to oil. The sun washed the surf and exposed miles of coastline littered with debris. Groups of bankers attacked this debris. Ants swarming food. She knew she was too late to find anything of importance, but she picked through the leftovers, searching for and finding a few pieces of lumber to take back to her stand of live oaks.

She would build a lean-to of her own. Touched as she was, she did not want to be beholding, even to Old Whaley, who came up behind her as she was hauling a waterlogged door over the dune.

"Made it through, did you?"

When she did not answer he grabbed the part of the door she'd been dragging. She was surprised by his strength: the door floated upward, its considerable weight evaporating.

"Good for you, then. And now you've set about building your mansion?"

"Thank you," she said.

"You don't need to thank me," he said. "I left you out here to die. You got no cause to thank me or anyone else on this island."

"Daniels," she said. "I suppose I should thank him for sparing my life."

Old Whaley laughed. "You put the fear in him. A God-fearing murderer. Now that's something to marvel at. I know for a fact that it was the portrait. He told it all up and down the island, how he saw the girl in the painting move her eyes. Said he heard her speak back to you. He'd just soon run a knife in anybody's belly as listen to them. Come to find out he's scared of a little bit of paint. Well, it makes more sense than him fearing a snake, I guess. But I know for a fact he kept the painting."

She'd brought it along to give to her father, along with five boxes of his papers, both personal and professional, to which he had entrusted her during his exile. Those papers contained his essence. They would restore his unfairly tarnished reputation. If Daniels kept the portrait, surely he recognized the value of what those tin boxes held.

"He kept it?"

"They say it hangs over his fireplace."

"Can you take me to his house?"

Whaley had been holding his end of the door effortlessly as they talked. Her request made him drop it in the sand.

"You'll be wanting me to believe it's true, what they say. For if you want to see him again, you are certainly touched."

"I didn't say I want to see him again."

"You're not talking sense. How long since you ate?'

It had been days. Two at least. The stomach cramps were so steady she knew the quarter hour by them. Whaley hoisted the door above his head and took off through the dunes. She understood to follow.

Inside his lean-to he pointed to a spot by the fireplace, tossed her a blanket, and set about heating up something in a black pot. While he worked she looked around the place, took note of the civilized touches—a shelf of leather-bound books, a music box, an oil painting of a mountain glen that reminded her of the wedding trip she took to Niagara Falls with Joseph.

"I suppose you subsist by robbing ships as well?" she asked him.

Whaley's laugh, low and deep in his chest, was without glee.

"Not a smart line of questioning fired at a man about to provide you with a meal."

"I'm growing accustomed to the men of this island contradicting themselves. Robbing and murdering, then taking me in, feeding me, offering me a corner of their homes."

"They only tolerate you because he's scared of you."

"Because of who I am?"

This time his laughter was filled with mirth, or mockery. "Who you are? He don't give a damn who you are. The more you carry on about your famous daddy, the more mad he thinks you are. If he really thought you were the daughter of that bastard, he'd of thrown you over same's he did your maid."

She thought of defending her father but realized, too late, how completely she'd exposed herself to Whaley. If her survival depended on hiding who she was, she was certainly found out now.

"All of what you see there I progged off the beach," he said. He ladled steaming stew into a bowl and brought it to her along with a hard and slightly molded piece of bread. She dipped the bread in the broth and devoured it, speared a potato and ate without chewing.

"You worry that I'll tell them you're not so crazy," he said.

She looked up at him, terrified suddenly that her every thought was obvious, transparent.

"Never mind that," he said. "He spared my life as well. I got here same way you did. Against my will."

"He boarded your ship?"

"Something like that."

Whaley studied her in the flickering light. She looked him in the eye, something she hadn't done to anyone since she'd arrived on the island. She needed to look the part. That meant no eye contact, appropriate body language—hunched back, drooped shoulders, a shuffling, sideways gait. Once a lady came to Richmond Hill to teach her how to walk, how to eat, how to converse. Her father paid the woman, though he swore he didn't—she found the account in his ledger. He said the woman came because she felt sorry for Theo, having lost her mother, who was supposed to teach her these things. But charity made Theo feel worse. She was relieved when she'd discovered the woman's name in the ledger. Thereafter she approached the lessons with a little more energy and interest. And now the lessons were truly paying off, for everything she had been taught she simply reversed.

"Well, it doesn't look like he's got you under guard either," she said, conscious of how liberating it was to be so rudely intrusive, now that she had so little to lose.

"They say he knows every pony on this island, every milk cow, every chicken. All these people are his spies. You think they volunteered to board you? Poor as they are? This island ain't good for growing nothing. Daniels supplies them with stock and the grain to feed it. He pays off the governor too. Not that the government's got dominion on these islands."

If there were no rule, no government, surely she had been forgotten. To distract herself from this thought, she asked another intrusive question.

"What was your trade before you were captured?"

"I was at sea."

"Ah," she said, looking above her. "I might have guessed carpentry, given the excellence of this structure."

"You make do with what the water washes up over here."

"I don't suppose the rest of them suffer someone like yourself taking the choice items."

Whaley smiled. "Progging for them is more a festivity. Especially if spirits happens to wash up. I've seen them feed liquor to an eight-year-old boy just for their amusement."

"I don't think they're all bad over here, Mr. Whaley."

"Call me Whaley."

"I will not. What would you call me—Alston?"

"I'd call you Burr," he said. He watched for her reaction.

She said, finally, "So you believe I'm who I say I am?"

"Why not? Everybody's got to have a father. He's good as any, I reckon."

Oh, but he was far better. Even in light of the misery they'd both suffered in the last few years—the duel, the treason charges, his exile and onerous return to New York—she felt blessed to have such a loving and honorable father. How deeply misunderstood he was now, how wide the discrepancy between his public persona and the father he'd been to her, eternally supportive and giving. She needed the world to see those papers.

"If they were all bad, these people," she said, "they would never have shared their food with me."

He seemed to look right through the layers of rags she wore, spy the jutting hipbones, the taut skin stretched over the ladder rungs of her ribcage. "Fed you like a princess, did they?"

"It's just that I don't believe people are either all good or all bad."

"I'd wager you keep better company than I do."

"You ought not to assume because my former station was a high one—"

He interrupted. "High? Daughter of the vice president? No, miss, I never would of said 'high.'"

"Let me finish, please," she said, smiling. She'd not smiled since before her son got sick. She told herself it had nothing to do with this man, everything to do with a limit to misery—a point crossed, after which the mind and heart seeks to vent its displeasure by becoming unexpectedly, blissfully surprised. "There are plenty of perfectly venal people in the circles among which I previously moved," she said, thinking of the man her father challenged to a duel only after the slander had turned personal and, she suspected, involved not only her father's honor but her own.

"Don't doubt you there," he said. "But you contradicted yourself. You said there isn't any of them all bad, then you said some of them is perfectly venal. I don't recall the exact meaning of that word but I'm going to venture it don't mean virtuous."

"I may well have contradicted myself," she said. "It's hard to think straight when you've eaten your fill for the first time in months. They say hunger makes you crazy, but I feel I had more clarity when I was in want than now, with this fire, this stew, this bread."

"A charming excuse," said Whaley. "Though I happen to agree with you: ain't no one all bad or all good. Daniels himself saved the likes of you. Which makes him a little less a villain."

This seemed a good place to ask again why he too was thought to be touched when he was obviously quite rational, even intelligent in his own way. But when she asked, he said, "You'll be wanting to bed down now. Take the tick in the corner there," he said, pointing to a bundle of moss and pine straw beneath what seemed to be a piece of sail.

"I will not take your bed."

"Nonsense. I'm not the one's been sleeping in the mud for the past three nights. I've got a blanket, I'll pull up here by the fire."

She nodded and stretched out on the bed. The pine needles felt as soft and luxurious as the finest goose down, but it was some time before she slept. Barring the couples who'd harbored her, she'd never slept so close to any man, much less a stranger. Joseph had his own rooms, and came to her in the night, and not every night. Whaley was close enough to touch. She could see his silhouette in the dying light of the fire. Could hear him breathing. She tried turning on her side, facing away from him, but that did not quell the mix of trepidation and excitement she felt.

But fatigue and relief not to be sleeping in wet sand, her skin raked by live-oak boughs shaken by steady wind, took over at some point in the night.

When she blinked open her eyes, Whaley was gone, but the fire had been revived, and there was a kettle boiling, a can of loose tea and a mug laid out on a stool cobbled crudely from progged planks. For the first time since she'd arrived on the island she slept later than her host. She made a cup of tea and sipped until Whaley returned with a load of wet twigs and, in a pail, two small fish.

"I reckon you're used to fish."

"I confess I would kill for a peach."

"Seems a trifle to murder over. Surely there's something you crave more."

She thought about it. For years her foremost desire was for the return of the bliss she'd felt when she'd been the mistress of Richmond Hill. And then she'd lost her son, which turned her want of a fine house and famous dinner guests childish and vain. Though he was alive still, coming for her surely, she'd lost her father after the duel and the Mexico scheme. But his glory could easily be restored. He suffered only from the usual male vanities. Envy. Pride. The failings of good men the world over. She had only a problem with his greed.

"My father made a deal with my husband," she said into the fire.

"Pardon?"

"A financial arrangement. For my hand. I can't say I was not given to the idea of marriage, or that there were not qualities in Joseph I admired, but my father was in trouble. He has always lived as if he were rich. He is not wise in business. We were going to lose Richmond Hill—the estate we used to own on the Hudson—and my father agreed to allow Joseph my hand if he would help out with the mortgage."

"A dowry," said Whaley in a way that made it clear he thought there was nothing terribly unusual there.

"No, not a dowry. An arrangement. A dowry is a onetime payment. This was not that. I have a bad habit of sneaking looks at people's ledgers. I saw the payments to my father, and they continued for some years after we were married. In fact, they continued far longer than the initial arrangement called for, as I finally confronted Joseph about it, and he told me that he'd continued to keep my father afloat out of pity."

"He lost the house anyway?"

"Yes," she said, turning to Whaley, who had cleaned the fish and was rolling them in meal to fry for breakfast. "But there were motivations, I am certain, other than financial ones. Political clout in the Southern colonies, where my father's enlightened stance on slavery doubtless cost him the presidency."

"Power changes a man. Even if they're not claiming to have heard women in pictures talking or moving their eyes, they lose touch with the rest of the world."

Feeling her face grow warm, she put down her tea, moved back from the fire. What angered her the most about his comment was the way he could have been either talking to himself, about someone else—Daniels, obviously—or listening, and understanding, all too well.

"If you're going to talk about my father, you could at least call him by name," she said.

"What your daddy's done or ain't done don't concern me nor anyone else on this island. You need to get used to that, or you'll drive yourself mad."

Whaley laughed at his joke so loudly that she nearly smiled herself. And of course he was right. Her father's illustrious career wasn't even news here, for the news, when it came, was months late and had no effect on the lives of the islanders. She wondered if, in fact, her father meant nothing to the rest of the country—wondered if she hadn't imagined the stares as she sat in the Alston family pew of the St. James Episcopal Church in

Charleston, or exaggerated the threat of shameful treatment that led her to choose, despite Joseph's protestations, to travel to her reunion with her father by sea instead of overland, which would have taken less than a week, opposed to the two weeks it would have taken her had there not been a light tied to the head of a nag. The thought of six days cooped up in a coach with strangers who would just know by looking at her who she was had led her to choose the ocean.

That she associated the ocean with indifference amused her now that her life—and the lives of everyone on this island—was so dependent upon what the sea delivered. Whaley's lodgings might be aesthetically lacking, but its roof kept the both of them dry and warm.

"Okay," she said, "I'll try not to drive myself mad. In the mean time, you'll help me build my manor?"

"Imagine I could lend a hand from time to time."

"And that portrait? You'll help me get it back?" She saw no need to mention the papers, for how could she trust this man she'd just met? Such a treasure might cause a good man to change direction. As he said, power changes a man.

When she looked up at him, his affable demeanor had darkened.

"Might as well take a knife to both our throats."

"I want it back."

"If that portrait went missing he'd search ever inch of this is-land until he turned it up. He'd catch you, and he'd kill you."

"It's all I've got from before."

Whaley handed over her breakfast.

"You got lots from before." He tapped his temple with a fore-finger. "Way more important than paint on a canvas."

"I don't know. I don't trust myself to remember. Not here, not as hard as it is to live."

"That only makes a memory stronger," he said.

Again she sensed some untold story. It was in his delivery at times, his sudden demonstrative surges, so noticeably impassioned given his phlegmatic demeanor. But now was not the time to press. It would take time, talking him into helping her get to her father's papers. And it wasn't as if she did not understand the danger. She had witnessed Daniels at what, for all she knew, might have been a routine Tuesday on the job, and it was as bloody and deeply evil a day as she'd ever hoped to witness. She stiffened at the thought of it and despite her attempts to push the memory away, it was as Whaley said: something about the island only made stronger that moment on the ship, when the door to her berth gave way and she tried hard to take her eyes off the woman in the portrait she thrust in front of her like a shield. But that woman would not break her stare, would not let her look away as her sweet French maidservant Eleanor, inches away, became two people, two sets of legs, one set unskirted from waist to knees, another bare from buttocks to boot tops. Theo did not look; she was not allowed to move her eyes from the gaze of the woman in the painting and still she could see everything, the man jerking atop Eleanor as he slapped her face and pried open her mouth to spit into it. Two sets of hands trying to pull the portrait from her arms. Her strength godly and omnipotent so long as she did not break the gaze. Finally three men pushed the two of them—herself and the woman in the portrait—topside.

Daniels had stood calmly among the carnage on deck. He was bare to the waist and there was an epaulet of blood on his shoulder.

"She won't let go her picture," said one of the men.

"Did you not try cutting off her arms?"

"We figured you'd want a taste first."

The bloody-shouldered leader reached out to her. She said to the woman in the portrait, *I am the daughter of Aaron Burr.*

"What'd she say?" one of the men behind her whispered.

"Said she's Aaron Burr's daughter," said the leader.

"The one what killed that fellow in a duel?"

The leader put a bloody hand on her shoulder. He said as he drew his sword that he did not care if she was the queen of bloody England.

She smiled at the woman in the portrait who said, Stay with me, Theo. I will not let them harm you.

I will stay with you, she said. Past the woman, beyond the gray horizon, a blue line of hills arose and in the middle distance the lushly treed forest lining the bank across the Hudson came slowly into focus. Smoke rose from the chimneys of Richmond Hill. Under a canopy of linden trees in the garden, she dined with her father.

I brought you this gift, she said to him. *I've come home to be with you now. Never again will we be parted.* She extended the portrait to her father.

"Let her go," said Daniels. A creaking as his sword found refuge in its leather sheath. She felt the fingers on her shoulder loosen and fall away.

"Go where?" said a voice behind.

"Take her ashore," he said. "She's our burden now. We cannot touch her because she has already been touched. By God."

God's touch might not save her a second time. Whaley seemed to know the man and his ways; she ought to put her trust in Whaley, not Richmond Hill or morning mist along the banks of the Hudson, not the sweetness of peaches or Chopin's nocturnes. Whaley was real. At this moment he was talking to her, in fact.

"Best get to progging," he was saying. He'd wrapped her some biscuits and a little leftover croaker in a cloth for her lunch.

She hesitated in the doorway to thank him, but when she did, finally, say the words, he waved her away. "Helps me too," he said.

"I don't see how. Now you're taking care of two. Twice as hard."

"Twice the rewards," he said, then he dropped his eyes in shyness. "We best not tarry now. Wasting good light."

She spent the day alone, scouring the coastline, pushing farther up the island away from the crowds. The farther she traveled, of course, the more distance there was to lug home whatever she found. So she made piles in the high dunes, lumber and some cookware—two pewter mugs, a lone piece of china—a strip of sail that would do nicely for a blanket, a few bottles she could use to fetch water. Within days she was lusting after not peaches but nails. Had the wind through the sea oats promised to bring her anything she wanted, she would have asked, hours before, for chocolate, books, Chopin. Now it was nails, a couple of hinges for her door, an ax, a saw, a hammer.

A week or so after Whaley brought her into his hut, he lay sleeping on the bed. That night as always he offered her the tick, but she would not hear of it, not that her refusal ever dissuaded him from going through the exchange the next night. Whaley's sleep-breath rose to a not-quite snore and rain pelted the piecemeal roof above her head, but what kept her awake was the thought of Whaley offering nightly his bed, the predictability of it, its link in a chain of daily occurrences she previously would have deemed quotidian. Ritual was just as important in her former milieu but it was understood so differently, as a pattern of society, a set of preordained rules observed by those who truly understood how life should be lived.

Civilization depended upon adherence to such a pattern, and perhaps for that reason she had always resented it. Joseph had his next-day clothes laid out for him by his manservant by ten the night before. His family always decamped for DeBordieu Island on the first of May. Four o'clock came and tea was served, dinner at seven thirty sharp.

Why not go to DeBordieu early this year, she asked Joseph, whose patience with such suggestions made her feel all the more fragile. Smile at her every word, humor her at all costs.

On this island there was nothing static or plodding about routine. Survival was predicated on things being the same: the sea yielding food and delivering materials adaptable to your daily needs, the wind steady enough to keep the bugs away but not strong enough to cause the destruction of which it was so easily capable.

This is what Theo was thinking, lying by the fire, inches away from Whaley, so close she could smell his sleep-breath, when the door blew open.

Whaley rose so quickly she saw only his blanket, flung across the room. Then he was standing by the fire, gripping a piece of wood the length and thickness of an ax handle. She looked beyond him to see Daniels's face, lit only by the remnant glow of fire in the hearth. He looked her over once before his eyes sought out Whaley in the smoky gloom. He seemed unconcerned about the makeshift weapon, as if he knew it would not be used on him.

Theo kept her eyes on Whaley. "It's my father come at last," she said, and curtsied low, her skirts rustling the tick. "Home to Richmond Hill. Oh, how they've missed me, especially the Missus Astor."

"Hush now," said Whaley, and she knew by the fierceness of the tone that he knew she was putting on a show, and because he understood she kept it up, speaking lovingly of peaches, cream, pinafores, her favorite quilt, a lazy cat tinkling the piano keys, until Whaley, responding to something else in the room she could not see, raised his stick above her head and let loose a string of oaths, her cue to cower among her skirts on the floor.

She hid her head in her arms and could see nothing, though this did not keep her stomach from clinching nor calm her quickened breath.

"Least you've got good enough sense not to touch her."

"She's already touched," said Whaley. "Just taking my turn sheltering her."

"Who asked you to take a turn?"

"Nobody asked. But everyone else on this island has done his share."

"You're not everybody else. The rest of them contribute. You don't do a damn thing but feed your face and grow your beard."

Whaley said nothing to this.

"What is that you're building across the dune?"

"She was sleeping beneath an oak. She'd of died had I not took her in."

Theo heard a yawn so protracted she thought it exaggerated. Then Daniels said, "I believe I will have me a dram."

"Afraid I'm out."

"You ought to be more afraid. Man lets you live on his property for nine years and you won't offer him a sociable drink when he stops in."

More silence on Whaley's part. Theo worried her ragged breathing was thunderous, that Daniels would feel her fear and know she was not touched, that she heard and understood every nuance of this conversation even through her nearly hysterical fear that Whaley, by sheltering her, had committed himself to certain death.

"You touch her, you're dead."

"I've never once even thought of it."

"I never asked if you *thought* of it. Not the kind of thing a man gives a lot of thought to."

"Some men might."

"You're not one of them."

Even through her fear, Theo understood from what was said that these men were more than passably acquainted, though it was impossible for her to concentrate on much more than breathing, and pretending that the intake and expulsion of air was something akin to a prayer: *Please don't let him kill Whaley. All I have.*

"No one else wants to harbor her," Daniels was saying. "The wives are all complaining. As if I'm not keeping them and their brood and their sorry husbands alive."

"Ungrateful bunch," said Whaley.

An intolerably long pause. "You'd think a man's tongue might get a little less sharp if he went months without speaking to another."

"Or a might more sharp, depending on the man."

"Still having that argument?"

"Which?"

"What kind of man you are?"

"I've near decided."

"I'm sure you have. No mystery what side you put yourself on either. You want to build her a shelter, might as well do it right. Come up tomorrow, get what you need. We'll not be there, but you know your way around. Take a nail more than you need and I'll be back for more than a friendly dram."

"When did I ever take even my fair share?" said Whaley, but the door had slammed shut before he opened his mouth to speak. She watched Whaley latch the door, cross the tiny room, and pull a jar from a pile of wood. He drank deeply from it. She could smell it from where she lay by the fire. She had not yet seen him drink. On this island she'd seen much harm done from men drinking in the dark. His drinking made her all the more tense, for he'd lied to Daniels about the whiskey and he seemed to be fueling something raw and fresh with each sip.

She huddled, still shaking a little, by the fire. So much had transpired in Daniels's visit that she did not understand, and yet she gleaned enough to know that there was something between these men, a vestige of a bond that, however tenuous or threatened by Whaley's taking her in, might well work to her advantage. Daniels invited Whaley to his compound. For supplies. And she'd knelt by the fire convinced that Whaley was about to be beheaded, that Daniels had come for her, that someone on the island had testified to her sanity.

Though she knew this was not the time, she could not help herself, for it was this night that Theo first realized how much Whaley had begun to depend on her company.

"He acted like he knew you," she said, watching him closely.

"Of course he knows me. Knows everybody on this island."

"No, I mean he speaks to you as if he really knows you."

Whaley stepped out of the weak light of the fire, back into the shadows of the room.

"You go to sleep," he said.

This made her angry—she did not care to be talked to like a child—until she remembered that it was his house, that she was, essentially, a child. Defenseless, useless, a dependent who contributed next to nothing to the daily toil of surviving on the island. And he was upset, not himself. Still, it was not easy to sleep when someone ordered you to do so, and she lay there listening to him breathe and sip his drink until the light seeped in beneath the door and around the chimney and she could make out his shadow still slumped against the far wall.

She started the fire, fetched his fishing pole outside, found the leather pouch where he kept his captured crickets, slung it over her shoulder, trudged off to the sound, flat and still in the dawn quiet. She'd heard him say this was one of the best times of day to catch fish, but she'd only been fishing from a boat in the Hudson, and she'd had someone else—an older cousin, a suitor—to bait the hook. It took a full twenty minutes to get the cricket to stay on the crude hook, and another thirty before she managed to pull in two small fish. She worked out the hook with great difficulty and put the fish in the cricket box and turned to go. This was when Whaley let out his low chortle, morning-congested but so sincere and delighted-sounding that she forgot all about the night they'd had.

He was standing atop the dune, drinking from their lone mug. "You fish like a madwoman," he said.

"These fish must be partial to lunacy."

"Right now they're partial to my crickets. Pull them out of that pouch before I don't have one last cricket to show for all my hours of cricket-trapping."

"But they're dead," she said. She was alongside him now and he reached into the pouch and pulled the fish out and crammed them unceremoniously in his pants pockets.

"Not quite yet," he said. "Takes them a while."

Back in the shack she insisted on cooking. Bemused, he allowed her to take over. She was making herself indispensable. She realized how reliant she was on his mercy.

Seated with a plate by the fire, Whaley studied his food and said, "You don't cook much for yourself do you?"

"I had servants," she admitted.

"I knew your husband was a gentleman," he said, "but what exactly is his trade?"

She chewed a bite of crusty fish, swallowed, amused at how bad her manners had become. She said, "He has several rice plantations."

Whaley nodded.

"And tea as well."

Another nod.

"And he is the chief commander of the South Carolina Militia."

Whaley's eyes widened. "Military man?"

"By virtue of his being governor of South Carolina."

Whaley's face showed such confusion—for he thought she was joking, wanted perhaps to believe she was joking, but was led on also by some shocking filament of truthfulness in her voice—that she laughed, rather crazily.

He laughed too.

"Governor, you say? That's good work if you can get it."

"Oh no," she said. "It's a dreadful job."

"I imagine I could get used to it."

"You'd be terrible at it," she said.

He grinned. "And why is that?"

"You can't walk around the governor's palace with fish in your pocket."

"And why not, if you're the governor? Who's going to tell you not to?"

"A host of people. And you all serve them, not the other way round."

"You sound like you're well shy of that role," he said.

"It's true," she said. She felt only a twinge of guilt in her words, for she felt at that point that she could tell Whaley anything.

Yet as she rose to clean the dishes, she realized they had not said a word about Daniels's visit. The marked shift in his mood, from his late-night drunken melancholy to this morning's alacrity, made her suspicious.

That night as they sat by the fire she said, "So are you going to take him up on his offer for materials to build my manor house?"

He tensed. "I'll not be beholding to that man for things I can pick up off the beach."

Before she could think, she pointed out how beholding they both were to that man.

"You don't know what you're talking about," said Whaley. "You ought not to say anything when nothing is what you know."

"If I know nothing, it's because you tell me nothing."

"Everything that goes on in the world is not your affair. Your husband is not the governor here."

"Fine," she said. "If you can point me the way to his compound, I'll go alone. I know it's up past the big dunes, on the sound side. Certainly his lodgings will befit his station. I'm sure I'll be able to recognize it."

"You go up there alone, you might as well slit your wrists right here and now." He withdrew the knife he kept sheathed at his waist, extended it to her.

Theo ignored the knife he offered, looked him in the eye. "You're not telling me something."

"What I already told you, you've not listened to."

She feigned anger, but she knew he was right. She hadn't paid much attention to his threats because she was too obsessed with recovering her father's papers. All she had to do was smuggle them off the island, get them in the right hands, and her father's reputation would be restored, for how tender and noble he was in those missives, how courageous and devoted a statesman and citizen did his journals reveal him to be. All the accusations against him would be exposed as slander; his plan for Mexico and the western provinces would be understood as advantageous to the common American good, much less threatening than French and Spanish dominion. And even if she were never rescued from this island, even if she spent the rest of her days the ward of a deranged pirate, pummeled by relentless, sand-laced wind, she would join her father as empress of his sovereign land.

That day the progging was fruitless; she brought home only items passed over by others: rotten timbers, strips of sail, rusted iron rings from busted-up barrels. Whaley looked at the things she dragged over the dunes and went back to plucking feathers from a tern, too busy to even pass judgment.

That night, while he snored softly a few feet away, she realized she would likely be dead now were it not for Whaley. Therefore it seemed only logical to put her trust fully in the notion that Whaley had been sent to protect her. Not by God, whose mercy was too celestial to concern itself with the assignment of earthly sentinels, but by her father, whose Aristotlean idea of love—a single soul inhabiting two bodies—had gotten Theo through many a night before she had even arrived on this island.

The next morning, as they sat drinking tea by the fire, breakfasting silently as was their habit, she said, "There's nothing left to find on the beach. I'm going to his compound today."

"You'd be better off walking into the ocean during a storm."

"I can swim."

"We'll see about that," he said.

She grabbed her ratty shawl and made a show of wrapping herself tightly against the elements, as if his resistance was also the cause of the wet gusts outside, the low clouds hugging the dunes. Spitting rain and high lonely call of gulls. Something in their song she decided had only to do with survival, for what would they sing about on such a gray day, in such a forbidding seascape, but sustenance? Their cry for food became, as she trudged through the thick wet sand, her own lament: *Why did I leave?* She had feigned fearlessness but now, alone, on her way to Daniels's compound, she remembered poor Eleanor's last hour, how long it had taken for them to bring her topside, how many of Daniels's men, in the interim, had disappeared below deck. Eleanor had appeared relieved when Daniels had finally ordered her flung overboard, as if every breath after what she had endured at their hands was eternal. *Just let me go to my reward, I'd rather open my mouth to the salty water and swallow, dear God let me go.* She was naked and bloody and hugged her ruined clothes to her chest and in her shame she did not look at Theo, not that Theo was at that moment capable of seeing her. How, then, could she remember so clearly Eleanor's last minute? In memory she had taken leave of her senses, but perhaps she had feigned that as well? Enough to fool Daniels once, and she had fooled him again when he'd appeared in Whaley's hut, but what would happen if it were just the two of them, if, in private, he studied her closely enough to know that no God had touched her, that if she were touched by anything it was devotion to her father and his cause?

The wind increased as she neared his compound, which was a good hour's walk from Whaley's hut. It stood on a rise, fortified by a stockade; smoke rose from the chimneys of the half-dozen houses built on high stilts above the sand. She took shelter in a nearby wood for another hour, her shivering induced as much from fear as cold. The gate to the compound was open but in the time she spent hesitating she saw not a living soul. Occasionally a dog barked and overhead the gulls kept up their song, but here it sounded less desperate, as if they'd been sated, as if they had fed off the obvious spoils gathered by Daniels and his men. And why shouldn't she too take what he had offered? If anyone approached her, all she had to do was string along a narrative of opulent nights at Richmond Hill. *Leave the poor touched soul alone.* Even if she were caught searching for her father's papers, she would be pardoned, for she wasn't in her right mind, and had she not already achieved impunity?

Breathing deeply, Theo picked her way out of the woods and into the stockade. One house, obviously Daniels's, stood a story higher than the others and was twice as wide, regally shingled in shaggy dark shake. At the far edge of the compound, past a well and a shelter beneath which the ribs of several half-finished skiffs sat on scaffolding, she saw a vast pile of lumber. Splintered remains of shipwreckage. Someone else's heartbreak, soon to be her salvation. But only as cover: the real bounty lay in the grandest of these modest, weather-beaten shacks.

The words that came in a steady rush as she moved past the lumber toward Daniels's lodgings were not the words in her head, though both streams honored her father, the articulated one nonsensically, the unspoken one meant to convince her that the risk was for good reason. *When I have those papers in hand, he will come for me.* This is what she timed her steps to when midway across the yard she saw only a low brown streak and then she was in the sand, kicking at the animal with the leg not lodged between its teeth and then Whaley was beating the dog off with a piece of lumber and the dog was limping off bloody and snarling.

A throbbing in her left leg beneath the knee. With each breath it hurt more. Blood soaked the shawl he'd ripped from her shoulders to staunch the wound.

"I didn't see it," she said.

"You weren't looking."

"You followed me?"

"Just happened to be over here on my own business."

She thanked him and he grunted, as if to say, don't thank me, don't even acknowledge me.

It wasn't until he trudged through the sand to the pile of sal-
vaged wood, grabbed a couple long poles, found a section of dry-
rotted sail, fashioned a makeshift sling to take her home that she
settled enough to ponder his arrival. She understood then: he
loved her. Why else would he have followed? As he dragged her
down island, she thought of how ignorant she had been of the
signs. Her back to him, nauseous and sweating from her wounds,
she collected and cataloged those signs in a manner so consciously
calculated others would have thought her manipulative. But even
before she arrived on this island, Theo had entertained a broader
view on this subject, about which she had devoted many hours
of contemplation while courting Joseph. Taking some small advantage of a man in love with you was, to her mind, allowable if
not exactly noble. What was love, in its incipient flush, but de-
lirium, temporary leave-taking, derangement of sense and emotion? What had it to do with another human being, their unique
traits, attributes, qualities? It seemed to Theo that those afflicted
might as well be under the influence of spirits. Certainly they
weren't experiencing any reality she participated in.

Therefore, using the situation to its advantage was not exactly
manipulating Whaley, only his heightened and patently distrust-
ful state of mind. The state was ephemeral; when he dropped back
down to lowly earth, when he *hurt* again, was able to feel things
dictated by cause and effect rather than some chimerical disen-
gagement with reality, she would adopt a different set of rules.

Back at the shack, he helped her inside, stoked the fire, fetched her water, washed and dressed her wounds. For the next week she lay recuperating from her bite, which Whaley kept plastered with a poultice of mud, hornet's nest, and unidentifiable herbs procured from an island widow known for her remedies. The pain grew worse and the poultice smelled foul and itched worse than any of the thousand bug bites she'd encountered on this island; her fever continued for a day and a half, but discomfort only exacerbated her scheming. She found herself energized by purpose, now that she no longer had to worry about survival, which was ensured by two things: Whaley's feelings for her and whatever he was hiding from her about Daniels. She thought again of Daniels's visit. So assiduously did she reconstruct it as she lay recuperating, almost always alone, Whaley out foraging for food or firewood, that nearly every detail felt different. To begin with, she was not scared. What was there to fear from a man who burst in on them in the middle of the night and then offered building materials? She'd sneaked looks at Daniels, noted the way he looked at Whaley, the way he looked at her. Flames reflected in his fierce blue eyes. In memory there was light enough to study him, to see what she needed to see, though a part of her surely realized that the fire was down to coals when he arrived, and that, had she bothered to look up at him instead of cowering on the floor, she would have seen only a profile in shadow.

Whaley doted on her as much as a man of his demeanor could be said to dote. He made sure she was comfortable, altered his routine to tend to her needs. When he was gone she missed him and this meant she felt something for him too, beyond gratitude, beyond the need for company. What she felt she would not let herself examine. As if feeling in the first place were something one could dissect. She liked it when he was with her, she disliked being apart from him. There were other things more worthy of her analysis. How she might retrieve her father's papers. How she might enlist Whaley's aid.

The latter she spent a good deal of time considering, even after her leg had healed enough for her to hobble about the cabin with the help of a crutch Whaley had fashioned for her from a live-oak limb. Ought she tell him now about her father's papers? Certainly he had shown no interest in helping her retrieve the portrait. She worried that the papers would not interest him either, for he was no longer of the world that valued what those papers represented: her father's greatness.

So began her pattern: she would winnow away at him with talk of her return to Daniels's house. Usually she brought it up at night, when he was both exhausted from his day's labor and more convivial, though rarely did he grace her talk of returning with much more than a grunt. She waited, and her leg grew stronger; she limped a bit, a nasty scar remained, but she needed to be able to run. She had a plan to distract the dog with food this time, but she knew that no matter how much food she took along, no matter how strong her leg, she would need Whaley. It would take two to keep the dog from attacking, and she needed a lookout while she searched Daniels's quarters.

But Whaley remained unyielding. After weeks of trying to cajole him, she announced she would leave first thing in the morning for the compound. After all, she said, Daniels offered, and she had no reason to think that the offer did not still stand.

He took it calmly, did not look at her when at last he said, "The dog who nearly crippled you's the only thing up there still stands."

"I've thought of that," she said. "I plan on taking along food this time."

"Whose food would that be?"

"With your permission."

"My permission means nothing to you. It doesn't matter what Daniels offered that night. He's not one to remember such and is certainly not one to honor a promise. You seem to have forgot all about how you met the man."

"I've not forgotten," she said, feigning insult. "But while we're on the subject of forgetting, you wish me to heed your warning about him and yet you're omitting what seem to be crucial details about your dealings with the man."

"For the last time, woman, I don't owe you anything. Especially not a lengthy accounting of my past."

She let her voice drop to a pleasant whisper. "I did not mean to suggest I'm owed anything. But how can I take seriously your warnings when you leave out what I suspect is some truly horrible, and likely pertinent, fact?"

For a full minute he seemed to look through her. Then he said, "I will tell you everything when I'm ready to."

"Fine," she said. "In the meantime I am going to build my house. With or without your help."

As if its weight were tremendous, he managed to lift his gaze to hers. There he left it. There was no light in his eyes, but nor did he look away. He seemed to have given up fighting something against which defeat was only halfhearted fantasy. His acquiescence made her think of Joseph, of how she had never felt for him that pure and unquestionable attachment she'd felt for her father. Love should shrink the earth, should do away finally with the soil on which feet are planted. Spirit only should rise and merge with that of the beloved. Whaley was so solidly structure, so skeletal, like the ribs of the shack he'd built, seen from within, shorn of the patchwork thatch that protected them from the elements. She'd never encountered anyone less concerned with the vanities with which it seemed her precious former life, and everyone in it, had been preoccupied. And yet smoke still rose from him, an essence of great mystery. Enough to intrigue her; enough to convince her for the time being that she was not solely manipulating him to regain those papers and set about restoring her father's rightful place in this world.

"You'll listen to me now. We'll settle this in a day if you listen to me."

He told her a man owed him a favor and this man owned a cart and had tamed one of the wild island ponies to draw this cart. He told her he'd make one trip when he was sure Daniels was off island and that he would fetch only a cartful and that after their return, she had to promise him never to go near the compound again.

An easier vow she'd never taken, as what need would she have of ever returning? If all went as planned, she would soon be reunited with her father.

WHEN THEY REACHED the compound it appeared even more deserted than the first time. No smoke rose from chimneys. A day gray and listless. Only an occasional breeze to rise from the surrounding sea oats a rustle like the dry cough of a croupy child. She sat in the cart while Whaley got out and, armed with a length of board and a thick piece of meat he'd procured from God knows where, searched for the dog. He whistled. He sneaked around the edges of the raised houses, stooping to look beneath the crawl spaces. At one point when he was out of sight, she thought she heard him call out a name.

He was gone a good while. When he came back to the cart, he said, "Locked him in a shed."

They went to work. When the cart was three-quarters full, she told Whaley she needed to excuse herself. Without a word he pointed to an outhouse on the far perimeter of the compound and returned to loading.

In the outhouse she held her nose and waited a few minutes, in case he was watching. Then she opened the door a sliver, saw that he was hard at work, oblivious. She circled around to Daniels's house, stole quickly up the back stairs. The house was

well designed to catch the breeze, though its features were bi-
zarrely incongruent. Much of it had been reassembled from the
staterooms of shipwrecks. The dark paneling smelled still of sea
grass, fish and brine, and rather deliciously of meat, fried, and
something vaguely garlicky. She passed a kitchen, several bed-
rooms, and finally, at the front of the house, a large parlor. Crude
chairs grouped around a massive fireplace. Above the fireplace
hung her portrait.

The sight of her face—years younger, so fresh and untainted
by the travails to come, the humiliation and unfairness that was,
at least, her life, if not the general nature of things—startled her
so deeply that she forgot entirely her mission. No longer did her
father's papers even exist. For all she thought of them they could
have been spread out, a carpet, beneath her feet. The portrait had
saved her life. Had it not the power to turn a murdering thief
fearful of the vengeance of God? Had Daniels not sworn up and
down the island that the girl in the portrait—her younger, innocent, hopeful self—had spoken to him as she had spoken to her? If
he revered it enough to hang in his parlor, surely he'd want it back
badly enough to allow her to be reunited with her father.

Her wounded leg ached as she carried the portrait down the
dark hallway. She was careful not to look at the woman in the
painting for fear that life in Daniels's den had turned her, that
she might, with only her eyes, bring Theo to harm. She slung it
under her arm and, when she was down the back stairs, lurched
across the courtyard toward the cart.

She did not see Whaley until well after she heard the hiss of the dog and then a silence as the dog came hurtling through the unnaturally dense and still air. She managed to toss the portrait out of the way rather than use it to protect herself, for it seemed to her that she'd used up all her chances, that the choice she made was final and fateful. She closed her eyes to the attack and when she opened them Whaley stood over her, though the dog was still on her. A blurry second and she realized: he had figured out her plan. He had discovered her gone and figured out where she was. He had let the dog out of the shed. Now he was watching her die. She understood then: love too had limits. People could love you so much that they compromised their every shred of dignity, the love they lavished would strip them to skeletal, but there were things you could do to make them stop loving you, even if they were eaten up with it, even if they said they would die for you. At some point they had to protect themselves.

Or maybe he did not love her. Or what if he did love her and was letting her die because he was the only one who ever loved her for who she was and what if he knew that she would never settle for such honesty because she was incapable of reciprocating? These were the things she wanted to have filled her mind when, years later, she thought of that afternoon when Whaley let the dog nearly kill her before he killed the dog and dragged her and the portrait across the dunes to a skiff tied to a sound-side dock and rowed them from one island to another.

IV

MAGGIE WHALEY
Yaupon Island, North Carolina

ONE OF THOSE NIGHTS not long after the last storm swept the island clean, Maggie sat with her sister on the steps of the church. Whaley was reading aloud her Norfolk grocery store prices. To Maggie this noise was as closely known as the roll of surf on the beach. Something settled so deep inside she hardly heard it, though her sister, to read her prices, trumped up a special voice, frilly ball dress compared to her usual wrinkled housecoat drawl.

The way her sister put on aggravated the life out of Maggie. Whaley'd sat in the same pew at the same little school Maggie had and learned from the same old mildew-ravaged books. They'd read aloud for the same succession of not-long-for-this-island schoolteachers the very same sentences that children off island doubtless mumbled without intent or comprehension, because what they smacked of, these teach-you-to-read sentences, was a world known and taken for granted by children everywhere except for Yaupon and the few left-behind places like it. Daddy's automobiles chugged up the driveway in these sentences, and snowstorms piled up and sleds navigated the piles of snow. Named dogs caroused around in the subject/verb/objects. Maggie and her brothers and sisters had always had a dog poking around up under the house, but not one of them had gone by anything but the color of their coat if they were lucky. Most likely: Hey Dog or Here Puppy. Reading those sentences along in the breezy, careless way the teacher did got away with Maggie. She thought about the damn things, what was going on in them, what they were trying to say. Dogs named Conrad or Judith sneaked up and licked her knees, tickling her while she read aloud in front of the whole class. She'd be reading and at the same time climbing up in Daddy's car and crouching back on the floorboards, afraid of going around in a hot steamy box but willing to try everything like she was known to do by everyone on the island.

Whaley was reading along in her prissy voice when Maggie spotted Woodrow coming across the creek. Maggie was all after-supper logy from half-listening to her sister call out how much a head of cabbage will run you up in Norfolk, but since Woodrow had come back across from burying Sarah he'd kept to himself, mostly down south near the inlet the storm cut, doing God knows what, Maggie had no idea. She left him alone, though Whaley kept after her to go check on him.

"Now you're all about checking up on people?" Maggie said, to shut her up, and it worked, though she could tell it was eating at her, Woodrow's disappearance. They hadn't seen a soul except that O'Malley who had brought the mail and some food over every few days. Maggie could have been sleeping and still seen a body come across that creek, especially Woodrow.

"Here comes Woodrow," she said, but Whaley did not look up. Maggie heard her voice hitch up a little and go even prissier, more what Dr. Levinson and them called Elizabethan: her vowels flattened and roiling like breakers across her tongue.

Woodrow took his time coming up the hill. He took a seat third row from the bottom. Whaley read her prices right on. When she stopped to fold up one of those papers in the tight way she had like she was taking a sheet off the line, Maggie said, "Crawl wrote and said you're going to be eighty this year, Woodrow."

Soon as she said it she wanted it back. How would she know what Crawl said unless she opened up Crawl's letter and read it. She knew that Woodrow knew what all they left out of the letters Crawl wrote, how they always stopped just shy of Crawl telling Woodrow he'd be over across to get him tomorrow if Woodrow would just say the word.

Woodrow didn't say anything for so long that Whaley went ahead on with her prices. Then he said, in the middle of Whaley going on about something called a blow-dryer, "Crawl don't know nothing about how old I am."

"Old enough to know better," Maggie said without even

breathing. She liked to tease Woodrow and he was known to take her teasing and smack it right back at her. Sometimes, sitting on the church steps, they fell into an easy rhythm of ribbing—even Whaley had been known to smile at their back and forth—and God knows if ever there were a need for some lightness, it was during that buggy yellow sunset when Woodrow all of a sudden returned to them.

But as soon as her words were out of her mouth here came Whaley with her own. Maggie didn't even think she was listening. When she was reading her prices it could hail and she would chant right on.

"Too old to change," Whaley said.

Ever after, Maggie remembered the moment as if she were still sitting on those steps. Slight land breeze winging in an odor of sulfurous marsh. Orange sun lowering itself over the trees to settle, like everything and everyone else, across the sound. The way Woodrow slapped distracted at his neck as if a bug had bit him, then pulled his hand away and opened his palm and discovered there wasn't any bug after all, as if the hurt he felt right then from her sister's words and maybe hers too (though she meant no harm by them, was only trying to engage Woodrow in a little trash talk) were deeply inward, as if what they had done to Woodrow, what caused him to say after a minute of tense silence, *Y'all ought not to have done me like y'all done me,* would thereafter and always be antagonized by the slightest thing they said or did or did not say or do, by even a bug bite, or the threat of a bug bite, by the wind.

Looking back was a luxury, a chance to tuck and tidy. The stories her sister told the Tape Recorders, especially the ones about her famous ancestor, weren't all sweetness and light, but they somehow managed to wrap up in a way that left Whaley bathed in light as holy as pink Yaupon dusk. What Maggie remembered thinking and what she thought at the time: the distance between was the Pamlico Sound separating their island from the rest of the world.

She did not think, as she ought to have thought when Whaley told Woodrow he was too old to change, You heartless bitch, what is wrong with you, you need to be sucking up to the man after what we've done to him, and instead you sit up there on your top step insulting him. She did not look to Woodrow, did not appraise his hurt or notice whether there was truly a bug on the hand he pulled away from the skin he slapped. She did not tend to Woodrow because, much as she hated to admit it, her sister's words—too old to change—made her think about herself.

Or rather of Boyd, of her life with Boyd.

She was forty years old when she met him, and he was twenty-four. She had heard of Boyd's arrival on island even though she did not see him up close until that day he showed up was leaking away in shadows. She was down island, taking her nearly nightly swim. She liked to swim unencumbered, but that night for some reason she kept her suit on, or what she called a suit: bra and panties.

She had her back to the shore, eyes out to sea, floating past the breakers in the mild after-supper surf. Pointing her feet to the horizon, sculling as the sun shot through her, touched her places with sudsy fingers. A little bit of heaven and the best bits of earth merged in her afternoon bask. So deep was her pleasure that she was oblivious when, occasionally, boys all the way up to grown men—kindergarteners to when they dropped out of school, usually not much into their teens—came to spy in the dunes above her basking spot, knowing as all the world did of her habit of leaving off clothes when the water was warm. It liked to killed her sister, especially because Maggie never once bothered to acknowledge her audience. She liked to think of herself as the model you don't get showed in school or at home. Boys needed to see the thing alive and full frontal so they at least knew what they were lying about when they went around bragging. She'd seen the pictures scrawled on the stall doors of the single bathroom in the schoolhouse. A nasty word for a woman's private parts spelled out in a spindly hand, an arrow lassoing it and pointing to a pitiful triangle. If she could help out with the anatomy, well, everyone on the island took a hand in raising the children.

She had her back to Boyd but she knew he was there. She felt his eyes on her, steady as the sun tinting her skin, but she did not turn to him. She kept her toes pointed out to sea. She did not want to appear any too eager, for she'd seen him down at the dock that morning and he was tall and rangy like she liked them. Who knew how long he'd be around? So many of the ones who showed up announcing they were on the island to stay were gone the first big blow. They lacked fortitude, Whaley claimed. The island was no place for crooks, drunks, liars, gamblers, philanderers, and other sorts of reprobates because these particular types were in need always of outside resources to sustain them. Whaley made it sound like only the virtuous could survive on their island. Maggie knew better, though it was true that to any more than make do out here, you had to know how to make peace with yourself, and with the weather.

Sometimes Maggie felt at peace; other days she woke up to find that, like the sand sifted away by the current, a part of her had eroded during the night and floated out to sea as she lay curled up against the wall, listening to her big sister's snores in the next room of the house her father built from washed-ashore timber.

Not long after Boyd arrived, word got around that he'd been born on island, that his father had drowned one day checking his pots up on the Albemarle when the wind blew up and the swells ranged all the way up the Alligator River. After the body washed up in Mann's Harbor two or three weeks later, Boyd's mama took him and his brother and sister across the sound to Harker's Island to stay with kin, then disappeared into the continent. Kept on going west, devoured by all that vast and dangerous acreage. Maggie was more than a little scared of it herself, which is why she'd never left. Maggie'd heard about the way people nowadays just kept on moving. It wasn't a war going on, but people sure were acting like it, like they were being chased, like wherever they were from had been taken over by the enemy. Pecking around like hens, sniffing out someplace safer, cleaner, wealthier, more jobs, less wind, more culture. People? Seemed to Maggie they wanted only everything. Wanted it yesterday morning at the crack. Though Maggie could understand the notion of something better down the road. She imagined she'd be the same if she took herself off island, always peering down the highway or out the window at the looming woods, wondering if there was another man, a better job, more money, less bugs or heat or snow. Because she understood the lure of Always Elsewhere, she was scared to death of leaving her island. She would not even let herself imagine letting any one desire drive her but the need for that crusty cake of sun and salty sea on her naked skin as she basked in the ocean. Maggie needed tiny shells stuck to her skin when she got undressed for bed. She needed these shells to rain down on the floorboards nights when she undressed, little bedtime chimes.

Much as she loved her island, Maggie was suspicious when people came from the mainland to settle there. More often than not they were running from something or someone. Boyd came to the island to fish, or so he claimed. He went straight to Woodrow to learn how. Back then, Woodrow had Crawl crewing for him. He'd bought a boat from the O'Malleys and contracted out to sell them most of what he caught. No one on the island would allow it, but Woodrow was the best waterman around. He could always come up with some fish. Whaley said he was lucky, but it wasn't luck because there wasn't any such thing to Maggie's mind and besides she'd had this conversation with Woodrow once and he said he didn't believe in luck either. He claimed the whereabouts of fish in the sea was a process of elimination, a strict adherence to the tiniest subtleties of wind and tide.

Why would Woodrow take on Boyd when he already had Crawl crewing for him? Years later when she got around to asking, Woodrow said, Black man couldn't say no to a white boy no matter what a yes might cost him.

Maggie used to believe that the quiet sinewy strength her sister admired in Woodrow was maybe just years of having to go round agreeing with white people. Instead of resilience, it was suppressed indignation. Her sister looked at Woodrow and saw pride, but she didn't respect it because she did not think it was hard fought for. It was far easier for Whaley to pretend Woodrow was a fine upstanding colored man, exemplary among his race, than to stop and consider who he really was.

Whaley never did see what Maggie learned too late: Woodrow had his jellyfish tentacles spread out every which way, feeling the world in ways most people would not dare. This did not mean he was fragile or weak. Maggie and Whaley would have died every day for years if not for Woodrow, who made it possible for them to live on the island long after every living thing but the mosquitoes called it quits. What he was, Maggie came to understand, was particularly sensitive. He could feel the approach of a storm some claimed by snuggling his bare toes in the sand off his front porch. He knew water. God knows he could pull flopping silver bodies from it with a hook or net. But these were learned things—not nearly so powerful as the brooding resolve so long misunderstood by Maggie, never understood or appreciated by Whaley. Maggie herself was not inclined toward this brand of sensitivity. She felt, and felt deeper, surely than her big sister. But before Boyd came and before he left, she wasn't one to put her feelers out for very long or for very far. She'd as soon shrug it off. Life on the island, despite its many and mostly long-gone pleasures, was hard enough without letting every little thing get away with you.

But then Boyd started coming around. Woodrow took him out between four and five in the morning and brought him in early afternoon, a full day's work, after which Boyd, being so new on the island, without a boat to tinker on all afternoon, nets of his own to mend, turned up wherever Maggie was: working her and Whaley's patchy little garden, talking to Grady and Ellie up at the store, taking her bask in the late afternoon sun. One day he turned up beside her in the ocean. She was on her back, feet pointed toward Portugal. Dressed in her "suit," her shift and sandals discarded on a dune. Boyd, near as she could tell, wore only a droopy pair of boxer shorts. He was well built, not too thin though, broad-shouldered, capable it appeared of heavy lifting.

She let him float awhile unacknowledged.

"I hear you're wild," he said after a while.

She heard a little fear in his voice, which made her like him— and what he said—better than if he'd come on all cocky.

"You must have been talking to somebody tame," she said.

He snickered. "That'd be about everybody on this island."

She put her feet down, jumped a coming wave, turned toward him for the first time since he'd appeared floating beside her.

"How do they act where you come from?"

He smiled and shrugged, and she understood him to say: "You got me. Harker's Island ain't much different."

"The young and foolish act young and foolish all over," she said, smiling at the thought of it, that insolent and selfish desire to make every moment feel better than the previous one.

"You're not exactly old."

"Not exactly, you say?" She laughed a little, but it was a forced laugh, conversational. "I'm nearly exactly old enough to be your mother."

This was nearly exactly true on Yaupon, where women fattened up with children in their midteens. Plus, at the time she thought Boyd was even younger than he was.

"My mama's ancient compared to you," he said.

She studied him until he turned to her, at which point he was smacked unawares by a wave. She rose above him, buoyant in the swell. She thought about his name—transpose two little letters and it would read "body." She shook her head, as if to clear the water from her ears, though there were thoughts, warm and shooting, she was really trying to clear.

"I mean she's not that old, but you're not nearly so old as she is."

"Don't worry," she said. " I know you love your mama. Let's go in before you drown," she said, windmilling away from him in a backstroke turned breast as the breakers receded and the water shallowed.

They sat in the dunes watching the waves roll golden in the declining light. He pulled a flask of homemade wine from the pocket of his jeans, and as they sipped he talked about growing up on Harker's Island, hearing stories about the home place, stories about his father the fisherman. He had been in the army— he'd joined right out of high school and had been stationed in Germany—and this surprised and pleased her, for he was so innocent, so tentative and nervous in her presence, and it amazed her that he could have done all that and still grow so scared around a woman that he let the waves slap him silly. Of course she was wise enough to know that there is no reasoning what scares you. People otherwise invincible can turn to quivering at the sight of, say, a spider. But it surprised her still to be a witness to it, this innocent cowering by a man who'd seen so much more of the world than she ever would.

Maybe it was the fact that their talk flowed so easily, that there was between them an easy and sassy friction—giving each other a hard time, trafficking from the start in smart-assedness and indirection—that made his age seem irrelevant in the beginning. She'd known so few people she could really talk to, and no men save for Woodrow, who mostly listened. She knew within minutes what would happen between them, for their conversation was as close to foreplay as she'd ever experienced, each sentence a shirt shed, a caress, until they were down to bare skin.

He put his hand on her arm. She let it remain. The sun seared through his veins, into hers. She said, "I'm forty years old."

"That's just math," he said. "I'm no damn good with figures."

"Too old to have a baby," she said. She wasn't talking to him anymore. If she had been talking to him, she wouldn't have brought up a baby here before they'd even kissed.

But he wasn't the least bit put off by the topic.

"Say what? My aunt had a baby at forty-three. Far as I could tell it only had one head."

She nodded, uncharacteristically assuaged by his dismissal of mere arithmetic. She wasn't that good with numbers either. Numbers meant less here than they did off island, where there were thousands of forty-year-old men, whole cities full of them no doubt, and yet how many of them could talk to her like Boyd did?

Here was Boyd and he was free and she was too. Neither of them needed to add, subtract, or study chromosomes.

But this did not mean that she could be with Boyd (who that day came at her with a salty, wine-scented kiss and she shrugged and smiled and met him halfway) without some worry. Her ex-husband, Ronnie, lived down island and often fished close to Woodrow, hoping to benefit from Woodrow's impeccable feel for the catch. If she took this boy to bed (and she knew already who was leading this dance), it would get out sooner or later, and Ronnie in his cups would come stirring trouble as he could be a jealous and mean bastard who, even though he was the one run her off with his whoring up and down the banks, wanted her to sleep forever alone.

More salty-sweet kisses. A hand on her breast, snaking down inside the cup of her bra, a thumb and forefinger pinching her nipple. She laid him down in the sand and said, "How long you going to be living with your aunt?"

"Until I move?" He pulled her toward him, hip-wiggling to position herself over that part of him in need of coverage. After five seconds of pressure expertly applied, she lifted herself up and away, made her point.

"One thing I'll say about being forty," she said, "is that it's no longer all that sexy to screw some boy up in the dunes."

"Sand all in your slits?" he asked, grinning like a preteen.

It was hard to believe he'd been to Germany just then. She had it in her mind that such travel turned you into someone out of one of those teaching sentences: Boyd traveled to Europe where he spent the summer studying artifacts of old. She did not think it was possible that you could cross the ocean and come back talking schoolboy playground trash right on, as if you'd spent the whole time drinking beer with your buddies. She must have transmitted this thought, for he immediately apologized and looked at her with such obvious fear that she had found him out that she was back to finding him endearing and surprisingly mature for his age.

"At least bring a blanket. If you can't get a blanket, a towel's better than nothing."

"When?"

"Next time," she said. She left him adjusting himself in his shorts, twitching about in the sand.

There was a next time. Soon after the first time. They met in the dunes at dusk, spread out on a nubbly chenille bedspread he'd lifted from his aunt's house. He was timid with her at first and maneuvered his body shyly as if he was used to performing in the pitch blackness, in cramped quarters—the backseat of a car, upside a shed in some neighbor girl's backyard—and for an audience indifferent to nuance. She let him work away his modesty before she slowed things down, took time for careful curious examinations, extended fondles and caresses, kisses in places he had obviously never been kissed.

Maggie wasn't exactly not nervous. It had been a year then since she'd been with Ronnie. She knew she looked better than most island women her age, a fact generally attributed by everyone but her to her childlessness. She did not like to think that babies would have ruined her looks. She'd seen some women get their hips back, a few even blossom afterward, take some color in their skin they'd lacked. She'd rather believe that some people are given their looks early and others grow into them. Whaley, when she was seventeen, had a figure used to drive every man on the island to throw themselves in the surf to save showing their obvious and attentive salutation. She hedged badly, banked on looking good forever; she went around with her lip as stiff as her read-aloud voice and did not pay one iota of attention to any man, and when in her early thirties she started down that lonely-as-hell-I-wouldn't-mind-settling-down road, her ass was flat and her high haughty look yonder breasts were gone to sag and she'd doubled her chin with lard and butter and worst of all was that her expression, which had always tended toward the sweet distracted vacancy of the unself-consciously beautiful, had turned into a look-at-me-why-don't-you wince.

Maggie might have fared better than her sister, but she worried about the effects of time, wind, and sun on her skin, surely sandpaper compared to the peach-fuzzy girls he'd been with. He'd been with a few, she could tell, though they had not taught him much. Or maybe he hadn't been willing to learn.

Now he was willing, and able. He grew looser and a little more confident with each rendezvous, but she hated the way they had to hide and sneak, hated even more the sand and the heat and the godawful tempest of bugs.

"Why can't we go to your place?" he asked when she mentioned it.

"I live with my sister."

Boyd made a point of exaggerating his habitual, one-size-fits-all shrug. Whaley had surely caught wind of them—the island was too tiny for her not to know how Maggie was spending her evenings. But so far Boyd had not come by the house and she'd not asked him up there because she knew Whaley would disapprove, as she did of every man Maggie had ever brought by there even as she tried to rouse a flirt, pulling and patting at her dress to tighten it. The roles the two of them played were pathetic to

Maggie mostly because they were predictable: tight, disapproving older sister; loose, boy-crazy younger one. Maggie longed for a little more originality, especially given the fact that they had a steady audience, that the whole island was a witness to their stale roles.

"You don't know my sister," she said.

"No, but I've seen her around. Down at the store some. Woodrow sells her fish."

"Don't say it," said Maggie.

"Say what?"

"Whatever you're about to say about her."

That shrug again. To Maggie it was beginning to represent all the weighty things he knew were out there but, because of his youth, wasn't up to shouldering, this gesture. But the thing she liked about him was that his heart wasn't in this carefree ignorance. Hell, his shoulder was barely in it. The shrugs were mostly flicks and twitches, the blade shuddering from some rippling nerve.

"Just that y'all don't much favor. That's all I was going to say."

Maggie looked out to sea so he would not see her gloat. She wanted Boyd kept separate from Whaley and all the silly childish things that had come between her and her only blood kin.

"Come on," she said. As they stood there was a rustling in the sand a dune or two back from where they lay naked on the chenille. High helium squeals of boys, spying.

"Oh hell," she said.

Boyd was struggling into his boxers, about to light out after them, but she stopped him.

"I know who they are. I'll put the fear in them."

"Don't doubt that," he said. He came at her, nuzzling her, half-interested, interest growing, but she turned away and dressed, a little bothered by his lack of doubt as to her ability to put the fear in these spy boys, a little surprised that she took so much to heart his surely idle comments.

"Where we going?"

"Just follow me."

At Woodrow's she knocked loudly at the screen door, in defiance of her sister, who when she wanted Woodrow would come to the door and stand close to it, not knocking, sending her white lady waves inside. She knocked loud enough to be heard, and Sarah in her apron, her hands a little bloodied from some freshly slaughtered game, responded in good time.

"Woodrow here?" she asked Sarah.

"Out around back," Sarah said, taking in both Maggie and Boyd with her characteristically slight and indifferent appraisal.

After Sarah was gone Woodrow all but said he did not believe Maggie cared much for his bride. But in fact Maggie wanted to feel close to Sarah. She wanted Sarah's affection and she courted Sarah in her own way. Whaley didn't like Sarah because she was a colored woman and haughty about it—*uppity* was the word Whaley used—but Maggie knew the truth about Sarah: she was a hard woman. Wasn't a warm bone in her body far as Maggie could tell. She figured Woodrow had to see a different side of her, but she knew that even Woodrow struggled with Sarah's moods.

Not one day went by that Maggie did not feel bad about what happened to Sarah. She had to remind herself of Sarah's miserly spirit, but in death those faults seemed to fade. Wasn't it the color of Maggie's skin that caused Sarah to look right through her if she looked her way at all? It wasn't personal. She was good enough for Woodrow to love, and he did love her.

They found Woodrow sitting on a crab pot, studying his hogs. He looked up, then right past them like he did most everyone, black or white. Only *living* things she'd seen him study were his boys or his grandbabies, that was about all aside from the horizon, the tide, oaks and yaupons in the yard to see if the wind was shifting, the lit end of those cigars he loved.

"Woodrow?"

"Right here," said Woodrow. If he was looking at either of them he was looking at Boyd, who was switching his head back and forth between Maggie and Woodrow as if previously separate parts of his life—work and lust—had just come together and he was caught off guard.

"Boyd needs a place to stay."

She did not look at Boyd. She didn't have to; she could feel his embarrassment.

"Do he?"

"On his own. I was thinking your summer kitchen," she said, gesturing toward the one-room, many-windowed outbuilding. A few years ago, before Crawl took off for Morehead, Woodrow had built Sarah a kitchen on the back of the house so she wouldn't have to traipse in and out of the weather. Then he'd fixed up the summer kitchen for Crawl and his off-island wife, Vanessa, to stay in, but Vanessa didn't last out the winter before she dragged Crawl back across the sound to Morehead. Since then it had sat empty and so far as Maggie knew it was the only empty structure on the island.

"What's Boyd thinking?"

"Boyd ain't," said Boyd, finding his voice and finding it creaky and low. "Obviously somebody's doing Boyd's thinking for him."

Woodrow smiled slightly, then nodded at the summer kitchen. "Screens is all busted up."

"We can mend them."

Woodrow looked briefly in her direction, and she thought she saw an eyebrow raised at her "we." Later she would get to know Woodrow's every twitch, his every syllabic emphasis; she'd learn to read him, which was as hard as learning to read Braille, for it called on a different sensory approach than she'd ever known before.

"Best soak them in kerosene when you get them patched," he said, seemingly to his hogs.

"How come?" asked Boyd.

"Keep the bugs away," said Maggie rotely, as if this trick was obvious to the world, not just their island where the bugs could make life miserable to outsiders especially.

"He have to share the outhouse with me and Sarah," said Woodrow.

That's no problem, she nearly said, but she caught herself this time. She'd best be careful, speaking for him, calling his shots, presuming to know what was and was not a problem for him. She knew that, left on his own, Boyd would have kept right on staying with his aunt, Virginia Balsom, who already had begun to spread talk about Maggie "corrupting" her nephew. Ginny was a vengeful cow who, soon as she heard what those spy-boys had to report, was liable to try and poison Boyd against her by dragging up every wrong thing she'd done in her lifetime. The times she got a little tight and went off with some ill-chosen man. There had been a few of those times over the years. Things got away with her sometimes when she drank. After a few drinks this overwhelming feeling of license, of entitlement, would begin its tug. Look how you live, the liquor would whisper, all shut up on this island, cut off from most everything that makes life worth the uphill trudge. Said every sip: You deserve whatever pleasure you can piece together tonight. The booze would strike cells in the pit of her stomach and keep on surging southward and when it reached her loins it was like a waiter was there to take her order. Tonight's the night, whatever you want.

Only she never let it get further than some sloppy kisses, some old boy equally as looped rubbing his hand up her stomach. Whenever she went off with one of these men, the booze would at some point blot out the desire it had awakened. She opted for drunk over laid every time. Wasn't any high moral wrangling involved either. More like that buzzer went off in her stomach, *Hit me baby, time for another patch,* and she'd push away whatever worked-up male she'd dragged out to the dunes, set off to douse her fiery nerves.

Boyd said, "I got a place to stay."

Straining again, not wanting to step in, not wanting even more for him to ruin everything, she said, "When Crawl or any of them come for a visit he can stay back at his aunt's place."

Woodrow smiled his okay, much as she was going to get out of him, and before Boyd could speak, Maggie turned and led him through the house and outside, calling good-bye to Sarah who had made herself scarce in some hidden corner of their neatly kept cottage.

"What in the world was all that for?" Boyd asked.

They were nearing the creek, close to the footbridge Woodrow had helped her father and the other men of the village build years ago when a storm washed out the previous one. She dragged him off the path and led him into a bowed shelter carved out by stooped and gnarled yaupons. The mosquito buzz sounded mechanized, like an outboard cranked up high. He slapped at his ankles as she pulled him closer, kissed what she thought of as some sense into him.

"I want you every night," she said. "In a bed, not on some borrowed blanket in the dunes where those little brats are going to be every evening now, waiting on a show."

"Hell," he said, "that's fine, but everybody's going to know it still. I mean, me living back behind the only black on the island so I can bed down with my woman?"

"Lover," she said.

"Do what?"

"Say I'm your lover. Don't call me your woman. That sounds like some trashy song on the radio, talking about your wo-man."

"Okay, lover," he said, laughing. "You really think it's better, me living over there behind them?"

"If you have a problem living behind Woodrow and Sarah, I believe we've got problems doing what we're doing."

"I like Woodrow," he said. He looked confused for a minute, as if trying to decide what to say. "I don't know that he cares too much for me. He's never out-and-out rude or anything, but most of the time we're out on the water he looks right through me. Sometimes he even tells Crawl something to tell me. Like I don't speak English."

"Woodrow likes you fine," she said. "That's just the way Woodrow is."

"Talks to my shoes if he talks to any part of me."

"You'd do that to him if you were black and he were white."

"Hard to say. I've never been all that good at imagining anything other than what I got."

Maggie filed this comment away, and in the years since he'd been gone, she trotted it out often, found ways to use it to justify what happened between them. She often felt she was the opposite—capable of imagining anything but what she had.

Six weeks after Boyd arrived on the island, his uncle Skillet from down at Harker's Island towed over a twenty-one-foot skiff he'd bought cheap off a retired waterman from Atlantic. Probably he did not want his nephew crewing for a Negro anymore, Maggie said, suspicious of such an extravagant gift, but it was hard to harbor suspicion, Boyd was so proud of that boat. Woodrow helped him get it sea-ready—the boat had spent a season set up on sawhorses in some old boy's backyard—and Boyd promised to take Maggie out with him after he'd bought and set his pots, borrowed from Woodrow a purse seine, hocked half his belongings for setup gear. Maggie'd spent plenty time out on the water with her daddy and brothers, and it wasn't something she'd dreamed of repeating. It was hard work and even half days could turn tedious, but this was Boyd and the boy was beside himself and she did dearly love passion of any stripe, the more intense the better, and they would be alone, no one around to look askance at her and her emphasis-on-boy boyfriend and what better way to see the sun come up than the way they did those few mornings she went out with him which happened to be smack in the middle of a big moon that made the sea foam shimmer, turned the spray silver. They would trade sips from a thermos of coffee as black as the sea beneath them. She'd tuck her hands up his shirt, cup the muscles rippling his rib cage. He was too giddy and

proud-nervous to interrupt his fishing with a little sunrise loving, but being out there all alone, salt breeze batting them as they
turned for home, got them so hot they'd barely get the boat tied
up before they'd walk run back to the summer kitchen, fling their
cast-off clothes at the blinds, and tuck into each other, inside and
outside, all of them and the whole shut-tight dead-aired cottage
awash in sea-pricked passion.

Of all the things she could have done, going out with Boyd
those mornings was what drew her big sister's ire.

"You think I'm here to wait on you while you're out on the
water all day long? It's not for me to run this house. Last time I
checked, Daddy left it to both of us."

It was just past noon when she returned—plenty of time yet for
whatever chores needed doing, and she told her sister so.

"That's not the point. You're making a trashy fool out of yourself, and of me too in the process. Putting that boy up in Woodrow's summer kitchen, my God. You got people in Meherrituck
talking about the boy lives behind the colored couple, got himself
an old lady lover."

"Let 'em talk is how I feel about that."

"I know good and well how you feel about everything. You don't
give a damn about anything but feeling good at the moment."

"Don't start, Miss Whaley."

"Don't call me that. I have a first name."

"No one's allowed to call you by it."

"We're not discussing what they choose to call me. We're talking about what they're out there calling you."

Maggie said nothing. She was folding wash off the line and the sheets were stiff and sun-warmed, and she held the cotton to her cheek and missed her lover, who in her mind had merged with other things she desired: sun and saltwater and dusk and that feeling of finally having found someone you wanted to spend all your time with.

Though this last part, well—she got to where she didn't trust it. She wanted him to stay and yet she worried she could not keep him. She did not think he was liable to give up everything you want and even need when you're young—excitement, loud fast nights, traveling (even it was off Harker's Island up to Raleigh or Norfolk or down to Wilmington, hell, these were places she'd barely been herself), and most of all, maybe last of all, other women. Say he settled with her. She'd be his first real lover—the backseat girls, the upside-the-shed-girls didn't hardly count—and he'd nearly be marrying the first girl he went with. She knew that's how it happened lots of times, but she'd seen a lot of unhappiness in those couples who had to get their parents to sign for them in order to cross over to Morehead and get married.

It was herself too that she didn't trust. She had a history, and he did not understand nor want to *learn* to understand history. No one does when they're young. Whaley loved to talk about how her namesake was so well versed in Latin and Greek, could read old dead poets in French, knew by heart the names of the British royalty and all the stories from the Bible. Maybe that's where Whaley got her taste for all the ancient things she lived to tell the Tape Recorders. But Whaley wasn't ever young, really. Not that Maggie was ever so young as Boyd. When she was his age exactly, she was stringing around with a married man as much older than her as she was to Boyd. But there was enough youthful innocence left to remember what it felt like, having to deal with the fact that this man she fancied she loved had slept alongside a wife he swore he could not stomach the sight of (how incredible she found this notion, how oddly repellent, so much so that she would not let herself ponder it even though her mind wanted to go there, like the sight of some washed-ashore half-pecked-apart tern you can't *not* look at) and had children in a world that should have been slate clean for their own offspring. She knew that sooner or later, her history would get to Boyd.

And perhaps there was something of the island itself, the fact that every second it was being taken away by wind and water at the same time it was being added to, grain by grain. This place seemed to have something against the notion of forever. Everything felt so *borrowed;* it was hard not to be skeptical of anything lasting longer than a season. But she got around to this reason lastly and treated it lightly, preferring to blame herself over geography and nature.

It wasn't that she was a bad person; it was that there was something bad wrong with her. Sometimes she felt like the wind blew right through her. The strangest things made her cry— the yellow suds ebbing around some storm wrack, a dead snake, the first few bars of a song overheard from someone's window as she passed by at night—but let someone she'd known all her life swell up with a tumor and she paid it no more mind than a mosquito bite. Her sister was always calling her selfish, but that was too easy. She cared about other people so much that she wanted to see inside them, to think their same thoughts. She just did not care to sit for hours in their stuffy parlors, talking about couldn't that new preacher hear their stomachs growling, why were his sermons so long?

Boyd, by comparison, was noble and believed in people's goodness. He wasn't so good he was boring, but he was a fine thing in this world and she got quickly to where it seemed just wrong to think she could have him.

Doubt kept at her, a whining bug in her ear even when she tried not to consider it. Still, when they were lying in bed, or walking along the island in the after supper settling down of day, talking their playful, idle talk, everything went away. Then there was only the two of them, standing alone and indomitable in the slight spray from the surf.

One Sunday six months after Boyd arrived on the island, he announced he was taking his boat across to Morehead that weekend to attend his cousin's baby's christening. This was the first time he'd left the island and would be the longest they'd been apart.

"Your cousin's baby?" she said. A breeze batted the curtains she'd sewn for the summer kitchen, where they lay sweaty and entwined.

"Yep."

"Sounds kind of distant to me."

"Y'all don't have cousins who have babies over here?"

"I doubt I'd cross the creek to go to their christening if I did."

"You don't want me to go," he said.

"Go on across," she said in such a sulky voice that Boyd laughed.

"Why don't you come with me?"

"What, as your date?"

"Yes, as my date."

It was her turn to laugh at the thought of tagging along behind him through a gauntlet of family, like some schoolgirl he'd met in the parking lot of Dairy Queen.

"What's so funny?"

"I don't think your cousin's baby's christening would care to be upstaged by you showing up with the likes of me."

"Why, is there something wrong with you?"

He meant it as a joke, she knew, but how could she take it as such, knowing that there was something wrong with everyone, sure, it was what made people worth speaking to, but at that moment even more than usual there seemed something *bad* wrong with her. Her sister knew it. She treated her like she was fragile, always had. Only Woodrow treated her normal, though Woodrow, who knew what he was thinking? Maybe his treating her normal was just his way of making an exception for her foolishness. She'd turned away from Boyd at the mention of the christening, and his hand lay heavy across her rib cage, and the weight of it seemed so constricting that she blinked back tears of pain. Then she went silly to stop herself from crying.

"I'm a leopard," she said.

"You're a *who*?" Boyd said, his last word wavy with laughter.

"Leopard. I escaped from a leopard colony."

This got away with him enough to derail the subject of her going across with him, but not for long. All week long he kept after her. All week, at his side or alone, she worried about his leaving, and was visited by dreams, waking or in fitful sleep, of a ghost she thought she'd long ago shed.

Growing up, she and Whaley had spent hours playing a game they called Dare, a version of hide-and-go-seek based in historical fact, island lore, myth, and the endless fascination they had for stories featuring female adventurers. After horrid fights erupted over who would get to play Virginia Dare herself—Whaley always claimed her right because she knew the history better, or "the Truth" as she called it (notwithstanding the fact that the story of Virginia Dare and her lost colony was considered America's longest-running mystery), while Maggie's claim seemed irrefutable in its simplicity: she was better at *being* Virginia, she could scamper up dunes barefoot to search the horizon for her grandfather's ships come to rescue them, she wasn't afraid of the forest like her sister, she would gladly get dirty and wet and brave bug

bite and even jellyfish sting—their mother intervened, demand-
ing they take turns.

The difference in the way Maggie and Whaley understood the
world was exemplified not only in how they played Virginia but in
what they felt the story was *about*. Whaley's version was pitched
to people like the Tape Recorders who were all about some stuff
happened four hundred years before they were born. So proud
even at that age, so convinced of her superior mind, so free from
doubt and resistant to the possibility that life was lived mostly
in the vague border between right and wrong, certain that the
island they happened to have been born on was the only place
on the globe for her to live, Whaley's Virginia was always up in
someone's face (well, Maggie's face, seeing as how she was the
only other one playing the game), lecturing about how she was
the first white girl born in the United States of America and her
grandfather John White was the true father of this country and
to heck with Jamestown and as for the Pilgrims, walking around
the woods with buckles on their shoes, they dressed like a nun
if you asked her and invented the most good-for-nothing laziest
holiday ever where all you do is sit around and eat, what a waste of
time. This was just the start of all Whaley's Virginia had to allow.
Whaley's colony never got around to ever getting lost, because
see, she didn't believe they ever did get lost. She believed the ones
who came back for them didn't look all that hard. She believed
she was blood kin to Virginia Dare, that there was not one drop
of anything but white blood in her either, all that hogwash about

the colonists fleeing the island on account of storms and going across and mixing with Indians, that made no sense, who would ever leave the island? Just because of some wind? Maybe a little storm surge?

The world according to Whaley, unchanged in the decades since they had last played Dare: why in the world would anyone see the world differently than she did?

Maggie's Virginia was not big on words. Her Dare played outdoors. Hours spent lying in the sand, digging in the tidepools for sand fiddlers, wandering the low wind-stunted forests. If at first Virginia loved her life by the ocean, enjoyed pining away for the return of her grandfather and the rest of her colony, the longer they stayed away, the less she missed them. Her fellow colonists began to seem timid to her. She had been born here; she was different. They struck her as too easily pleased. This New World was to her a humongous loaf of bread, hers for the feasting, yet the rest of them were content to nibble like mice on the crust she would just as soon tear away and leave on her plate like a ravished bone. She wanted off island.

She began slipping into the forest. Just feet away from their stockade the scrub dropped away and wide paths appeared, spacious meadows with sluggish, murmuring creeks, moss-dripping cypresses, deep shadows pierced with soft yellow light. Daily she wandered with no particular destination. Friendly Indians took her in, taught her things: how to dam a creek with branches, chase fish into a pool where they could be easily speared. They gave her corn to plant, and beans and squash and pumpkins. They loaned her a hoe made from the vertebra of a bear. They taught her to grate nutmeg with a conch shell, how to track deer through the woods to find salt licks. She came to know polecat and muskrat, learned to spot a moccasin dripping from live oak amid a tress of Spanish moss. Rattlers are more poisonous on the hottest days, her new friends taught her; the severed tail of an alligator will wiggle right on for hours.

Virginia came dragging Maggie off island with her all hours of the day during that week before Boyd went across. So distracted was she by Virginia's bold and exotic adventures she felt some part of her was already in motion, as if she had spent the day out on the water and was feeling still the pitch and roll. But the part of her that wanted to leave behind everything was fearful of the place people never come back from. If she said as much to Boyd, he would say, I came back across, but he'd only been born over here, not raised, he'd not known it long enough to become it. Woodrow had gone across too and come back, Boyd might claim, but there again he would be right in fact and wrong in Truth, for Woodrow Thornton hadn't ever left this island even when he was up at Bayside welding for the Coast Guard those two years during some world war, even when Sarah had him staying with some of her people up in Norfolk one winter. Maggie knew what slant of light Woodrow saw against his lid when he blinked his eyes, she knew it was sea breeze he breathed. Much time as he'd spent out on the water, Woodrow's heart had never once left the island.

Instead of explaining it all to Boyd—how could he understand a grown woman giving herself over to waking dreams of a girl weeding a garden with a bear's backbone—she just pouted. The grown-up part of her understood he'd be back over in three days time; smothering him, she knew, was going to backfire big-time. But there was Virginia coaxing her into ghostwoods, and the notion of all that land, all those people bunched up in knots all across it . . . Maggie shut down when she thought about it. Have a good time, she said, though not in a way either of them knew her to mean.

She watched his boat slide out across the inlet, which was glassy and greenish that day, slick as it gets, and without even going home, or back to the summer kitchen, she made her way to Harvey Lockerman's house and bought a pint of that white liquor he made every winter. Boyd's the one who left. He might have said he wanted her to come along, but once she got over there and people started talking their nasty gossip, he'd wished he'd left her back over on that island.

Several men were crowded into Harvey's root cellar, passing pints and smoking and smelling like the catch of the day. She paid her money and took her pint and went back to the summer kitchen and opened all the windows and sipped the white, which smelled of yeast but tasted of turpentine. By the third stout patch she sloshed into her jelly glass, a curious molecular reorganization took place in her heart, rendering all her flaws and mistakes noble and altruistic and all the misery she felt the fault of Boyd for leaving, her sister for treating her like a slattern, the island for being stuck hours out in the ocean.

Another drink and she was blaming her great-great-grandfather who sired a family here on the island and kept secret his other family across the ocean. And her own daddy, who got rich off a shipment of whiskey that washed up on Sheep Island during Prohibition and spent the rest of his days drunk off what he did not sell. She liked to think—she *enjoyed* thinking—that what Whaley called her sorry streak came directly from this side of the family, with their ruddy Irish coloring and their love of singing even though not one of them had ever been known to read a note.

Wherever it came from, it had needed to be got out of her system. She could get it out by herself, but it would go a lot quicker if she had some company. She went back up the road to Lockerman's. The party had moved from the root cellar to the backyard. Harvey's wife and his wife's sister had joined the men but were sipping instead of slashing, and when Maggie came striding up the lawn, her steps deliberate and counted out so as not to let on how drunk she was already, the women traded glances Maggie could decipher even through her fog. When she took a seat, they slipped off inside the house.

It was late afternoon before it was even lunchtime and then it was dusk and the mosquitoes blew up from the marsh and had at her bare arms until she was nearly welted. A boy she knew from school, a Railey who had moved off island but was over visiting

Harvey, told her he had something inside the house would help soothe those bites.

She knew what that something was but followed him inside anyway, filed right past the women who were listening to the radio in the kitchen and stopped talking to stare her out as she stumbled on the threshhold.

She pushed him away after he'd kissed her down to the floor of the front porch. She said, "I'm hungry, I'm going home." Of course he followed her halfway up to the house, trying to talk her into some more of his bug-bite remedies. She treated him like she treated the bugs who maybe because of the liquor were on her like they'd never been before, swarming her, bleeding her leechlike.

Whaley was off somewhere, thank God. Maggie went to the kitchen and started making some oatmeal, about the only thing she could find that did not require a lot of knifing. She was slurping it up at the kitchen table when Whaley came in from the store. She could tell from the way Whaley did not look at her that she knew at least some of it.

Whaley made a noisy fuss of putting up groceries. Then she leaned against the counter, her arms tightly crossed, and said, "Least you waited till your boy was off island."

"He drinks himself, so what?"

"I'm not talking about the drinking, though God knows you ought to leave it alone too."

Maggie decided to ignore the "too." "When was the last time you saw me drunk?"

"I don't keep count of your actions, but if you want credit for acting like you ought to act, you'll not get it from me."

"That's a simple way of seeing it," said Maggie. "And a god-damn self-righteous way too."

Whaley said, "You know I'm right."

Maggie said, "Oh do I. You always are."

Whaley unfolded her arms, wet a rag, and swiped furiously at the countertop. "I don't have to listen to this mess."

"Did it ever occur to you that some people don't feel the same things you do? You think something awful's got to happen for somebody to feel sad. Somebody's got to die, or lose a child, or there's got to be a fire or a flood. Even then you don't hardly let somebody grieve before you claim they're wallowing. Well, guess what? It don't work like that. Some people can't control how they feel. They just feel bad for no reason and they deal with it best they can and it would be mighty Christian of you to show some support."

Whaley squeezed the rag until water ran down her arm.

"All I do is support you. While you screw some boy in plain daylight for all the children on the island to watch and run up and down telling everyone how they saw the two of you going at it in the dunes. I support you while you run off and get drunk and throw yourself all over Barry Railey, who's got a wife and three young'uns up in Suffolk . . ."

"Who said I threw myself at him? Mary Alice told you I threw myself at him?"

"Don't even go denying it. Mary Alice told me the whole story not a half hour ago."

"I don't have to listen to your mess either," said Maggie. She rose from the table, carried her bowl of oatmeal to the sink, sloshed water in it so wildly that a stream from the pump ricocheted off the basin and sprayed over her shoulder, onto the floor. Whaley was upside her, grabbing the bowl, *gimme that, you're not even fit to wash a dish,* and Maggie was all over her sister then, slapping at her with wild loping swings, pushing her back upside the counter, both of them crying, Maggie's hair streaming wet with tears and sweat and then she was outside, running down to the creek to Woodrow's. Sarah was sitting on the porch listening to her gospel songs on the radio, Maggie could hear the sleek, sexy guitar chords chugging along underneath the swelling chorus praising God in heaven.

In the summer kitchen she lay down across the bed she shared with Boyd and said his name. She wanted him with her and she prayed a sobbing prayer to God: *Please bring him back to me I won't ever run out on him I will be faithful and good to him and forgive me for what I did to my sister who I know loves me in some long-dry place in her heart. If you just bring him back, please God don't let him leave me.*

He came back late that night to find her passed out in her clothes, the screen door carelessly ajar and the summer kitchen aswarm with mosquitoes. He lit a fire in the trash burner Woodrow had installed for Crawl and his bride and pulled down the storm boards on all the windows and lit one of the El Reeso Sweets he'd brought back for Woodrow. He stripped to his shorts and sat sweating and blowing smoke defensively around the room. He let her sleep. When she woke she was thirsty and her skin was ravaged by bites.

He was lying beside her smoking.

"Hey baby," he said.

She rolled right over on top of him and was out of her dress in seconds. Later, lying parched and eaten up with mosquito bites and remorse alongside him as he smoked, she wanted him to ask her to go across with him, so she could say yes, for she would have then, and she would have made him leave that very evening, before she could feel better and change her mind. But he didn't ask. He seemed removed, distant, in a way she'd never seen him before. As if a part of him, his heart—the important part—had remained off island.

"I'm sorry," she said. "I messed up."

"What happened?"

She sighed. "Can we open some of the windows now?"

He got up and busied himself with the storm boards but did so reluctantly, as if cooping them up in the sticky heat with the mosquitoes she'd let in was part of her punishment.

"You don't want to tell me," he said from across the room.

She was holding a sock she'd dipped in water to her head and breathing hot and fast.

"I just don't like it when you're gone," she said. "I'm sorry."

"Quit saying that. I know you're sorry. I can tell by looking at you that you wish you hadn't done it. Thing is, what did you do?"

She reached for the water he'd brought in, drained the glass, stared defiantly at the emptiness as if willing it to refill.

"Had a little too much to drink," she said.

"I can see that."

"Slapped the hell out of my sister."

"Well," he said, "isn't that something you'd do stone sober?"

"Think about it all the time."

"I used to beat up and get beat up by my brothers every other day."

"Stops usually when you get into your twenties, though, doesn't it?"

They had a sad laugh over this. In the wake of the laughter she considered telling him about Barry Railey. Chances were he'd hear it, for if Mary Alice went and told Whaley down at the store, everyone had heard it by now. On the other hand, maybe he wouldn't hear of it, and would it not be better this time if he didn't know? Wasn't it hard enough for him to come back to find her smelly and pathetic?

"I've got to get up at the crack," he said. "We better get to bed."

The next morning, after getting up with Boyd to accompany him down to his boat — hugging on him so long and hard he had to gently pry her fingers off his shoulders—she was struck with terror that everything seemed about to crumble. What she wanted more than anything was for him to reassure her that things were going to be okay. Boyd seemed both unnerved and flattered by her neediness. He was willing to nurse her back to normalcy, but she could tell he found the whole process unpleasant.

When she got to the house Whaley was sitting on the porch with her coffee. She would not look at Maggie when Maggie took a seat beside her.

"I'm sorry, okay?"

"Okay what?"

Maggie had no answer for this, though she understood the question.

"I would tell you what happened with Barry Railey if I thought you wanted to hear it."

"Spare me," said Whaley.

"All right. I'll spare you, but what you're getting spared is the truth."

Whaley looked at her full-on for the first time that day. "You need a bath, Mag."

For the next week or so, Maggie was tentative and shy around both Whaley and Boyd. She spent hours weeding the garden and cooked dinner for Boyd every noon when he came in off the water, more to take her mind off things than at attempt to redress her wrongs, for Whaley'd just as soon let it go than speak of it again, though she'd never forget—Maggie knew her sins were tallied in that place where her sister kept score, a book of pages filled to the margins with black slants—nor, heaven forbid, forgive. She just had better things to do than listen to Maggie's mess. What else was there to say about it in Whaley's view but I'm right and you're wrong?

With her sister she knew where she stood. Boyd kept her guessing. Had she been asked, say by little Liz, who was known to ask her such, whether she liked a little mystery in a man, she'd surely have said, Oh hell yes, sign me up for the deep end, the more I knew them the more I need to be wanting to know about them, and it would have been true, for she'd never been with a man whose head and heart she didn't have figured out in a flat week, not to mention other parts of their body it took less than a day to understand. Now, though, with Boyd—it felt like he was pulling away from her a little each day, not so dramatically that she could see it in his eyes or hear it in his voice or God forbid feel it in his touch but detectable still in a way that got away with her terribly just because it was so slight, like the way the island itself was drifting every day a little bit southward, though to stand on her porch or, she'd heard, to fly over it in an airplane, it looked the same as it always had, ever since she could remember, ever since Whaley used to take her by the hand and lead her down the lane to see their aunt Mandy, who would let them dress her cats up in rags she swore belonged to the famous daughter of the vice president of the United States of America. And the island looked the same as it did when the vice president's daughter set foot on it, and yet it was a different island, or rather it was in a different place.

That was how it was with Boyd. He was the same but in a slightly different place. Wind in the night had picked up and moved tiny parts of him, the equivalent of sand grains, atoms, molecules, droplets of water they claim humans are mostly made of.

Maggie stood looking at him one afternoon as they mended nets in Woodrow's backyard. He had his shirt off and she was admiring the ropey muscles that had strung up across his back and shoulders since he'd been out on the water. Well, that's good, she thought. At least there's more of him for the wind to take away. Might take a while longer than it would have when his rangy self first set foot on the dock.

"I know all about that time with Barry Railey," he said.

She was stretching the net out, standing across the yard from him; there was some wind that day, and at first she thought the wind had picked up his words and twisted and mixed them, for he remained bent to his task until she did not respond. He looked up at her quickly, saw something in her eyes, dropped his own eyes to the net.

"Whaley told you?"

"Don't matter who. Matters who didn't."

"What you heard is a lie."

"Really?" He put down his end of the net, lit a cigarette, picked up his work again.

"I didn't throw myself at him if that's what you heard."

"But you went off with him?"

"I was with him, yes. And I let him kiss me before I came to my senses and stopped him."

"What made you come to your senses, Mag?"

Maggie looked across the island toward the ocean. More than anything she wanted her bask, the water on her shoulders, liquid heat and sea foam frothing around her.

"You're the one ran off to do God knows what across the sound. I don't like it when you're gone. It doesn't feel right over here."

"I went to my cousin's baby's christening, Mag. I was gone three days. I asked you to go with me. Asked you more than once. I'm going to ask you again to come across with me, for good, but I'm not going to keep asking you over and over. We could never *be* over here. It just won't work. You won't let it. You're scared of your sister. You don't want anything to change. I have to stay in some black man's outbuilding. You get to come across the creek when you want, and then you cross over and who knows why you act like you do over here, but you do, Mag. As long as we stay over here, you're going to keep getting in the way of us."

The woods Virginia led her through were a damn lie, Maggie thought, like the forests she'd seen in kids books, the pictures alongside the teaching sentences. Where was the brush and scrub so thick you had to hack at it with a machete to clear a path? In Virginia's forest the trees were high and far apart and friendly animals frolicked in deep blue shadow that flickered with sunlight through leaf canopy, and raccoons were sweet-eyed and never rabid, and snakes never hid beneath rocks but basked atop them like the tourists came to Meherrituck to burn their skin lying half-naked on the beach. This is the way Boyd would paint it over there too. A fat lie to get her across. What would keep her contained in Morehead or little Washington or wherever else over there he wanted them to settle? Even the islands had bridges to the mainland and all that coming and going, all those roads and intersections. He was dead wrong: she could never be what he needed her to be over there. She could never stay still.

"No *place* is going to keep people who love each other from loving each other."

"You know this how?"

"Beg your pardon?"

"I'm just asking," said Boyd, "how you happen to come by that particular bit of wisdom."

"You want me to have done everything in order to know it? Some things you just know. You don't have to have experienced them."

She was lecturing him. In her tone she heard something that terrified her: her big sister's sanctimony.

"Well, if you love me, you can love me just as good across the water."

"What about your family? I thought you came across to be where your father was raised?"

"True enough. But then I fell in love. I might would stay if it weren't for you. But we just cannot *be* over here. You won't allow it."

"So you're leaving?" She turned away from him, dried her eyes on her T-shirt.

"I don't know," he said. "No."

"I don't know either," she said, and then she felt it burn through her, the spite, the very thing that led her down to buy white liquor in some old boy's root cellar the moment he pushed off the dock that day.

"Seems like if you're going to leave me, well, seems like it'd hurt a lot worse then than now."

"So you want me to go?"

"I don't. But I feel like everybody's against us. Everything and everybody."

"You," he said, dropping his end of the net in the grass.

"What?"

"You seem like the worst enemy we got."

He got up and went inside, and she stood waiting for him to return—thought maybe he'd gone in for his shirt to protect against the gathering bugs, or had gone in to fetch himself something to drink—but he didn't come back and she did not go to him. Instead she went home and slept alone, thinking he needed to be without her in order to understand how much he missed her.

She let him be for the next few days. It wasn't easy, but she coddled the guilt he made her feel by calling her their worst enemy, and she spent her hours having conversations with him in her head, constructing arguments to prove wrong his notion that everything would be fine if only she'd come across with him. If at first it bothered her that her primary example of why leaving would be the end of them was well over four hundred years old, in time she came to see Virginia's story as important to their own as Genesis in the Bible. It came first, and everything after was a continuation. Think what would have happened had Virginia just stayed put on this island where she had everything she needed. Greed's what led her to go across, and greed and vanity and pride is what killed her and the rest of them too. Talk about an original sin. Think about those Tape Recorders coming across wanting to know what it is to live here on this island, and Whaley spouting her history of ancestors and recipes and ways to ward off bugs when the truth was that me and you, Boyd, maybe we aren't even real people struggling with how to love but just another installment in a story started when some girl got restless and tired of the people she'd grown up with and lit out for afar. And look what happened to her. Boyd. Look what happened to all of them.

By the time she crossed the creek to knock on the door of the summer kitchen the conversation had gotten so huge and convoluted she didn't think she could bear its weight anymore. Might as well get it out there, in the air.

It had been three days without a word. She'd stayed close to home, avoiding her sister, who for once seemed to sense her sadness enough to give her wide berth.

No one home. Coming up the lane she ran into Woodrow.

"You seen Boyd?"

"He across over to Morehead."

"Oh yeah," she said, pretending to know all about it. "How long's he going to be gone now?"

Woodrow looked at her full-on, then past her to the bridge his great-great-great-grandfather, master builder, had built over the creek. He seemed to study it awhile, as if trying to figure out how it had withstood the years of storm surge and wind when half the houses on this island were storm wrack across the sound. At least Maggie decided he was pondering such, as it was far more palatable than thinking he knew exactly what was going on with this pathetic old white woman been left by her younger lover.

"I believe he said he'd be back today or tomorrow, one."

"Thanks, Woodrow," she said, chipper as all get-out, though she wasn't two steps away from him when she bit her bottom lip to keep it from quivering.

He did not come back that night, which was understandable as the sound was choppy that evening and he was too green on the water still to risk much in the way of weather. But the next day the sound was flat glass and he did not show up the next day either, nor the next. By the fourth day without word, she was despondent. She went down to the store and bought herself a pack of cigarettes and let herself in the summer kitchen and sat in an old rocker of Woodrow's and smoked. She didn't eat. She barely went to the bathroom. Once someone came and knocked on the door—Woodrow or Sarah—but she didn't dare open it, as the only person she wanted to see would not need to knock.

She was still waiting, noon of the sixth day, when her sister got the key from Woodrow and blew into the room.

"Carrying on like this ain't going to bring him back."

"How would you know? What do you know about love?"

Whaley came and kneeled beside her. She reached out to run her fingers through Maggie's wild, wind-tossed hair, but Maggie pulled away.

"Surely you didn't think he'd stay."

"Because I'm an old hag, right? That's why you think he left me?"

"Well, think about it. Surely the boy wants young'uns, Mag. You're not about to do him much good there."

"I can have a child if I want to. It might kill me, but I'd be willing to try."

Whaley turned away. Maggie thought she was crying. It took a few seconds to identify the soft sniffling as muffled laughter.

"Get out," she said.

"I'm sorry, Mag. It's just, you're not seeing straight."

"You're the expert. You've got so much experience in these matters, I don't know why I didn't come to you first."

Whaley sighed and got up to leave. At the door she said, "He's down at the dock, by the way."

Maggie waited until her sister was gone. She tidied up the summer kitchen and washed up a bit and even made a point of stopping by to talk to Sarah, who was watering her garden and regarded Maggie with a little less suspicion and disdain than usual, as if Maggie's obvious desperation (she was sure the entire island knew of her self-imposed solitary confinement, the reasons behind it) softened her a little.

Boyd was washing his boat. She stood ashore, watching, waiting for the men hanging around the dock to notice her presence. One of them caught sight of her and said something under breath, and all of their heads turned at once, and then his pals filed past her and he was alone in the backlit dusk, time of day she always allowed to the two of them, soft settling bask before the mosquitoes emerged from the marsh and took over the night.

Already they were biting, but she never felt them. Why was this day her hardest on earth? She had lost her mother early on to cancer, her father to a slow ghastly alcoholic decline; her brother had drowned in the inlet when she and Whaley, ten and thirteen, were supposed to be looking after him. She'd had a husband beat her with a hairbrush and tie her hands to the clawfeet of a bathtub, spread jelly on her, and leave her caked and naked, baking the day long in the July heat, yet she'd never felt so low as she had while waiting for Boyd these last few days.

"Where've you been?"

He looked past her, up toward the village, which was dim and hazy now in the settling night. The water in the inlet was growing slick and black. She felt he was about to slip under its sheen and she reached out to hold him and he met her embrace but turned his face when she went to kiss him, offering his cheek.

"I got me a place over in Morehead. Down in the Promise Land. Near my sister Bonnie and them. Guess I'm going to fish out of Morehead for a while."

She would not look at him. She thought of Whaley, of the way she'd said, "Did you really think he'd stay?" as if the whole island knew the moment she mixed herself up with this boy how it would end. This did not feel like any end, though; it felt like the beginning of some new and hardly tolerable state of being in which air was precious and hard fought for and she cursed a girl dead four centuries who should have just stayed put.

"You guess," she said. It came out something between a croak and a whisper. "What do you mean, you guess?"

When he did not reply she looked up from the shallows and said, "There's not much guessing involved in going across and renting a goddamn house."

"Okay," he said, his voice weary and yet slightly fearful too. "I'm going to fish out of Morehead."

"For a while," she said. "Before you said, for a while."

"Maggie," he said, and touched her elbow in a way that made her feel like she was being steered, led along, like she'd stepped out of line.

She shook him loose and said, "Maybe we had more talking to do?"

"You coming with me?"

She looked at the sun dropping toward the water and thought, if I could just see across from here, if it was possible to stand on the dock over there and see the steeple, or smoke from Whaley's chimney, or the ghost forest down southside.

"Is this about Barry Railey? Because what you heard . . ."

"I don't care what you did when you were drunk one day. I care what this place does to you, how it makes you feel."

"You're telling me how I feel now?"

"You never answered my question yet. Are you coming with me?"

"Is this your idea of a discussion? You repeating the same question?"

"It's down to yes or no," he said. "I told you I wasn't going to keep asking. I'm leaving this coming Saturday."

If she never answered his question, if she kept it hanging in the air, would Saturday come?

"Well?" Boyd said.

He did not understand what he was asking her to do. How could she explain it to him? How could anyone tell somebody else what it was to *be* over here? Her sister preferred to warrant her loneliness by laying it all on men, their fickle nature, their love of what's between legs, their laziness and general dishonesty, but Maggie knew that Whaley too did not so much choose her lot as submit to the wind, not whatever it blew her way, but the fact that it was going to blow. That was the only fact Dr. Levinson and them need record.

"You just don't know," she said. "Don't understand."

"I know I love you more than I love any spit of sand and sea oat. I know you don't love this place so much as you need it to make you feel miserable right on."

"There you go again, telling somebody what they're feeling."

"I'm thinking what I'm hearing here is not a yes or a maybe," he said, and he went back to swabbing the stern of his boat with a rag.

This was a Wednesday. She thought she'd see him one last time, and on Saturday she sliced some cucumbers and soaked them in vinegar and hot chili pepper like he liked them and sliced some cold chicken and some of Whaley's thick bread. She iced some coffee and made a cherry pie. Whaley watched her cook all day. Late, in the waning light, she came upstairs and knocked on the door to Maggie's room.

"Might as well eat it if you're not going to take it down there to him."

Maggie didn't say anything. She lay with her back to the door, facing the sloping wall of the dormered room.

"You're not hungry, Mag?"

She'd lost weight, maybe a little more than was good for her. She'd always been proud of her hips, never minded nor complained about the spread of her thighs. Now she felt bone when she sat, felt the drained-away flesh like a phantom finger lost in an accident.

"Been picking all day," she lied.

Whaley made a noise in her throat, as if she did not believe her but did not have the energy to argue with her lies.

"Just tell me when he's gone off island," Maggie said to the wall.

"You can't lie in bed for another whole day."

"On second thought, don't tell me," she said. "I'll know."

Her sister made another one of her disapproving sound effects. When she lightly shut the door, Maggie considered how this exchange qualified as nearly tender. Surely it would be the most sympathy she could expect from her sister, who she knew to be biting her tongue.

She kept it mostly bit for the next few months. A winter of near constant squalls. The clothes dried inside, hung and hampered everywhere—the backs of chairs, the stair railing. Maggie went around in a ratty old white T-shirt Boyd had left at the summer kitchen. The shirt smelled of him still, or maybe she willed it to; she wore it to sleep in and she wore it to garden in and she wore it even to church, and in the cold winter winds she went without a bra and wore it upside her skin so that he was the one next to her body, Boyd, she felt him on her all the while.

Her loneliness was of the low-grade don't-ever-leave-even-when-you're-sleeping variety. She moved like a night crab around the island, jerky and nervous among the people she'd grown up with, skittish, intolerant of the kind of small talk that she'd once been so good at.

Whaley said: Find God. Maggie ignored her, but she tried. She prayed, and her prayers stretched out desperate and needy for longer and longer increments until they linked verbs at noon, the entire day one single waking prayer. She wanted to feel what she'd been promised, which was deliverance from the pain of longing. But she did not feel a thing except tired of carrying around a one-sided conversation in her head all day long, and when she complained to Whaley, her sister told her she was a fool and selfish to expect results from God. She was seeking atonement, deliverance, her sister told her. This would not do. You have to put yourself in God's hands, ask to be an instrument of his will.

She felt worse for having tried and failed to find, through God, through prayer, a way out of her misery. Some of the dumbest people she knew were smart enough to get religion. Her failure to understand how God could help her out of her pain made her feel twice as inadequate as before, when she'd gone around having an imaginary conversation with Boyd all day long instead of her heavenly maker.

She went back to talking to Boyd all day long. She'd walk down island where the wind had leveled the dunes to a crisply rippled flat. There the wind blew so loud she could yell hard at him and not be heard by a tern pecking oats alongside her.

Sometimes she would leave off talking to him and just dream. It kept her going, this elaborate day-or-night dream—she entertained it whenever, would will it no matter the sun or moon—of Boyd appearing again on the island. She'd look up from whatever in this dream occupied her—mending a fishing net (a chore she associated always with him) or weeding the sandy tomato patch out behind the summer kitchen, something, whichever, and there he'd be. Out of nowhere having showed up on this island he'd fled because she would never leave it. He'd not say the things people say in this fantasy Maggie was smart enough to know she shared with every sick-hearted sucker ever pined after someone who left them. Nothing obvious like I'm back, or You were right I could not live without you, or Let's begin anew my darling. Nor would he say something smart-ass flirty like You missed a weed, toeing an anthill with a brogan, grinning his shy crooked smile. In her dream he said nothing because there wasn't anything to say.

She tried to say nothing about him to other people. She knew that restoring her dignity (what little of it she could restore on this island where everyone stored in their head, along with the middle names of their children and the fifty states and their capitals, every time she'd ended up kissing someone not communally recognized as hers for the kissing) depended upon pretending he—they—never happened. She tried to never speak his name aloud.

Sometimes, going along, she'd nearly double over with shame. For she'd withstood life on this island that drove grown men, war veterans, sobbing for their mamas. She'd spent a night lying in six inches of cold water while the wind plucked a steeple from the church where half the village was riding out a nor'easter. She'd seen a boy she loved in grade school—little Tommy Bellamy, not but eight—brought in from the surf with both his legs chewed to bone below the knee, strings of pearly muscle trailing down from this thighs, his eyes crazy eternally open from the shock of one minute swimming along in the shallows with his buddies and the next dragged into a bloodred whirlpool by a rogue great white. She'd seen drownings, people she'd known all her life, hauled in accordion-bloated. Her own kin stretched out in the sand, blown up by a wind could care less what it delivered.

To be laid low by his leaving—sometimes, walking along, the very idea of it would get away with her so bad she'd nearly buckle. Never speaking his name to any soul (least not her sister) would at least keep them from knowing how scarred she was. But there was one person with whom she allowed herself the risk of talking about Boyd. Well, not talking *about*. Woodrow, being Woodrow, word-stingy, unreadable, never said much. But he listened. She felt okay talking to him about it because he felt things himself he'd never share with anyone on this island, even his Sarah. And because her sister would disown her if she knew she was telling her private deepest business to a colored man, however hard-working and indispensable he was to them on the island even back then.

"You ever see Boyd over in Morehead?" Maggie asked Woodrow one day. Her face ablaze in the asking, like she'd been out in the sun all day long of a cloudless August dog day. Woodrow was scrubbing bait slime from his boat. She knew he'd been over to Morehead to see Crawl, knew he'd carried Sarah over there and left her. Crawl's wife was about to deliver a grandbaby, Sarah had been packed up and counting the days for weeks. Later, when it was only the three of them left on the island, Maggie wondered if Sarah being off island that day she went down to the dock to talk to Woodrow, to speak her long gone lover's name aloud, was what allowed her the courage, the freedom, to ask Woodrow if he'd seen Boyd. Later, she'd wonder: Is this why Sarah had to die? So she could indulge herself on a subject she'd have been far better off to leave alone?

Woodrow said, more to himself than to her, "Seen him the other day."

She waited for more, though she knew that was all. She asked a question, he supplied an answer. She got used to it over the years, mostly because she had to—there were only three of them left on the island, finally, and here's how it is with three: two against one. She spent many the year feeling closer to Woodrow than she did her own sister. She wanted to know his insides, wanted to know what he felt about things. How he got through the days in that head of his, poling his skiff out to meet the mail boat, fishing for their supper, smoking his cigars, listening to Whaley read out her prices, what was he *thinking*? She'd never got so worked up about what was in a man's head. Tell the truth, she didn't care to hear what was in most of them's heads. She'd been with quite a few who couldn't tell her, not because they didn't want to or didn't know how—likely scenarios both—but because there won't nothing up there but blood and cotton balls.

"Where?" she asked.

He went on with his hosing down.

"He fish off Shackleford sometime."

Maggie felt her face stretching, hard red brick. One little bit of information and she felt as vibrantly alive as those first few weeks they spent together.

"Will you carry me across?" she said.

Woodrow came closer to a stare than she ever remembered.

"I need to see him."

"Lay eyes on him? Or *see* him see him?"

Another first: he'd never asked her questions so personal and, for him, direct. She knew exactly what he meant by *see* him see him. She knew Woodrow was remembering the noises coming out of his summer kitchen back when she used to meet Boyd there after the boats came in. She knew what he did not want any part of.

She said, "Lay eyes. Just talk."

Woodrow was back to what Whaley thought of as cigar store Indian Woodrow. But she knew he was thinking, processing, feeling. She wondered was he thinking, old Maggie can't take not having her way. Still, something told her that Woodrow was on her side. He might not have suffered in the same way she had (and he might even agree with Whaley that ninety percent of Maggie's suffering was of her own stubborn making), but she trusted him finally to understand her need to just lay eyes on him, talk to him.

What she wanted most of all was for Boyd to look inside her head like it was one of those ant farms a teacher brought onto the island once and see, as if through smudgy glass, her thoughts tunneling around each other. They every one had his name on them.

And he would know, just by looking at her, just by the sight of her climbing onto the dock, that he was right: they could not *be* on the island, and she could not be there without him.

"Will you take me, Woodrow?"

"What you gone tell Whaley?" he asked after the time it took him to light a cigar stub in a little wind.

She knew then that he'd do it, but only if she could come up with some reason to satisfy her sister. Woodrow sold Whaley fish, he odd-jobbed around the house, he had dealings with her that, fickle and ornery and hateful as she could be, she'd just as soon take and transfer to someone else, though it'd be pure spite to do so, for she knew good and well that Woodrow dealt as honestly as anyone up and down the banks.

"Female trouble," said Maggie.

"Doctor comes to Meherrituck, you know that, every third Tuesday."

"Can't wait," she said, clutching at her stomach.

Woodrow shook his head at her lie.

"What?" she said.

"She's a woman too. How you think you can fool her with that?"

"She'd near about rather hear me talk about Boyd than go on about my private parts."

Woodrow said, "Me and her both."

Maggie laughed a little, encouraged by his smart mouth.

"So?"

"I got to go back over there to get Sarah next week."

She felt her breath go shallow. "Woodrow, I mean, I'm asking a favor I know, but Sarah, she . . ."

"Sarah won't say nothing to you about nothing you do."

"I'm not worried about her saying anything."

Woodrow waited for her to tell him what she was worried about, which made it harder for her to do so.

"She doesn't much care for me, I know."

"Sarah cares for everybody the same," he said. "Except her family. She takes care of her babies. They come first to her, them and God."

"I just worry that, you know, she'll think . . ."

"Whatever she thinks, you won't hear about it. She ain't gone say nothing to you, Miss Maggie."

"I swear I wish you'd call me Maggie."

"I swear I wish a lot of things," said Woodrow.

Maggie wished a lot of things herself. This she had in common with Woodrow but not her sister, who was all the time saying she did not wish for what the Lord had not yet provided. One thing Maggie knew Whaley wished for, though, was for her little sister to act right, which was to say, act like *she* did. Well, no matter how hard she tried, this island was not going to let Maggie act right to suit her sister.

It was a risk, going across. Maggie thought of Virginia, safe one day at her home here on the banks, the next thing anybody knew the lot of them, all her kith and kin, lost and presumed dead. Not unlike Maggie's great-great-great-grandmother, her ship boarded out from Diamond Shoals by thieves, everyone aboard murdered but her. Because she was not right in the head, they spared her life? One not-right-in-the-head woman gets herself and her whole colony lost, another gets saved. Well, Maggie couldn't sit around studying the fates of the dead for clues to what she would do. All she'd be able to come up with was a contradiction, and she'd die bitter and alone trying to decide which story to trust.

When Whaley was up at the post office Maggie packed a bag and hid it behind the shed, an ancient cardboard suitcase with leather flaking off the handle and gathered pockets along the sides for God knows what, she had never seen anyone use the thing, since she had a working memory it had sat up under the gable in the attic. Rainy days she and Whaley had filled it with baby clothes and wash cloths and paraded around the attic as if disembarking from the train. What wayfarer had brought it there and why had he left it behind? Surely it belonged to no kin of hers.

The pockets she filled with sharks' teeth and sand dollars. Between her two good dresses and her Boyd's T-shirt she layered pictures of all her brothers and sisters taken at a backyard oyster roast when her father was still living, a picture of the house itself, all spruced up with sod on the lawn and flowers in the window boxes, another of the village taken from the front steps of the church just before the Ash Wednesday storm of '62. She had to slip these out of picture frames, which left empty glass for Whaley to find, so she hid them in the sea trunk in the spare bedroom and prayed her sister did not notice before she left. Toting the suitcase out to the shed, she cringed at its contents: pictures and shells, some underwear, a certificate she'd received for four years' perfect attendance Grades 3 through 7. Things a child would take when running away from home.

She'd have told Whaley if she thought Whaley would find some way to react other than hateful. Female trouble? Her sister wouldn't have pried. It was true that, as she said to Woodrow, Whaley'd nearly rather hear her go on about Boyd than to have to listen to her get gritty-specific about her insides. But she didn't want to even *not hear* her sister respond. Whaley would know she was lying and yet she'd not call out her lie and this was every bit as bad as her pitching a fit. Hell, it would be worse. Maggie didn't want to hear it, she figured why should I put up with anything from Whaley, it's my life, my time, not like I'm punching a clock for her.

She knew she was damned either way: tell her and suffer her silent indignation, don't and pay big later on. She chose down-the-road but it was just piling on another layer of anxious.

She sat up front. Woodrow smoked his cigar. Thirty minutes into the two-hour crossing the sound churned up and the boat slapped at the chop. She wore her daddy's old oiler over a not-quite-Sunday dress. It kept her dry, but inside the heavy rubber slicker she was boiling in the humid summer morning.

She didn't even try talking to Woodrow in the boat. But she didn't need to talk to him. Agreeing to carry her across could only mean he approved of what she was up to. This is what she told herself anyway. He wanted her to be with Boyd, Woodrow cared for her, and for Boyd—she'd been knowing that, despite Boyd's all the time claiming Woodrow hated him, treated him like some dumb green white boy. Boyd didn't know Woodrow like she did.

Woodrow would have said no to Boyd right off had he not cared
for him, despite the fact that it was a little harder for Woodrow
to go around turning down requests from white folks wanting to
learn how to fish. Woodrow would have found a way or would
have shamed him so bad out on the water—dumped him over
in a turn or had the poor boy pulling his back out wrenching up
pots the wrong way—that Boyd would have quit on Woodrow.
Woodrow was surely one of the best watermen on the banks, but
he wasn't the only one. Boyd could have found another tutor and
Woodrow could have sent him off to find one.

Obviously he wanted them to be together. Maggie decided he
liked having them back of his house in the summer kitchen. Up in
the bow, taking the spray head-on, Maggie smiled at the thought
of the summer kitchen once again housing rambunctious love.
Out of her head and up into who knows where went the knowledge gained during her time on this earth. Crossing the sound
she was ageless, whatever age you were when you were about to
regain love lost to you. No numbers affixed to it. No words for it
either. Just fine spray, a fountain of it, and sun on her cheeks, one
of those little windows in time when she felt so slackly warmly
comfortable in her body that it hardly existed.

Never damn mind that when Woodrow motored up the waterway to where he docked, she was wet, salt-crusty, smelly. Never
mind Crawl, there to meet him, shocked if not outright scornful
at the sight of her. Never mind she had no real plan for finding
Boyd, didn't know where he lived, didn't even know if seeing him

was better than somehow being seen by someone who knew who she was and would pass along news of her triumphant crossing.

Crawl helped his daddy tie up the boat. Didn't no more than nod at her, then Woodrow joined him on the dock, and they were walking away when she called out, "Wait once."

Crawl kept right on walking. But Woodrow stopped and turned back.

"Y'all know where the Promise Land's at?"

Crawl pointed the way. Ten blocks of small shingled cottages back of Arondell Street, hard by the railroad tracks. Some of the cottages were brought over on barges from Diamond City when the villagers fled Shackleford Banks, leaving it a ghost town after a bad hurricane at the turn of the century. The natives dispersed into the mainland, a colony lost. Signs of their former life—upturned dinghys, crab pots, gill nets—clogging their sandy cocklespurred yards. Looked to her like a banker didn't know what to do with grass. Four out of five had just let their grass die or raked over it, one. She read this as a sign they missed home. All of them pining to return, knocked back across the sound by storms, hunger, poverty, only to end up on this patch of crabgrass and cocklespur.

No, Maggie told herself, she was seeing the mainland through Whaley's eyes. Whaley with her fear of anywhere off island would sharpen her words and slash away at this place until there was nothing left of it but stubble.

Early afternoon and she saw no one out in the white-hot sun. The men were at work on road crews or at the canneries. The women, she figured, were cleaning house or cooking or tending to the children. She was starving. She'd borrowed a few dollars—well, ten—from the jar where Whaley kept the cash she saved. On a corner stood a grill, filling the neighborhood with the smoke of fried meat.

Inside a line of men sat at the counter drinking sweaty cans of beer, not their first, judging from slump of the shoulders. Most of them swiveled slightly on their creaky stools as if they needed to feel the sway of water beneath them even on land. She hesitated in the doorway, her arm about out of her shoulder socket from lugging her suitcase through the streets, the huge floor fan pushing her hair, dress, smell of sweat and salt right back outside.

The men studied her with hard red faces until, because she failed to blink, they turned away. Maggie wasn't used to not knowing soul one. She remembered the last time she'd been off island for any significant length of time—years ago, she was in her late twenties, already ancient to be unmarried, a spinster. She'd traveled with a girl she'd grown up with, Cleo Austin, to Elizabeth City to visit Cleo's cousins, who lived in a three-storied seemed like to Maggie mansion overlooking an arm of the Pasquotank River. They stayed a week. Days they'd wander in and out of the stores, looking at dresses and toys and cookware and even farm implements and tools in the mercantile and feed stores, and every night they attended dances in a bandstand by the river or went to church or strolled up and down the esplanade. She'd met a boy who wanted to marry her—he'd claimed so the third time she'd danced with him—but he was red-haired and scrawny and his last name was Sheep and his first name was Myron and he was her age and lived right on with his mama and unmarried sister and even though she could not claim any more independence, she knew from looking at the way he hitched his pants well up over his hips and the fat tortured knot of his tie that she'd be marrying his mother and sister and that they would find her (and she them) intolerably lazy and dull.

A buck-toothed boy wearing a dirty apron and a pencil stub behind his big ear was in front of her with his little pad. It had been years since she'd been in a restaurant. She had nearly forgotten how it worked.

She nodded at the man on the stool next to her.

"What he's having, I guess," she said.

The boy blinked and slid his nervous eyes to her neighbor's plate, then looked at her with his open, pimply face.

"Looks good enough to eat," she added.

"Cheeseburger steak," he nearly yelled, printing it out slowly in big blocks across his pad. He was gone, the swinging kitchen doors batting up a breeze as she forgot to tell him, Bring me some sweet tea.

Five minutes later a replica of the plate next door arrived in the boy's shaky hands. She made him nervous, plainly. He'd gone away and bent down beneath the counter but was back with a sweat-beading bottle of beer.

"I didn't order that," she said.

The boy shrugged a bony shoulder at the man next to her.

"What he's having. That's what you said."

"I meant food."

He stared, dejected, at the beer. "But it's done been opened."

Maggie sighed. "I reckon between the two of us we can find someone to drink it."

"Yeah, but he'll make me pay for it out of my wages and—"

"I'll pay for it, shug. Bring me some sweet tea."

He shot off without a word. The steak was so tough and taste-less she smothered her plate in ketchup. Chewing, Maggie felt her eyes watering, her throat closing. What in the world was she do-ing across over here, eating a hamburger steak like she had a clue? The horror she felt then was crippling, a seizing so much worse than nausea or backache, for such things passed but this futil-ity stretched itself thinly out across time continuous, it remained in her blood like something handed her by God, a part of her, unshakeable, nothing to do but muddle through it. Only a few things had she found would make it fade. One was a bask in her sun-warmed surf. Another was leaving off whatever she was doing and going down to the docks to see if she could find Woodrow, for Woodrow, even when he was in his most removed of moods, taught her some things. It wasn't what she naively used to call his quiet dignity, for Woodrow was not perfect, he had his faults, blind spots, resentments, hurts. No, it wasn't his strong silence but something more complicated she had no name for.

Woodrow was with his family now. She wasn't about to go

snooping around Colored Town asking directions to Crawl's, where Sarah would treat her like a stray cat.

Everything caught up with her then: the sneaking away, the useless suitcase, the sun reflecting off the water, hot salty wind. Sweat streaked down her sides, dampening her dress. Her throat was rusted shut. Where was that boy with her sweet tea? She felt the men staring, heard the stools creek as they swiveled her way.

One sip of beer to tide her over until her tea came. She curled her hand around the bottle, shocked by its iciness against the oppressive air of the diner.

And then it was the next afternoon, and Maggie held her head in her hands, staring at a fish hook floating balefully in an inch of water in the bottom of the boat, which rocked wildly, setting off a lurch in her stomach, as Woodrow helped Sarah onto the seat beside her. Maggie could not lift her head. Snippets of the last twenty-four hours arrived out of sequence and truncated by thunderous pain in her forehead, lobe, stomach, pride, what little dignity she'd ever had. Sarah, scrunched tight on the seat beside her, felt towering and rigid compared to Maggie's doleful slump. Somewhere in the middle of the sound, out of sight of both mainland and island she both dreaded and longed for, she would collapse from shame into Sarah's lap. Sarah would hold her shoulders, stroke her dirty white-lady hair. Would not say a word. Would let her cry and babble and even drool onto her skirt while the piecemeal images took slow root in a murky sequence.

Beers appearing on the salt-strewn counter before her, half-

eaten and abandoned cheeseburger steak pushed away and heaped
with cigarette butts from the smokers who'd pushed in close to
engage her in wild trash talk, then, when she declared loudly after
four or five bottles of sweaty beer what she would not do to get her
hands on some sweet homemade wine, invited her over to some
old boy's body shop where he had him a little something set up.
Sweet as mother's milk was this wine of his. She remembered sort
of thinking as she gathered her father's oiler around her shoulders
and stumbled to the bathroom that this was it, dividing line; if
she went for the wine she would lose everything she'd worked for,
she'd never get him back, her life would be over. But then, she'd
never had a chance. Never even had a plan. Come across with a
trunk filled with seashells and photographs and eat hamburger
steak? The thought of it shamed her into leaving the grill, three
drunk fishermen in tow. When they arrived at the body shop,
home of sweet-as-mother's-milk wine, the day grew dimmer, the
memories disassociated. More men standing around wide doors
wheeled open to expose the bays where dented cars sat ignored.
Someone handed her a tumbler, the wine sweet as threatened.
Glen Campbell on the radio. He was a lineman for the county.
A crowd of men coming and going, Maggie the only girl and not
a girl, a grown woman too old to be laughing and grabbing cigarettes out the mouths of smelly fishermen in off the water on a
day grown too hot to fish. She'd let slip back at the grill that she
was over from the banks and nearly all the men had family somewhere up the chain or had fled the banks themselves, a whole lot

of Do you know I bet you know, though she did not bring herself to tell them she rarely got off her island except a few times a year to Meherrituck. She did not mention Boyd for the longest time. When she did, not one of the men claimed to know him. She thought this odd, given the fact that the Promise Land was filled with transplants from the banks and everyone knew everyone and there weren't but a dozen families over there anyway, someone was bound to know him, Y'all lying to me, she said as she began to suck the wine down like it was going to get her what she wanted, who she wanted, Y'all do too know Boyd, and someone asked her what he was to her and she smiled and said, Friend, slyly, and someone else said, What you doing getting friendly with a boy, try a grown damn man on for size and then there was some dancing and soon she found herself sandwiched between two men obviously eager to see her in the so-called office of the body shop which featured for furniture a sprung-cushioned seat torn from a bus, its Naugahyde ripped and patched with duct tape, the coiled springs visible between the worn cushion and uncomfortable as hell when they pushed her down atop it and began their zipper music which she drowned out with screams which they tried to silence by filling her mouth with their flesh.

She did what she had to do: used teeth to get out from under them. Remembering the taste of blood, metallic, sharp, she threw up over the side of the boat, Sarah holding her shoulders, stroking her hair as she heaved, offering her water when her stomach was way empty, when she had nothing left inside her except shame, fear, and worse, the memory of what happened next.

Tearing crazy drunk and disheveled through the streets of the Promise Land, screaming his name. Everywhere children and dogs. Her dress torn, her eye blackening, and a little blood staining her cheeks. Who knew where her suitcase was? She could not remember running from the body shop, how she managed to elude four drunk men, three or four more in the work bays; she could only surmise they let her go out of fear. She could imagine, later, that they had nothing at all to fear, for all they had to say, what they surely would have said had she managed to end up in the police station to press charges against instead of the opposite, *She wanted it, hell, she asked for it, she knew what the story was once we left out of the grill, she promised us all a slice,* on and on in the impudent imagery of men talking about sex, slices, pieces, pokes, lays, all their idiotic words for things they didn't understand.

And someone—a stunned mailman—told her where he lived. What he did not tell her was that he had moved in with his sister and her family. She found out quickly enough, knocking the door nearly down, crying out for her Boyd. The door slivered open and a woman holding a sleeping child, who favored Boyd in the set of the eyes and the slope of the nose, took one look at her face and shut and bolted the door. Which did not make Maggie go away as desired. Made her bang louder, call his name in a register so low and wild with want and need that it set dogs to howling, touched off a siren even. Which drew closer. Which stopped in the street in front of her.

At the police station she went slack. The wine began to wear off and she slipped into a near catatonic state. Soon and swift came the shame. There was one boy policeman who talked to her sweetly enough to get the name of Woodrow out of her, and then Crawl. He wrote it down on a sheet of paper and went away to confer with his higher-ups and in a few minutes came back to the cell where they said they were holding her for her protection (for when she told them what had happened at the body shop they went a little easier on her, treated her a bit differently than when she was simply drunk, disorderly, disrupting the peace of the Promise Land) and said to her, "Captain says this is some nigger."

"Captain ought to know there's another name for them."

"You sure now, ma'am?"

Maggie looked up at the boy. He seemed younger and very far away.

"Sure about another name?"

"Sure you wanting us to call this fellow?"

"Fellow is an improvement. He's a man. It's his daddy brung me over here, and if I know Crawl, it's his daddy will come and get me out of this goddamn oven."

"You need to be watching your language," said the boy policeman.

"Y'all need to be arresting those drunks that tried to kill me."

"Hey now," he said in a voice she assumed he felt was soothing. "No one tried to kill you."

"You were there?"

The boy looked at his sharply shined police-boy shoes. "I'll call this man if you sure you want me to."

"It's call him or stay here. I imagine we'd both prefer you call him."

For the couple hours it took Woodrow to arrive, she lay sweating and shaking on the bunk. She asked for water but no one tended to her. Shaking, retching, nearly dying of thirst, she realized that the moment she gave them Crawl's name they assumed she really did go down to the body shop with the idea of, as her escorts said as they held her down on the bus-seat sofa, fucking the lot of them six ways to Sunday, for what woman innocent of such charges would call a nigger to come pick her up out of jail?

She imagined they treated Woodrow even worse when he arrived. She knew they subjected him to all kinds of questions, treated him as if he were her pimp. She knew also, though not from anything he said for he said nothing to her about it, ever—she knew that the things they said to him got away with him, hurt him, deeply.

BACK ON THE ISLAND in the slow wretched weeks after her return, what got away with her the worst, what kept her eyes to the ground and her cheeks streaked with dampness, was not anger at the men who'd had their drunken way with her, or the thought of what Boyd felt when he came in off the water that day to hear from his sister about the crazy old woman liked to beat her door down calling his name. What she'd done to Woodrow— Sarah too—came in time to cause her mind to switch back and forth between two opposite notions: thereafter she would never venture farther from home than the post office (for it was easy to blame for the terror that seized her that day at the lunch counter *not* the way she had of thwarting over and again some slim shot at contentment, but instead the wider world, the vast and un-confined lie that had seduced so many before her starting with the first white child born on these shores) or, more terrifying but maybe more what she deserved, she needed to leave again, and this time for good.

Woodrow'd been sweet enough to carry her across. Sarah'd stroked her wet forehead as she heaved over the side of the boat. Now neither of them could quite raise their gaze higher than her waist when she encountered them on the lane. She could not bear this eye-avert for the rest of her life.

But instead of Maggie having to leave, everyone else left. What it came down to was the three of them sitting on the steps of the church trying to figure out what in the world's a blow-dryer. Sarah dead and gone, Crawl nearly given up on ever getting his daddy away from his white women. Even the Tape Recorders skipping a season now, Dr. Levinson too old to go without power and light for the three days or else sick of the mosquitoes, or maybe he was sick of hearing Whaley tell the same old stories. Maggie never thought she'd miss the Tape Recorders, but when they did not come that year she thought, Hell, now that everybody's gone and most of them dead, now that it was only the three of them left of this island, she might could tell the real story of her life.

But no one was interested in this story. Least not Whaley, who pieced it together from folks coming and going across the sound. Maggie sure didn't volunteer it, though in some ways she did not have to say a word. She'd disappeared for two days, Whaley knew Woodrow to be over in Morehead fetching Sarah, she knew Boyd lived over in the Promise Land, she wasn't so dumb at math that she couldn't add. She liked numbers, her prices, what things cost. Plus all she had to do was look at Maggie to know the whole sordid story.

Maggie went about trying to forget again, tried all the things she'd tried and failed before: prayer, work, endless hours in the after-supper surf. The village was overrun by ghosts. Sometimes Maggie would wander down to the schoolhouse and find her seat on the third row, sit and listen to teaching sentences until the room and finally the entire island filled with all those who'd fled after the storms came battering. Mostly, though, she just accepted the way things were now. Tourists came over now of a weekend, O'Malley Senior had started up a damn near business ferrying them round-trip from Blue Harbor. They brought cameras and took pictures of the two old white women too stubborn to leave and their colored protector. They asked questions, silly and maybe even a little mean, How y'all stand these mosquitoes, how come you stayed when everybody else fled this godforsaken place? The undertow of their curiosity seemed to Maggie judgmental if not contemptuous. She and Whaley and Woodrow were becoming a kind of freak show, one of those quaint stories about human resilience Maggie sometimes read aloud from the Norfolk paper. They smiled, waved, stood for the pictures, but underneath pasted smiles lurked the ways they got away with each other. Only three of them left on this island. Why could they not put it aside?

That lovely night on the steps of the church with Woodrow and Whaley, it came to her why. Had to do with the Tape Recorders, she decided. Which story to tell them, whose story told it best? Once, little Liz got Maggie started on the subject of men, love, what it was like living your whole life where the pickings were so slim that some took up with cousins and others—her sister being one—went without. Maggie was just about to tell it then, the real story of this island, the only one that mattered: that boy's beautifully muscled and sun-browned back as he lifted his pots onto the dock when he came in off the water, the afternoons in the summer kitchen, his pleading with her to leave her island and what happened when she sort of halfway tried.

She kept quiet, though, for her sister's sake. Whaley had her story. It had to do with weather, wind, water, quaint customs, recipes, yaupon tea. Mostly it had to with history, by which her sister meant their great-great-great-grandmother, Theodosia, daughter of a famous murderer. That was Whaley's idea of a story to tell.

She went right on and told it too. And Maggie stopped short of filling a tape with how bad she hurt over some boy years ago, even though sitting that night on the church steps, Maggie knew her story explained life on this island better than anything out of Whaley's mouth. God bless Whaley's soul. She had her own hurts, surely. She'd never put them down on tape, though. And if Maggie was to tell her side of it, it would by God last, would linger forever across time like the pink cloudy sky shrouding the rising sun of a morning, which is why she'd never tell it. To hell with it. It was already out there, whipping Whaley's newspaper, in the wind.

V

THEODOSIA BURR ALSTON
Yaupon Island, North Carolina

THE FIRST THING SHE saw when Whaley brought her home to the cottage he'd built while she was recuperating with a widow down island was the portrait. In a gesture Theo might have found mocking had she not owed him her life, he'd hung it dead center of the front room above the fireplace. It had been damaged in the crossing, its canvas torn in the high right corner, the colors bleeding and fading from exposure to the sun, its frame stained with her blood. Later, she would learn that he'd used the painting to shelter her from the sun, that she lay bleeding in the bottom of the leaking skiff, an inch of bloody water washing her wounds with salt, and anyone who might have come upon them hugging the sound-side shore of the banks, moving slowly southward, weaving in and out of the marshes, would have pondered the absurdity of this haggard boatman rowing his cargo of portrait.

She said, hobbling into the house, "I'd think you'd rather not have to stare at that countless times every day of your life."

"You would think?" He was busy stowing the items the island ladies had donated—old dresses, a bonnet, a tablecloth, rags, really, but she was glad to have them—into a lidless wobbly chest.

"Beg your pardon?"

"You said, I'd think. *Would* think. Never you mind the thinking about what goes where. It ain't much choice, is it, since we don't have nothing and got nowhere to put our nothing."

She knew by his grammar that she'd angered him. He knew she preferred he not speak to her as he would a barmaid.

She said, "I'm sorry, Whaley."

He said he knew she was sorry. He said in the way people say, "I know you're sorry," which makes you understand how pitiful you would be to them were they in the mind to pity you. He lit a fire, went out. She sat in the one crude chair he'd built and did not look at the portrait. Instead she studied her body. She'd spent hours since the moment she'd come to in the widow Royall's cottage observing the scars and bruises across her arms, legs, and neck, for they kept fresh the debt she owed Whaley. Another reminder was the throbbing in her bones when the sky turned dark and a storm whipped across the island, a new sensation since her injury. Lingering pain she accepted without question, for it was so vastly preferable to the things she'd wasted time worrying about in her other life. She remembered once at DeBordieu an afternoon of incessant worrying over whether Joseph's family might take offense if she did not come down to dinner that evening.

Now the weight of what she had done hung over everything. He'd hardly looked at her when fetching her from the widow Royall, who, like every other woman on the island who had come to take turns sitting with her and helping dress her wounds and attending selflessly and often brusquely to her condition, assumed they were married. "Yonder your husband comes," she'd said when she'd spotted Whaley making his way up the lane to her cottage. "He's a sturdy one," she'd added, hint of a smile so slight in her choice of the word "sturdy" that Theo did not know whether to appear appreciative or embarrassed.

So too did every exchange she'd had with Whaley that day seem fraught with ambiguity. She was relieved when he went out, but as soon as he was gone she wished for his return. He was gone all day. She set about stowing her few hand-me-downs in the single bedroom that appeared obviously lived in—his clothes on the floor, a blanket on the tick, a conch shell filled with whale oil and a stringy wick on the table—picked at a bit of supper from some salted mullet and biscuits he'd left for her by the fire and waited up for him in bed. But when he came in, well after dark, he stayed in the parlor.

She caught him undressed to the waist as he lay down on a pallet of rags by the fire.

"They think we're married," she said. "Every last one of them referred to me as Missus Whaley. So you might as well sleep in the bedroom. Alongside me. Because we're married and that's what married couples do."

She'd not planned on behaving so boldly, though she knew whatever she sacrificed would not come close to equaling what she owed him. That was one way, an obvious way, she might make amends. What surprised her was how she felt no shame, inviting this man to her bed. In the months she'd been away from him, he'd changed greatly. The Old Whaley nickname no longer fit, for he looked younger than she assumed he was, just shy of forty. His beard was graying but it was cropped, his hair had been trimmed, and the muscle he'd put on while building the cottage bunched across his back and shoulders.

She did not think, until after she made her offer, of her own body, of how distasteful she might appear to him. But what he said next pushed the thought out of her mind.

"I believe I know what married folk do. I've been married this past going on eighteen years."

"You're married?"

"Four children too, God willing they prosper still."

"But why did you not tell me before?"

"You never tried to be my wife before."

Now the shame arrived. She wanted to retreat to her bed, but she hurt too much to move. Sometimes her injuries burned wildly and anew, pain triggered by guilt over what she'd done— her vanity, her selfish prideful clinging to her past—and how it had dragged Whaley away from the life he'd managed to cobble together after whatever catastrophe he'd endured had deposited him on Nag's Head, left him to Daniels's charge. Even though she felt wrong asking—it really wasn't any of her concern, despite the fact that their new community thought them married— she wanted more than ever to know everything about him. She wanted to know the names of his children, their ages, who they favored. But she could see by the way he stood that they would not be talking about such things.

She said instead: "Why are we stopping here, Whaley? We're only a couple islands south of him. I know because I made the widow Royall point it out on a map. Less than a half day's sail in a good wind. It's unsafe, stopping here. Why did you not just leave me here and keep on to the mainland?"

"Because I don't fancy spending the rest of my life running. And because I damn near let you die already."

"You saved my life."

"After I turned that mongrel loose and watched a good half of the blood in your body stain the sand."

"I don't blame you for that. I put your life in great peril. And all for my father's papers."

"I don't care to hear what it was you were hoping to find in his quarters. We've other things to think about now."

"You think he's looking for us?"

"I think he'll never stop."

He'd moved into the light. Theo understood, looking at his

body in the half-flickering light, that she was right—there were limits to love, and his had been reached that day. Yet he'd stayed here, waiting for her to recover from her wounds.

"I'm sorry to hear you're married."

He looked at her strangely. "It's not something ought to make you feel sorry for a person, generally. Besides, you're married yourself."

"I think it unlikely that I am going to reunite with my husband," she said. And she stood there waiting for him to make the same claim about his wife.

Instead, he said good night. For the next few weeks he worked in the yard building simultaneously a shed and a boat. He admitted he knew little about boatbuilding and so he hired himself out as an apprentice to the best boatbuilder on the island, learning what he could, bartering time for scrap lumber, borrowing tools to work on his boat by firelight. Theo spent the days fishing in the sound for supper, digging for clams, planting a garden, helping out island women with their chores in exchange for items she and Whaley had no means to procure. They could not have survived without the help of the islanders who never once questioned her arrival on this island so near death, never once asked how she happened to get attacked by a dog, or other obvious questions: where she came from, who she was running from.

Theo was amazed by Whaley's pluck, the way he went about hammering together a new life on a new island. His ability to land anywhere and make do—she had never known that in a man. Her father certainly liked to think of himself as resilient, but there was something in her father's ego that would turn any attempt at a comeback into an unqualified failure. *Had* turned: she thought of his Mexican Empire scheme. As for Joseph, he was the governor, but had anything happened to him, had they taken away his money and his land and his houses and his slaves, he'd starve within a week. He knew nothing of how hard it was just to live. Of course, neither did she until she mistook a lamp tied to a horse's head for a ship's beacon.

Whaley kept to himself. He was gone when she rose in the morning and often not home when she went to bed. He finished his boat and took it out on the water in the mornings, and in the afternoons he dug clams or cut cedar to sell as posts across over to Morehead. She grew gradually stronger and able to work in the garden of an afternoon, though she still limped even with her cane and felt sometimes, in public, the unflinching attention of island children, which made her feel disfigured. Aside from the women who sometimes stopped in to check on her she had no one to talk to save the cow Whaley procured from God knows where, she never asked. She named her Nora, after one of Joseph's sisters. To Nora she told stories of Richmond Hill. The night she alone entertained Chief William Brant Thayendanega, Mohawk leader of the Six Indian Nations. Nora seemed to have a passion for Horace, whose odes, recited while Theo milked her, had a curiously calming effect. Curious in part because they were so badly mangled. All she had to occupy her hours were memories and yet a fog was blowing in off the sea, overtaking the priceless past she'd kept so vigilantly alive. Each day she lost a little more of herself.

One night she woke from sleep in a panic. A presence in the room. She felt it before she heard breathing. A dream in which she understood she was dreaming but could not manage to force herself awake. Her head on the pillow as heavy as an anvil. Her mangled appendages useless by her side. Daniels had come for her. He'd already dispensed with Whaley, all stealth and silent steel, a knife across the throat as Whaley slumbered in the front room, beneath that portrait Daniels had come to retrieve. She tried to form some words, not of supplication but an offering, Take me now, take the portrait too, though whatever propensities you have allowed it are patently false, it has no power and it never spoke to me, it was all a misguided act to fool you into thinking I was worth saving, it is only paint and a battered frame, technically amateurish and not even a very good likeness.

Then Whaley said, "I need you to wake up."

The bones in her neck creaked as she raised her head from the tick. In a bluish light from the moon she saw him leaning against the wall, a blanket wrapped around his shoulders.

"I have something to tell you now," he said.

She swallowed and nodded, her relief that he was alive mixed now with trepidation, for whatever he had to tell her was middle-of-the-night weighty.

"I've not been honest," he said.

She waited. Her own breathing, shallow and ragged, drowned out his, though, anxious as she was, she knew there wasn't anything he could tell her about himself that would make her not care for him. Had he been hired by Jefferson to assassinate her father she would have come in time to his side of it. Yet the fact that there was something to make him cower, render him so dejected, bothered her, for it meant he wasn't perhaps as inviolable as she'd thought him.

"Ten, eleven years ago, I was in the West Indies with a crew out of Hull. We were ambushing supply ships running to the islands, Spanish galleons mostly. Daniels was down there too. He claimed to be the grandson of Teach. Blackbeard, they also call him. The math is off by a good half century, but when you get to know the man, you believe that part of his story more, for if Teach was as black of heart as he was of beard, Lord God the blackness at the core of Daniels.

"We'd put in at a place named Cortez's Cay. Laying out for a fleet of French ships headed for Martinique. I was second mate by title, but the captain, my mother's brother Clarence, was a day and night fall-down drunkard, so it was me mostly captaining that ship. We'd dropped anchor in a cove and set up camp awaiting the fleet to arrive. Second night on the island one of the crew caught something trying to steal our food. They brought him into the tent I shared with my uncle and the equally besotted first mate. He won't nothing but sunburnt leather and bone. Wild-haired, blackbearded like his so-called granddaddy. Uncle Clarence tried to get him talking, but he just spat and swore until Clarence ordered his skinny arse hung and his dirty black throat cut."

"What was he doing on that island?"

"Daniels isn't one to explain a lot about his past."

"You two have that in common then."

What annoyed her most was not what he had left out—she hadn't exactly told him everything about herself either—but what he had led her to believe: that he too was touched, if not by God then by Daniels, God of these banks.

"We have more in common than I care to admit."

She could feel the heat of his shame, how bright it still burned.

"I figure he got chased there and somehow survived, or else—and this is more likely—the bastard ran afoul of whoever took him on as crew, got tossed overboard, or left behind to die. Myself, I was a thief, I had no problem killing an entire crew in order to get my hands on a few hundred dragoons. But kill a man because he was hungry? I couldn't stand for it.

"My uncle was a drunk and a middling sailor. Daniels knew the islands. He'd been asea since he was ten years old, pirating to hear him tell it for nearly that long. That and his famous granddaddy's only thing I ever heard him tell about his past. Long as we kept Clarence full of liquor, he'd never even notice Daniels was still around."

"You came back here with him?"

"He knew he'd of died that night or starved to death on that island had I not saved his hide. I never meant to spend the brunt of my life in the company of Daniels. I never meant to abandon my family for these pitiful dunes. But I guess at a certain point— around the time I run into Daniels—I had already started to realize I couldn't very well go back and pretend to be these young'un's daddy again. Or that woman's husband. Not after all I'd done.

"By the time we got back up here it'd been somehow decided: he'd set me up with my own boat. He claimed to have three ships at his ready. Turned out he had a barely seaworthy one and a half. He didn't lie about one thing, though—he said he'd take care of me for saving his life, and that he did."

"So what happened between you then?"

"We made a lot of money together, for one thing. I had a house in his compound, a couple of women I called wives—weren't no more than girls, really. Eventually Daniels did set me up with my own ship. What it come to was, you know how they say you can choose your own death? I never believed it. I'm not much when it comes to fearing any God, but I do believe when it's time to go you're gone. You don't get to sit around deciding which door to take. Only it seemed to me, all that time on a ship with my uncle, watching him drink himself to death, he was going to die drunk sure as he'd lived every day of his life past the age of ten with liquor sloshing in his belly. And he didn't have to die like that. He could of chose not to. Name your poison, they tell you. Well, you can also name the medicine to take that'll cure you."

She nodded sympathetically but still had to stifle a smirk. Was he suggesting that, since he stopped thieving, he would be allowed to die a not-thief? It did not seem her place to point out the ridiculousness of his point, yet when she looked up, his eyes were on her and he seemed to read her thoughts.

"You're wondering how it is I think I can live with all the wrong I done? I guess most men like me think they're going to go down accountable for it no matter, no sense in fighting what has turned out to be your nature. I could easily accept that what I did those years with Daniels is my true nature. Or I could start doing some good or at least quit doing evil."

That his admission, his sincere desire to change his life for the better would turn her stomach was nearly as distressing to her as the notion that she was only a part of his atonement. It was not love; it was rehabilitation. The old Old Whaley would have unleashed the dog and let him devour her; the newly reformed Whaley would stand above until she was maimed, then pull the dog off in order to right his wrongs. Not love but something akin to business, a transaction rendered on a payment long overdue.

"You've not told me what happened between you two."

"I stopped robbing ships. I left my house in the compound, left those girls I called wives. I told Daniels he could take my share of it, told him I was tired. He thought it was God behind it all. I believe he fears any god could lay claim on you—or that picture of you—but not a god I could turn to in order to deliver me from my thieving ways. That God he's got nothing but hate for."

"And he left you alone?"

"So long's I stayed to myself, on his island. He said he'd see to it I'd never starve, but I told him I didn't want his help. Said I'd make do somehow. Fine, he said, only one thing: if you try to leave the island I'll kill you."

"But you saved his life," she said.

"And I stopped doing evil and he hated me for it. He could tolerate watching me turn myself into the village hermit, but returning to my family, going back to the life I'd left—he could not allow that."

"You give the man a great deal of credit," said Theo, "by assuming that your reformation would make him feel guilty about his own immorality."

"That's a generous way to look on it," said Whaley. "I suppose it's not that complicated. He's superstitious, what it is. All I know is, only way he could cut me loose was to turn me into a island eccentric, tell his people to steer clear of me, let me alone, ignore me. That way he could keep on controlling me but give me the illusion of freedom."

"Well, you're free of him now," she said.

"I'll never be free of him."

Whaley rose from the corner of the room, struggled up out of his dejected slump, as if telling his story had made him feel only worse. She wanted him beside her and she said so, but he left the room without any sign he'd heard her.

They lived together as man and woman sharing shelter and some meals, going their separate ways each morning and keeping separate counsel, revealing only those parts of themselves that pertained to the business of survival: firewood, seed for the garden, could he maybe find her some tallow for new candles? In their stolid exchanges, Theo imagined at least the beginnings of an intimacy between them, something shared, the two of them against the wind and tide, inviolable elements that made life on this island a daily and vigilant calculation. She wished for more. Joseph was a blur to her now. Since they had arrived here on Yaupon, that life was even more murky. Even her son, Aaron, whose death had seemed so insurmountable, was only a vestige of grief. She could not even remember his voice. Even, finally, her father. There was no washed-ashore bottle stuffed with parchment lined with his loopy scrawl arranging a rescue. Should some party arrive to retrieve her, her scars would have rendered her unrecognizable. If not the scars, her limp, the blotchy complexion of her neck where the widow Royall had sewn the skin back crudely. Her once regal posture, weakened by years now of constant wind. Like the tree the island was named for, she bent to survive.

At least she no longer resembled the woman in the portrait. Not that she ever looked above the hearth, though her little cottage, built for the two of them, grew as grand to her as Richmond Hill, as adored. She did not like to stray far from it. One day after supper she was down island cutting palmetto fronds for a new broom. Climbing a dune she came upon Whaley washing himself in the surf. She'd not seen him since breakfast. His back was lit by the last brilliant glow of the sun. What compelled her to stop and stare was not governed by thought. All those years in her youth spent in assiduous study, her father training her to be the smartest woman in America. No Latin came into her head to guide her, no quotes from posthumous philosophers. Sturdy Whaley in the sun-glistening surf; he was her husband and she was his wife.

That night she lay awake in the bedroom, restless under a thin nightgown, muscles taut, skin nearly feverish. Every drop of blood in her body pooling below her waist. She closed her eyes, she opened her eyes, same image preventing her from sleep: Whaley's sunlit back, surf breaking over his shoulders. Every time she decided to throw back the blanket and go to him, the thought that he might be repulsed by her scarred body kept her imprisoned in the bed. In time she heard his sleep-breathing, light snores, the pallet rustling as he shifted. She would just sit by him and watch him sleep. The fire was down to ember. Maybe she would just lie alongside him for a minute. He smelled of woodsmoke and faintly of saltwater. One minute she was watching light from the dying fire tint his skin and the next she was kissing his neck and saying how sorry she was to have taken advantage of his kindness and put his life in peril.

"Hush," he said, pulling her closer, searching out bare skin beneath her night clothes. And she smiled. Her father had not raised her to smile at a man commanding her not to speak. Fleetingly she thought, my father is dead now, and then she did not think of him again that night, and she thought of him less and less during the years that followed.

Phillip came first. He came out screaming and huge, with Whaley's blue eyes and his father's distrust of stillness. Dear God, you were only the slightest part of my moral education, I scarcely know how to appeal to your eternal mercy, but please let this child live. Never again will I waste time craving peaches. She promised to treasure these people who took her in half-dead, hard women to whom she owed her life. About their lives she knew nothing at all, for they were not warm or convivial, did not waste time with gossip or empty ceremony, yet in their brusque way they were the kindest people she'd known, for they helped each other out without prejudice or condition. After Phillip was born, they had her up in a couple of days, canning, helping to mend Whaley's nets. He needs your help now, they said, and she was waiting for him nights when he came in off the water.

A year later there was a girl, Amanda Jane, and finally another boy: she named him Alexander, after her father's nemesis, as if to ward off the weight of the past, though she did not admit such to Whaley. He was good to the children, though he spent so much of his time away, fishing, working on his boats, or hiring himself out to others. As the children grew older she had more time to devote to others, and she worked hard to become one of those women she'd admired when she'd first arrived, silent and bent to the task at hand, pleasant enough but also stoic, held back. So convinced was Theo that this was the way one ought to live life, that she became zealous about her new direction. She was the first to arrive at the house of an islander in need, the last to leave.

"You'd be best to spend more time at home," Whaley said to her one day. "The children need you."

"They get on fine."

"I need you then," he said.

"For what?"

He looked at her funny. She'd surprised herself, saying this, but now that it was said she thought she might as well pursue it.

"Why do you need me, Whaley? What do you need me for?"

He looked at her sideways, slyly, reminding her of those mornings she first spent in his hovel, when they delighted in their shared status, wards of the State of Daniels.

"Nothing in particular. Everything you do around here, somebody else could do. Chores and all. But what I need you for ain't particular."

"You're not making any sense."

"Dammit, I can't put it into any sense. I can't say how, exactly. I just know I do. You want me to make something up or you want me to leave words out of it?"

She'd never had a man admit to feeling something for her he could not articulate. She'd never had a man admit to needing her, though surely men had; Joseph needed her to be the daughter of a famous man, the wife of a governor. Her father needed her to make him feel as if he wasn't a total failure. She'd confused these needs with devotion, and only Whaley, in his fumbling but sincere way, could make her understand how she could be needed for nothing at all, and everything.

Thereafter she spent more time with her Whaley and her children. Only the portrait remained from her life off island. For years she'd avoided the sight of it, though she knew it was there, silted with grime and dirt, dimmed by smoke from the poorly drafting chimney. I found it in the dunes after a nor'easter, she told her children. But Mother it looks like you it's your eyes your nose, they said when they were still young enough to say unchecked what came into their heads. Before she gave up trying to educate them about the ways of a world she had come to renounce and turned them into a team of proggers. Fan out and scour. Don't come home empty-handed. Silly babies, of course that is not me.

It was only an innocent question, the child had every right to ask it, the resemblance was still there even if Theo did not feel as if she even inhabited the same body as the woman above the hearth, though for weeks afterward she felt a niggling guilt. She'd meant to discuss with Whaley what to tell the children about her past, and his, but there were fish to catch and clean, a garden to tend to, old ornery Nora to retrieve from the marsh and milk of a morning. Had she ever managed five minutes free of pressing chore or needy child to discuss such a thing, Whaley was not good at discussing such. After all, she'd known the man over a year before he had spoken of his wife and children.

Some old island salt who claimed to have once walked across the inlet during a hard freeze said in her presence that the island stayed put but was always leaving. Every grain of sand underfoot different from the ground his father stood upon. And what of her? Her humors were the same, but the molecules that made up her scarred body were nearly all new. Why bring up the past? She understood, stinging from the innocent query of a child, that the portrait would only haunt her household. She'd taught her children not to put stock in tales of ghosts and haints their friends loved to tell in the dunes at night, passed down from their parents and beyond, some of them set in the fens and moors of another windswept island. Why hang a portrait of a ghost above the hearth?

But before she could put her mind to the task of disposing of the portrait—for it was not so simple a task as throwing it in the inlet, too much blood had been shed for it to be discarded among the dunes—her energy was taken up with the living.

The day that Whaley brought home Hezekiah Thornton was hot and windless. Theo remembered the conditions always as they seemed summoned by the vitriol of the words that passed between them. It was the worst fight they ever had, and the last one.

Hezekiah was dark, thin, and slightly stooped. He stood in the yard with his hands clasped in front of him as if he'd been towed to the house with a rope.

"This is Hezekiah," said Whaley. "He'll be helping us out with some chores."

Hezekiah half-nodded when Theo glanced his way. He would not look Theo in the eye. They stood sweating in the merciless midmorning heat. Whaley brushed past her, disappeared inside the house.

"Where do you come from, Hezekiah?"

"Over across the sound, up around Somerset."

"Oh yes," she said, pretending to know the place he mentioned.

"Pardon me," she said. Then, turning for the door, she invited him up on the porch, out of the sun. Another half nod.

Inside she found Whaley calmly eating his dinner.

"Who is that man?"

"Hezekiah. Like I said, he'll be helping out for a time."

"The children are perfectly capable of helping out."

"You seem bound to keep them in school all day."

"We cannot afford to keep that man."

"He doesn't appear to eat much."

"Where's he going to stay?"

"Shed for now. We'll build him a cabin directly."

"Where'd he come from?"

"I'd wager Africa."

She was pouring water from a pitcher into a mug to take to Hezekiah. She slopped a good mugful on the floor as she slammed the pitcher on the table and turned to Whaley.

"You did not buy that man?"

Whaley chewed, swallowed. "How many slaves did the governor own?"

She knew the number: nearly three hundred, counting those who worked the rice farms, the various houses, the governor's mansion.

"That has nothing to do with this man."

"It's got something to do with you, though. Let's suppose I wanted to support my wife in the manner in which she was formerly accustomed."

"I'm not your wife. And that man is not our slave."

"You've not heard me call him such."

"He's standing out there like he expects to be horsewhipped for looking me in the eye."

"I believe you might have scared him. Truth be told, you scare me sometimes."

"You get rid of that man, Whaley. Take him back where you got him. Or I will take my children and leave here."

"Leave?"

"Don't doubt me."

"Oh, I don't. Just, where are you going to go? Home to Charleston? Back up to New York? Your daddy's likely dead, and as for the governor, I'd wager he's found himself another wife. I believe you might be standing in the only place left for you. Unless you and your portrait are still thinking this is only temporary."

Whaley went back to his plate. She saw no use arguing with a hungry man. She tried to remember the last time she and Whaley had quarreled. Some years ago, when he'd asked her to spend more time at home, confessed he needed her, though he could not say what he needed her for. She'd acquiesced then, but she would not do so now. She poured another mug of water and took it out to Hezekiah, who was waiting in the sun where she'd left him. She handed him the water and told him she'd bring him something to eat, and for the rest of the day she ignored her husband, who worked with Hezekiah on fixing up the shed.

That night she sat up for hours in the parlor, thinking of things to say to Whaley, shaping her argument against his owning another person. Chief among her reasons was one so obvious, so irrefutable she felt silly saying it: after all they'd been through, all they'd sacrificed in their lifetimes, the things that had been wrenched from them—home, family, children, whole *lives*—how could he possibly put someone else through the slightest anguish, and for profit?

Worry addled her wounds. She felt the scars across her body, remembering the day and a half she lay bleeding in the bottom of the stolen boat, or what Whaley'd told her about it: her blood mixing with the wash in the bottom, Whaley afraid to bail the blood out for fear of drawing sharks, his attempts to hug the shore should the boat start taking on water, his fear that Daniels had alerted his charges up and down the banks to be on the lookout for them, that land was no less safe than sea.

Whaley woke her. He was stoking the fire. Pink light winging in off the ocean. She roused herself from her thin sleep, in the rocking chair, her muscles stiff and creaky from an awkward night's slumber.

"I'll make you some breakfast," she said when he did not speak or look at her.

"I packed something already," he said. "You get to bed."

"Whaley," she said to him when she saw he was moving toward the door, without a kiss or even a look her way.

He stopped. She hesitated, as if waiting for something other than herself to usher in the apology. But what had she to apologize for? He was the one who ought to know better than to try to pay money for human life.

"Yes?" he asked.

"You're taking him with you?"

"No. He'll be at work on his shed."

"He'll need breakfast then? I'll see to it," she said, glad to have something to say, something practical, a statement of fact. But when the door eased shut, her worry returned, and she tried to understand this paltry exchange of words as a start, if not exactly a triumph. She could talk sense into him. He'd listen to her, surely.

Meanwhile she went about fixing breakfast for Hezekiah. She found him sawing logs in the sideyard.

"I've got your breakfast ready."

The blade eased to a stop in the log. He stood, holding it awkwardly, shielding the sun with his free hand so that he might look vaguely in her general direction.

"It's on the table."

"I'm obliged if you can bring me a bit of bread," he said.

"Nonsense. There are cakes and some jam and eggs and side meat."

"I won't be needing all that."

"Mr. Whaley told me before he left to come and get you when it's ready."

For the next ten minutes she uttered hundreds of words in negotiation to Hezekiah's dozens. He did not want to accept her food. He'd just take a slice of bread, a little side meat, thank you. She wouldn't hear of it. The food would go to waste, she said. She could feed it to her children, he said. They get plenty to eat, she said. He smiled over her shoulder and she turned to see the children watching their standoff from the back porch. She shooed them inside and followed them to the kitchen where she made up a plate and had Alex take it out to Hezekiah.

All day long she listened to his work—sawing, chopping, hammering—while thinking of arguments against his presence in their backyard. She'd expected Whaley home after lunch. Usually when it was this hot the good fishing was over by noon. Of all the days for him to dawdle. Likely he was off helping someone else, when she needed him here at home. She grew more anxious by the minute, not because she missed him but because she was eager to have it out with him while her arguments were still fiery and fresh.

When the children came home from school, she sent them out to play, as she was beginning to get worried, and did not need them afoot in her kitchen as she fixed supper. The sun dropped over the sound, and the wind kicked up a little, lightly, from the southeast. Nothing to worry about. He'd ridden out far worse weather.

The next morning she paced the parlor, accompanied by Hezekiah's incessant hammering. There was no school that day, so she sent the children out to help Hezekiah, too distracted to worry about whether they'd be a bother. Midday and no sign of Whaley. She laid out the noon meal and told Phillip to feed his brother and sister and take a plate to Hezekiah and hurried down to the inlet, where she spent the afternoon at the dock, waiting for the boats to come in, asking everyone if they might have seen her husband out on the water. Maybe he's across over to Bath, several of the men suggested, which annoyed her, as she'd not abandoned her work to solicit speculation from men who did not even bother to stop unloading their catch or swabbing their skiffs to answer her query, deliberately phrased so as to require a yes or a no. Simple enough, yet these men either evaded the question or suggested in the aversion of their deep-set eyes, in perpetual squint from years of sound-mirrored sunlight, knowledge of certain catastrophe.

Walking back through the village, she was besieged by disastrous possibilities: he'd slipped, hit his head, drowned. The boat had capsized in a squall and the chum had drawn sharks. His heart had given way, the sun and heat had stricken him lock-limbed, speechless, and parched. Once past the church she timed her footsteps to Hezekiah's hammering. Occasionally he would stop, but the pounding continued, taken over by her pulse. If Whaley did not return, would a similar rhythm keep her attuned, in step, moving forward? Many was the time she might have given herself over to despair or ennui, endless the hours when she fought away the sleepwalk of the touched, only to tether her movements to Whaley's coming and going, his devotion to quotidian ritual. At the time she had not considered what sort of love this was. But now that he was gone it seemed far more than survival, this measured cadence they'd managed to share.

At the top of the rise she saw the ribs of roofline, Hezekiah silhouetted against the afternoon sun, her three children cheerful factotums at his feet.

"You may go," she told him after sending the children down island to hunt for turtle eggs.

"Go where?"

"You're free."

Hezekiah was standing on a low rung of a ladder, which required her to shade her eyes to see his face.

He said, "Mr. Whaley never bought me."

Her confusion must have registered in her shaded eyes, for he did not bother to climb down before he began to explain his presence in her life. Like all the other island blacks, he had been brought over to lighter ships. Now that the trade had moved north to ports with easier access, he and several others were being sold down at the dock when Whaley happened to have come in off the water.

"He paid the man cash money, but as soon as we were back up off the inlet he told me I could go on back to where I come from. Last place I lived before they brought me over here was Somerset, up by Columbia. I didn't have anybody back across over there so I asked him to give me some work, said I'd work off what I owed him. But he said no, said if I was going to work I was going to get paid for my work. He said, 'You don't owe me nothing at all. Somebody else owes you and yours, and I wish I could live long enough to see you compensated for your suffering.'"

Only the last word registered, and she found herself repeating it silently as she swallowed and tried not to believe that he'd planned this. But it was too convenient, his bringing home Hezekiah, then disappearing. And insulting to both Hezekiah and herself. Leading this poor man to believe that his actions were motivated by a moral compass. And not trusting that she could make do, in his absence, with the children.

The most egregious insult of all was to himself. What right had he, who had survived so much and managed to regain some goodness and decency in his life, to taint the sanctity of his soul?

For the next few days the anger she felt toward Whaley alternated with shame for allowing herself to believe him capable of such cruelty. Hours plagued with constant and multiple irritations: Hezekiah's hammering (she finally asked him to go down to the sound and fish for their supper, just for an hour's quiet), her children's questions (where is daddy when is he coming home did he come home last night), the lies she delivered in answer to their questions (your father had business across the sound he'll be back soon) and—the most intolerable annoyance, the one that kept her from more than a quarter hour of sleep, that needled her day and night—the fear that he had returned to his other family, that he'd booked passage on some British-bound ship, leaving her here to deal with a situation that, she scarcely wanted to admit, was after all her creation. It wasn't as if he'd have ever started a family had they stayed in that place now called after the head of a horse, the two island wards wed on a wet dune in a ceremony attended only by sand crab and tern, after which they'd set about filling their ramshackle lean-to with unfortunate offspring certain to suffer from their parents' afflictions, her deliciously comical delusions of grandeur (daughter of a vice president, wife of a governor) and his eccentric and uncivilized dress and behavior. No, this life, this island, even if she were honest, these children (for she was finally the one who gave herself to him, who decided to indulge the misconceptions of the islanders who thought them married and perform wifely duties that no man would refuse)—all of what they shared was her doing. Maybe he never wanted it. He was just too good to let her die. But just because he had saved her life did not mean he loved her.

She took to talking to him aloud. At first the children asked her who she was talking to, but after a day or two they began to cower. Phillip, eleven years old then, seemed to sense his ascension to some new authority. He kept the younger ones fed and bathed and made sure they did not acknowledge their mother when she said aloud to long gone Whaley, You ought never have killed that dog or Do you really think she'll want you back after all these years?

On the fourth morning she looked out of the window in the summer kitchen and saw Hezekiah strolling into the yard carrying a pail of water. She was at his side, her arms freckled with flour, in seconds.

She told him he was welcome to stay in the shed until he found other lodgings, but that there wasn't any way she could pay him.

"Whaley never thought of that, did he?"

"Beg your pardon, ma'am?"

"Call me Theodosia," she said, not kindly. She did not want to be shrill with him, but he was a part of the plan.

"Where did he go?" she said.

"Where did who go?"

"You'll have to fend for yourself. Did he expect you to stay around forever making sure we don't starve? Is this his idea of what freedom is?"

Hezekiah stood stiffly before her, still holding the pail of water.

"I will not have it," she said. "Think of the position he's left us both in. I am unable to compensate you, which makes my dependence on your help criminal, an affront to God's laws, and though he paid you and purportedly set you free, he expected you to remain here, in service to us."

"I believe I'd be more comfortable calling you Miss Whaley," he said, but it was clear that he was trying not to say something else.

"As if that is who I am," she said. "Ever was."

He said nothing. They stood there in the high sun, sweating. The part of her that noticed and pitied his obvious discomfort was a sliver compared to her anger, which made her ancient wounds ache as if Whaley, by abandoning her, by tricking this poor man with false promises of freedom, had unleashed Daniels's dog again.

Finally Hezekiah said, "I didn't have nothing to do with him leaving out of here. He never said a word to me about it or any of his private business. I told you the truth. He said, 'You don't owe me nothing.' He said he hoped he lived long enough—"

"I have work to do," she said, and returned to the summer kitchen.

This wasn't an excuse. She had twice as much work to do now that the burden of feeding and sheltering her children fell upon her only, for employing the assistance of Whaley's replacement was unthinkable to her. She'd not ask Hezekiah for a thing, just to spite Whaley's scheme. She chopped wood and set nets and cleaned fish and weeded the garden and scrubbed the floors and as she worked she was plagued by a recurring image of Whaley's return to his real wife. She saw him loping up a long lane in the English countryside, saw him turn hesitantly into the court-yard of a tidy cottage with a roof of abundant thatch. A stained-aproned woman feeding chickens glanced up at him warily and without recognition. He called her name. Sarah? Abigail? Only the name changed in the scene, which repeated itself incessantly, moving from yard to the parlor where the faithful loving wife fed her prodigal husband and then into the bedchamber where Theo could not bring herself to turn away from the details of their intimacy. To block this nightmare, Theo tried to conjure her own return to The Oaks, but she could only make it as far as the infernal and malarial swamps, which steamed with wintry fog.

A week after Whaley disappeared she went out to milk the

cow. Nora, as was her habit, had strayed with several other cows into the soundside marsh, where she grazed for hours, neither budging nor bothering to lift her head in response to Theo's call. Theo lifted her skirts and picked carefully through the oyster and clam shells lining the shore. Soon the bottom was hard packed and ridged by the current, and her feet, exhausted from a hard half day's work, felt as if they were being caressed by the slow pull of the tide, which was just beginning to rise. She stopped, stood still for a minute. The day was warm but the sun's disappearance darkened the waters as thick clouds streamed lazy and low. The thought of what she might look like to anyone happening along ashore nearly made her smile. Her mind cleared and the water washed away all her pain. No scars on her legs and arms and neck, no weather-triggered aches, no worry about how to feed her children, what to do about Hezekiah. She dropped her skirt and moved forward slowly, letting the water work its magic. What a treasure is this blankness, only sun and warm water and the rasp of the grasses in the intermittent wind. But she needed milk. With Whaley gone, the day was so much fuller, which was the way she struggled to make sense of his absence, as an annoyance, for this was easier than giving way to grief. The mounting catalog of all that she must accomplish before noon made her sigh at her laziness and trudge awkwardly ahead, calling out to Nora, the water fighting back, thick and resistant, until she stepped from firm sand into a patch of soft mud. When she stopped sinking the water rose to her waist. A foot in front of her a clump of sea oats sprouted, but as she leaned forward to pull herself out of the mire she lost her balance and pitched face-first into the water. The effort it took to right herself sucked her under a good half foot. Nora and her companions stood nearby, grazing with the unhurried and implacable dignity of cattle. Simply breathing soaked Theo's forehead with sweat. The chambers of her heart constricted. She'd heard of this happening to island boys, the tide rising, a death so slow and patient. She'd rather the sword of the pirate, the feral attack of a watchdog. Who was going to save her this time? Since she had gone years without regular prayer or thoughts in the general direction of heaven except to sometimes mumble a plea for rain to save her garden, or a request for a storm to divert its path, calling upon God to rescue her with his touch would only damn her.

The tide rose to her rib cage. Thinking of her children orphaned, both parents disappearing within days, brought tears. Her high cries for help had turned thin and hoarse by the time Nora and her companions, repelled by her yelling, lumbered out of the water onto shore and disappeared over a dune. More clouds blew in, no longer delightfully slow and white. Graying, then black-hearted. Increasing wind whipped the water into a steady chop. She grew chilly, then freezing, the water up to her breasts. She tried to turn to face shore, but the simplest movement sucked her under farther. An eighth inch was a precious plenty. Shivering, reciting the names of her children, the things she loved about each—Phillip's bossiness, Amanda Jane's prissiness, Alexander's eternal sweetness—she watched a barnacled bottle bearing a message from her father float idly by. She let it go. He was dead, or perhaps the emperor of Mexico. It hardly mattered now, the water at her shoulders.

Then a frigate appeared so close she could see the muzzles of cannon from below deck portholes, dispatched two men in a dinghy. She saw them between waves, there and then gone, the truth and a lie, her blank present and her peopled past. The rower had his back to her; in the stern a man whose face, when she finally placed it, wrestled her to the floor in front of the fire, a wintry night in Whaley's old lean-to. Daniels's eyes, steel gray and unblinking. Then she understood, and what washed over her from the neck down was not seawater but shame. How could she ever have believed Daniels would leave them be? She sobbed Whaley's name and those of her children, so dear to her, all she'd accomplished in this world, then closed her eyes to what might happen next.

When she opened them the water was flat and sun-touched. Her shoulders were exposed to the sun, and then her breasts, and finally her elbows. Behind her she heard the sibilant disturbance of water by rhythmically orchestrated oar. When he was in front of her, Hezekiah extended the oar to her, but rather than grab it she said, "I need you to pull me out, I've not the strength to do it myself," and after some hesitation, he drew the dinghy close enough behind her to hook his arms around her just below her bosom and hoist her into the boat.

She lay there, exhausted, remembering her arrival on this island, similarly incapacitated at the bottom of a leaky boat, and when she could breathe again she cried out for Whaley.

"We have to find him," she told Hezekiah, "they've come to harm him, we've got to dispose of that portrait, it's all my doing, as ever my thoughtlessness is to blame."

"Hush now," Hezekiah said, but she could not stop talking, and when they reached shore she had told him everything: her father, the duel, Joseph, the head of the nag, Daniels sparing her, Whaley taking her in, her return to Daniels's compound, the scars across her body. Hezekiah looked to shore and rowed while she talked. Bent to his task, he appeared burdened by the facts she imparted, though she knew he was listening. She knew that he heard her. He had come for her, after all.

"Whaley sent you to find me," she said.

"No ma'am. The children came home from school and you never did come back. I seen you leave out this morning and I figured something happened. I borrowed this boat and I'm hoping whoever it belong to don't discover it gone."

She said, "Will you help me find Whaley?"

He'd helped her out of the boat and dragged it up under a wax myrtle where he'd found it, out of the way of the tide.

"You need to get back and tend to those children."

"You'll help me find him," she said, careful to issue only statements.

"Get yourself dry, get you some food and water in you," he said, as if he were listing everything she needed to do before he would help her plan her search.

But that night when she had calmed her children with a lie about where she'd been all day (she claimed she'd been checking her crab pots in the sound and fell in a hole), she sat up late by the fire, disturbed not by dream or nightmare but by a waking recurring image of Whaley's hands, crudely hacked off below the wrist, fingers permanently curled as if clawing their way somewhere, left on the doorstep for anyone—her children, Hezekiah, passersby—to discover. In the morning her children filed into the parlor to find her ashen and awake in her chair.

"Where did the woman go," Alexander said, pointing to the blank space above the hearth where the portrait had been.

"Never you mind," said Theo. Sometime in the night she'd looked up to see the woman's cold eye on her and in a fit she scarcely remembered by daylight she'd taken the portrait off its nail, wrapped it in a sheet, and slid it behind the wardrobe she'd asked Whaley to build for her. She sent the boys out for wood, asked Amanda Jane to fetch her some matches, then, when the fire was stoked, gathered her children in front of it. During the night she'd decided to tell them everything: Richmond Hill, Charleston, her father's disgrace, his exile, the trip to New York, Daniels, her own exile as a woman touched by God. The dog mauling, their arrival on island. She'd even planned to tell them that she'd never married their father, that he had a family across the ocean, that she'd had another son. And that their father was a thief, however long retired. For even if she went this far, she would still be withholding the truth. She couldn't very well tell them that their father had died because of her vanity, that she had sentenced him to death when she'd stolen that portrait, for who would they be in the world if burdened with this knowledge? How would they ever love themselves, and who would they find to love them if they had no love for themselves?

She said none of this. She said what she'd wanted her father to say to her after her own mother's death. "Your father was very proud of all of you. If you ever doubt this, or doubt his love, you need only to ask me and I'll remind you of how much you meant to him."

Then she made breakfast and told them to go outside and see if Hezekiah had chores for them. When they were gone and the house was quiet she washed the dishes, which is what any other woman on this island would do if she'd lost her husband. She wasn't alone; she had her family, and the islanders would take care of her, so long as they believed her husband had died at sea. But what if his handless corpse washed up down island, bloated and bobbing in the marsh? She found herself wishing sharks had found the body, crabs had picked it apart by now.

What a thing to wish for. Yet it did not torment her, her need to keep secret at all costs the true story of how she arrived on this island. Whaley, after all, had his own secrets; surely others on the island were equally careful in presenting to the world some expurgated version of their lives. More was at stake than her integrity; the truth would damn her children, for she had come to know these islanders well, and she suspected that, according to their arcane but rigid ethical code, her husband's crimes—ransacking ships, stealing cargo, kidnapping, maybe even murder—would be far more tolerable than her own. But vanity, ego, pride—if elsewhere these were trifling infractions, here they would doom her and her children after her.

Thereafter she concentrated every waking moment on appearing to the island as the widow Whaley. She monitored every word out of her mouth, suppressing her erstwhile occasional lapses into fustian diction for sentences so simply blunt they sounded to her like shovel thrusts, ax blows. Ceaseless toil without complaint was her salvation. She shocked herself sometimes in how little she allowed herself to express the slightest pleasure. Her children brought her joy in the very fact of their survival rather than in the qualities and values by which her first child Aaron would have been judged: fine manners, intellectual curiosity, sophistication. The boys she raised to work hard and provide for their families; Amanda Jane she schooled in keeping house.

As her children grew up, she kept an eye out for any behavior the slightest bit effete or entitled, but they acted always as if they were in every way *of* this island. Wind blew away any pretense or affectation, any indulgence she'd failed to squelch. If you were to survive life on this island you had to understand the positive and even recuperative applications of wind. But what if it came back, her former frivolity, in her children's offspring? What if it skipped a generation, or two? She thought of a great-grandchild cultivating, say, her love of Chopin. This was not an unpleasant thought, so long as Theo was not around to witness it. She would not be; already she'd lived miraculously long, given her two near misses with death. She only wanted to live long enough then to see her children settled. Of course she would not mind outliving her lies—it might be her only chance at impunity if there was indeed a life after this one—but she expected to take her secrets with her, for what good would it do her children to know, so long after the fact, who she really was.

Better off for everyone to keep up the lies. Her boys were good boys. Hezekiah took to them and they to him. They fished with him and he taught them carpentry, a particular skill of his, and both of them married island girls and built houses in the village and took to the sea like their father. Amanda Jane was a bit more trouble to Theo. She was an idler and a dawdler, and if you asked her to do something once you'd be better off telling her again and then a third time to grow on, but she eventually met and married a boy from Elizabeth City, though within years she was back at the island with three towheaded babies, having shed her husband back up on the banks of the Pasquotank for reasons that Theo never completely understood. Not that she asked that many questions. She'd not prepared the girl for life off island.

Even though she told him at least once a week since Whaley's disappearance that he was free to leave, Hezekiah stayed on in the shed, though he added rooms and a summer kitchen and, five years after he showed up on her doorstep, married a sullen young girl named Violet. Her family had been around since the port was thriving, her father had been brought in to lighter ships, though Theo only knew this by hearsay; she knew nothing of the lives of the other island blacks, who lived off by themselves across the creek.

Theo knew she would not be welcome at the wedding but she spent the day baking pies, which she had Amanda Jane carry back to Hezekiah's house as soon as the couple returned to their new home.

"Hezekiah said tell you thanks," said Amanda Jane when Theo quizzed her about her errand. It bothered her deeply how Violet resisted her attempts at friendship. She knew it bothered Hezekiah as well, for there was a desperation behind it that all three of them recognized as having nothing to do Hezekiah and his new bride, with the here and now on this island. She was trying to rectify some past sin. Joseph and his hundreds of slaves.

Violet never took to her. It was difficult for Theo, seeing Violet coming and going, working alongside her sometimes in the garden plot they shared, having her every offering rebuffed or ignored, but she came to accept Violet's attitude as her just due for all those years of taking for granted the women and men who waited on her day and night.

Storms hit the island, one after the other. A hurricane opened a new inlet up the banks. Pea Island they called it. Ships took to docking at Manteo. Trade fell off; people began to trickle away. One stormy autumn the church was washed away in a nor'easter but rebuilt on the highest point of the island, its steeple visible a mile out to sea on clear days, pointing everyone who came to the island toward God in heaven.

The injuries Theo had suffered at the hand of Daniels's mongrel turned her limbs arthritic and it grew harder for her to stand. She sat on the porch entertaining memories. Since she could remember, even as a small child, the moment just before she fell asleep had been characterized by an extreme and even painful wakefulness. Never had she been one to drift off; like a terror came this intense few seconds wherein she felt so vividly alive it made her body ache, her heart fearful. Was this a nightly harbinger of the clarity rumored to precede death? She longed for such lucidity, for the memories had begun to collide and confuse. Some days she'd lost her first child with Whaley to swamp fever. Others, her presence on this island was due to her rule as empress of Mexico. After Jefferson sent an army to depose her, she'd been sentenced, like Napoleon Bonaparte, to imprisonment on a remote island.

One moment, however, remained untainted and clear. Out one afternoon to milk her errant cow, wading into the water, the sound sucking her under, Daniels holding her there while the tide washed from her the hopeful fantasy that Whaley had returned to his wife and children. Thereafter she knew without doubt that Daniels had come for him, that he would one day come for her. She'd readied herself that night, though she'd tried to buy time by hiding the portrait behind the bureau. The space above the hearth she avoided looking at as vigilantly as she had when it was filled with the likeness of her, for the ghost of that portrait—a rectangle against which the whitewashed walls had darkened with soot—terrified her nearly as much as the portrait.

Fifteen years passed, then twenty. Perhaps he was dead, Daniels. No, she would know if he were dead. She would feel it as she had felt, finally, that day she'd gone after Nora, Whaley's death. Her father, her legal rightful husband, Joseph—if they had passed on to some other sphere (and surely her father had by now, likely Joseph as well), she had felt nothing of it. She could not even summon shame over the nothingness she felt about the man who had groomed her to be the most highly educated and socially adept lady in America. Stray phrases of Latin and occasional snatches of Beethoven notwithstanding, that part of her life had been eclipsed by the long wait for Daniels to come for her at last.

One of the boys or Amanda Jane came by daily to check on her, but it was Hezekiah, living right behind her, upon whom she depended the most. He'd given up fishing for carpentry and most days was just out back of the house carrying on with his hammering and sawing. Two or three times a day he'd come to the back door and peer through the baggy screen down the hallway to where she sat in the parlor. More often than not he'd find her dozing. If she were awake and heard him she'd say one of two things:

"How many times do I have to ask you to come round front?"

Or: "Is that my coffin you're slapping together out there?"

Sometimes Violet would send Hezekiah over with something she'd baked or some leftover from their table as it was clear that Theo rarely bothered to eat unless someone brought her something by. Theo would always ask Hezekiah in to sit. No ma'am got to get back over to the house, he'd say. One day she would not take his no.

"Sit a bit. Please?"

It was winter, clouds hugging the coast to where she could not see thirty feet. She heard the sea but all that was visible was the final roll of water on sand, the part that delivered and took away.

"Right much a mess out there today," said Hezekiah.

Theo did not respond. Weather was not what she wanted to talk about. For weeks she'd been waking in the night to feel Daniels in the house. She heard his boots on the floorboards in the kitchen. The smell of his rum breath would linger in the hallway.

"There's but one thing on this earth left for me to do," she said.

"Yes ma'am," said Hezekiah, nodding. His words were not pitched in the interrogative, but in agreement, as if by agreeing he would not have to hear what that one thing was. His presence since Whaley's disappearance had brought such rewards: even though their exchanges were rote and terse to the point of curtness, quick and simple exchanges concerned wholly with wind, tide, crops, chores, he had become as dependable as the houses he framed, which were known the island over for their sturdiness in the harshest blows. Yet they were not, could never be, close enough to confess to each other any intimacies, and even last unfinished business would likely seem to him too personal.

But she needed his help. He'd built himself several fine boats, at least one of them seaworthy enough to ferry her up to Nag's Head.

He listened to her plan without comment or the slightest shift in posture or expression. When she was through he nodded so slightly she thought she might have imagined it.

"You'll take me then?"

"No ma'am," he said. "I'll not."

"And why not?"

"If that man was wanting some picture he'd have come for it long time ago. You delivering it and yourself too is not going to bring Mr. Whaley back here, nor put anybody's mind to rest."

"You speak so confidently of what you think I seek to gain. But the truth is, I've not even considered what might be gained. It's more that a score has been long left unsettled. I am the one he ought to have come for, not my husband. My husband, though he may have in another life stolen freely from others, did not take anything from Daniels. I am the one who took that painting, and for no sound reason. I was after my father's papers. I thought that if I held them in my possession I would be rescued and that, papers in hand, I would make my way to Washington and return my father to his early glory and promise."

Hezekiah was silent. She knew him to sometimes let folks talk themselves out. She'd seen him do it with Alex, who Hezekiah had taken on as an apprentice carpenter, though of course they had to pretend that Hezekiah was working for Alex, as it would not do for a black man, free or not, to serve over a white man, even on the island. Alex always had a better way of doing things, was forever insisting on his own way (a trait she traced to her own father's stubbornness, for surely he did not get this from Whaley), and she'd seen Hezekiah listen to Alex's plans with a patience that allowed Alex to talk himself inevitably toward the realization that his plan was inferior.

She felt he was up to the same with her, slowly feeding her enough rope to entangle herself in both word and deed.

"You realize that there are other boats on this island."

"Yes ma'am. Plenty of them. Most of them a might more seaworthy than mine."

"I will ask someone else."

He nodded at this too. He let her words settle between them, long enough for her to drift into an anxious dread of what would happen if she turned up at Daniels's compound. She tried to remind herself of how her father had always favored Thucydides over Herodotus and even her beloved Homer, for in the work of the latter two the divine presence of the gods was ever present on the battlefield. Thucydides, on the contrary, understood the events of the past to have been instigated by the choices and actions of mortals. His Peloponnesians marched into battle with confidence not in some divine protector whose will would decide whether an arrow might find their flesh but in the rightness of their own cause.

Her cause—restoring her father's reputation—had twice led her to be mauled by vicious dogs. Had it not also cost Whaley his life and deprived her children of a father? So many years had passed without a thought of how deeply wrong she'd been to serve so valiantly as a foot soldier in her father's army. Poor devoted Joseph had suffered and might be suffering still.

If there was justice those papers went down with the ship and had long since been devoured by salt.

"I know that I cannot make right the way it all happened," she said at last.

"No ma'am," said Hezekiah.

"All I wish," she said, and then she did not need to say any more as the wish, like the wind filling the sails of a doldrumed vessel, grew so vibrant and vivid that there was no need to articulate it, for surely Hezekiah saw it too. She was in the water, in the sound, but the tide was not rising and she was not stuck in mud but firmly footed and in control of the net she cast. What it brought back was bountiful: all the sorrows she'd caused others, and those she had caused herself, reined in and dragged ashore and packed tight and taken not back—I cannot make right the way it all happened—but away. For her to deal with. The weight hers alone to bear.

Now her cheeks were dry. Beside her she heard Hezekiah fidgeting. He had his chores. She had some of her own.

"I've kept you, Hezekiah, from your loved ones."

He'd been watching her closely. During her long silence, she could feel his steady, vigilant gaze. He seemed to see something different in her, or at least she imagined so, for instead of nodding his head in agreement, he shook his head no, which, she realized, he did not have to do. Her gratefulness was disproportionate to the slightness of the gesture, for anyone else might not have even noticed the nod. She would have liked to have thanked him, and for the next few months, until Violet found her crumpled dead under the clothesline, a basket of wet sheets on the ground beside her, she kept trying to find a way to thank him for that afternoon when he talked her out of empty and egotistical sacrifice without saying a word. But the time was never right. Had the moment arrived, he would have been embarrassed. Still, she felt it so strongly that the morning she walked out to hang the clothes on the line, it had become that one thing left on earth for her to do.

VI

WOODROW THORNTON
Yaupon Island, North Carolina

TOTING DEBRIS FROM HIS kitchen down island the day he got back across from burying Sarah's how Woodrow discovered the new inlet. In his mind it was Sarah cut the island in two. Sheared right through the marsh, snipped with the thick of the bigger blade the tangly roots of the myrtles, dredged five fathom of sand with her sewing scissors.

It had to be a reason for his sweet girl to die holding in her hand some scissors. Sarah had a reason for everything she did, and she expected Woodrow also to know always why, to think what he wanted before he did what he did. But Woodrow did not always know why. Hell, some days he just did what he did and did not expect squat to come from it. Not knowing why never got away with him like it did Sarah. There lay the difference in the God they prayed to, or the one Sarah actually prayed to and the one Woodrow started out praying to before some other side thought snagged him and left him feeling all the more a hopeless sinner. Sarah's praying left her knowing why: God's will, that's why. Even if it was something seemed like to Woodrow so simple— four people left on this island and how come they couldn't just look after each other—even if it made not a bit of sense, it wasn't to Sarah a mystery as it was the direct opposite, a fact, the way God made it.

So every morning Woodrow rose early and walked down to that good-for-nothing-but-birdshit southside, trying to figure out why she'd died holding those scissors. Took longer than it ought to— a couple days—for Woodrow, crouching in the marsh shooing mosquitoes with an El Reeso he'd got off them O'Malley's, to see what he ought to have known the moment he came up on the inlet: Sarah was wanting Woodrow where the sisters were not. Now she'd given him his own island, somewhere for him to hide out and not be bothered by the beck and call of two old white ladies had let her bleed to death on the floor of his tacked-on kitchen.

It did not matter at first that his end of the island lacked a house, a dock, easy access to the channel, an acre of graze for what livestock the storm had not killed, fresh water, more shade than a scrawny wax myrtle. Acres of dune is all, some spindly sea oat, crabs crawling around like they had somewhere big to be at. Sarah's hand had made it—Woodrow did not take it as far as God, he'd as soon stop with Sarah—and Woodrow, in her honor, was going to make it his. He left off fishing to prog for whatever washed-up timber he might use to build a shack across over there.

But mostly he would make a little pile in the dunes of whatever the sea brought him, didn't really matter what, he wasn't what you call picky, and after he'd dragged a few pieces of waterlogged plywood to his pile, he'd lie back and watch the birds.

Hours Woodrow spent down there watching gulls, terns, pelicans, glide down the coast, light on a wave as if it were all of a sudden brought to a halt and turned sand dune. Woodrow envied a bird. He was a boy when the brothers flew their first plane up the banks at Kitty Hawk. There was some news that everyone on the island heard and had something to allow about, though only thing it had to do with any of them was that they might have caught some of the same wind had lifted that machine off the dune. Wasn't like any Lockerman or Midgette or Pollock or Whaley was going to go buying a ticket, flying up to New York for the weekend. Woodrow's mother thought it was devilish, this business of a man acting bird, disrupting God's own order. Sarah, too, put it down as foolishness. But Woodrow did not see a single thing wrong or ungodly concerning it. Afternoons lying across some sea-warped plywood on that slice of the island Sarah had made him, Woodrow flew so low above the water he'd wake to dampness above his lip, a moustache from the spray. He could not climb a dune without wanting so badly the breeze to lift him up and sweep him across the water.

He'd had these flying dreams before, back when he heard about the brothers' machines, when he figured he might as well dream. Not as if he'd ever climb his black ass up in a real airplane.

But now it didn't seem to be about bird or plane. More like he wanted off, wanted across; more like this slice of Sarah's could not hold him.

Another thing for Woodrow to not understand. He skimmed the waves and wiped the spray off his upper lip and said, I do not understand one bit of what has been delivered me. As for the sisters, he had no idea how they were getting on. Someone surely was seeing to them in his stead, lest they starve to death or sit bickering on the steps of the very church could have saved his Sarah's life, Whaley moaning about not having any grocery store ads to read aloud, Miss Maggie talking about where's Woodrow at, I need to see Woodrow, find Woodrow for me, not because she needed Woodrow, not because she had anything true or pure to relate to him or because she wanted to ask him how was he feeling was there anything she could do for him and God is my witness Woodrow Thornton I am sorry and so is my sister about what we let happen to your sweet Sarah, every waking moment I wish it was me the wind had took instead of her. No, it was more she needed him because she was tired of her sister. She needed something between her and Whaley. O'Malley could bring her over a big piece of plywood to put up on the church steps, serve the same purpose.

Sometimes he would come home past dusk mosquito-bit and hungry to find a stack of letters from Crawl and the rest of his children, but he did not need to know how to read or have them read out loud to him in order to know what was in them. He'd get him a High Life he'd iced down that morning and sit out on the porch holding the cold can to his cheek and in the other he would hold those letters. Up from the creek the tree frog song would rise, spreading across the yard like fog and here come the lick right off those envelopes and there go the words, out into the marsh, same ones and sweet ones but same ones, over and over, Daddy how you doing, how you holding up, for a line or two before We got room, you don't need to bring a thing, come on over on the next ferry, or Crawl would be talking about I'll be over across tomorrow to get you, Daddy, you can help me out at the club.

Spinning ball, said Woodrow to the night crabs crawling. High Life.

One day he could not go back to that place Sarah had made for him. She would just have to not understand. He could not live off down there by himself. Well, she'd say, the white women make you feel more alone than the birds, but what it came down to was the three of them on this island that every one else had fled.

He went out on the water that morning, brought his catch to their front door. Whaley was as polite as she knew to be but clearly put out by his standing right there on her front threshold after thirty-odd years of coming around back. Seemed like to Woodrow she'd turned whiter in the face and way whiter in the hair. Maybe he was blacker from his days of lying back and smoking sweets and flying low over the breakers.

"I'll meet the mail boat," he said.

"That O'Malley boy's been bringing it by occasionally," she said.

Boy? thought Woodrow. O'Malley's nearly as old as she is.

"I'll meet him directly," he said.

"Well, I know he'll be obliged not to have to make the extra trip over here," she said, but he wasn't listening. He'd caught sight of that picture behind her, the one Maggie'd told him Whaley wrapped up and toted up the hill to the church during the storm. The one thing she'd saved; instead of Sarah, a picture of her ancestor roundly said to be a lunatic. Woodrow could count on his hands the times he'd looked at it. Certainly he'd never been invited in to stand around in the parlor and study it. The woman in the picture looked like she'd already left her body, but in her eyes was a sweet satisfaction of having finally understood something her great-great or whatever Whaley was to her would never fathom.

Whaley watched him staring. What, she said with every inch of her visible body; What, she asked, without saying squat.

"I reckon y'all favor some," said Woodrow.

Woodrow didn't even bother building on again, just set his cookstove right up in what Sarah used to call the parlor, piped it into the chimney, lived in one room. Most nights he slept in his chair. He had everything he needed right alongside his chair where he sat evenings by the fire when it was too cold or raw to sit out on the porch. He had everything he needed and yet his life was filled with lack. What went missing when Woodrow set up in the so-called parlor were all the things made his life more than just shuffling around his down-to-one-room widower's cottage, fetching dinner and the mail for his white women sisters, trying not to let anything anybody said or did or didn't say or do get away with him, doling his words out like coins the week before payday. The kind of life the Tape Recorders already had Woodrow living, no noticeable emotion unless you count indifference, no love, no hate, just hard work and evenings so quiet his voice box rusted shut. Finally Woodrow had become the type of person the Tape Recorders had been making him out to be since they'd come across with their tape machines and their questions stuffed already with the answers and those beekeeper hats they took to wearing to keep the bugs off of them.

One evening Woodrow crossed the creek to join his white women on the steps of the church. They saw him coming but acted like they never did. He climbed up the steps, sat and listened to Whaley read aloud her prices.

Maggie said, "Crawl wrote said you're going to be eighty this year, Woodrow." She said this before she ever read the letter itself. Skimmed ahead to switch out the parts she couldn't bring herself to read, the parts where Crawl tried to talk some sense into his senile daddy, convince him that providing for two old fussy white women wasn't any of his. Whaley, sitting on the top stoop, had her flyers spread out and was not listening to a word of

Crawl's letter nor anything out the mouth of her sister. When she had her advertisements spread out across her lap on the church steps where the three of them would sit just like people in town will linger after supper to watch traffic and call out to neighbor women strolling babies, she was just not there. Had a two-storied green bus come chugging across the creek, she wouldn't have lifted her head to grace the sight with her reading glasses. Woodrow thought at first she was preparing to go off island by teaching herself what to expect to pay across over there for a pound of butter. But after a while he figured the flyers were part of what kept her here. She'd spit the prices out like fruit seed. She'd get ill at a bunch of innocent bananas for costing highway robbery, she would read her prices like Maggie would read the letters to the editor, taking sides and arguing with every one of them, My land the way people live in this world, she'd say every night when it got too dark to read and she folded up her newspaper like the Coast Guard taught Woodrow to fold a flag, that careful, that slow, like a color guard was standing at attention waiting on her to finish.

"Crawl don't know nothing about how old I am," Woodrow said to the water, to the wind, to the sand fiddlers, to anyone or anything but the company he was keeping at that moment in time.

"Old enough to know better," said Maggie.

"Too old to change," said Whaley.

They weren't talking or even listening to each other, and down the road Woodrow might just decide they weren't really talking to him either, for what they said they could have easily said about themselves, Woodrow figured when he let it settle and studied it. But at the time the words just spilled out of their mouths and hung there, and the white women, sisters, moved right on through time continuous, though Woodrow, to whom they had supposedly been speaking, *about whom* their comments were supposed to be describing, was stuck down on the birdshit southside.

"Why can I not just come across," he said to Sarah that night as he lay talking to her in the dark. He told her what the sisters said and he listened to what she had to say back. Their conversation was surf on the beach, claiming ground and then receding, sea listening to the land, then offering more words, steady rhythm into the night.

How come you let what people say get away with you so much, said Sarah, and Woodrow never did answer because she knew how bad people could hurt him with their words. Woodrow just hurt. They'd both been knowing that. And here he was on this island with no one left to hurt him anymore but Maggie who was too sweetly dizzy in the head to hurt much and Whaley who Woodrow thought he knew every which way she had of hurting him but she was good for coming up with a new one.

Sarah had snipped him off his very own island but he could not stay across over there.

"Y'all ought not to have done me like y'all done me," said Woodrow. I've seen dogs done better, he started to add, but what he said was more than he'd said in months. More, maybe, than he'd ever said to anyone in his life.

He got up and picked his way through the laid-out advertisements, down the steps of the church. The village he walked across
to home that night looked just as it used to be when he was a boy,
the two stores stocking shoelaces and bolts of colored cloth, the
old hospital and the post office with over fifty boxes in the walls,
little glass windows Woodrow would peek through and pretend
he was looking right inside something mysterious—the innards
of some complicated machine, some smart so-and-so's brain—
like he was being offered a sneak at the way things worked in
this life.

High above his head the church bell chimed out the hour like it
used to when anyone on the island had anywhere to be at. Down
by the dock island boys, squealing, seal-slick naked, splashed in
the inlet. Whatever he said, it wasn't going to fill his lack or make
him spread his mess out of his lone widower's room. He felt bad
for saying it, for even though Maggie, who was eat up with guilt,
born with it the way some children come into being with two extra toes, would like as not beat him across the creek to apologize,
he'd not hear mention of it from Whaley one way or the other.
She'd think him weak, though, for saying it out loud. All those
years he'd known her he'd heard her only once say she was sorry,
in the church that day Sarah laid across the altar kerchiefless and
what Whaley really meant by sorry was It's awful what happened
while you were gone, how the wind took Sarah, I feel for you.
Not: I'm the one done this, Woodrow Thornton, as God is my
witness will you ever forgive me?

Spite keeps that woman's motor running and that's all, Sarah used to say. Somebody cut the spite off and you might as well start sawing on her coffin. What he'd said—y'all ought not to have done me like y'all done me—was just shoveling coal at her spite. But if you don't say anything, Sarah said to him that night as he lay in bed talking to her, you stay her back-door nigger right on.

When she talked like this Woodrow hurt even harder for not taking her off island when she wanted to go. Last time they'd lived off island had been in Norfolk, in the nineteen and sixties. Everybody carrying on. Army off fighting someplace he'd never heard of, trying to beat somebody people told him never did do anything to any United States of America in the first place. White boys growing their hair long and putting all kinds of mess down their throats, women walking down daytime streets wearing an outfit you used to have to buy a dirty magazine to get a peek at, colored people, his own children even, bushing their hair out and taking new names made no sense to the sound. Crazies popping out the windows of tall buildings shooting presidents and preachers, mobs lighting cities on fire. We're going back across, said Woodrow, and when Sarah tried to tell him wasn't anywhere else safe left in this world, Woodrow said he favored wind over hellfire, said he'd rather let the wind or the water take him out than die choking in a high-sky tower with a brick lawn and blue lights streaking the night instead of the sleepy sweep of the lighthouse over on Meherrituck.

"I reckon I better get to work," Woodrow said to Sarah when

sleep would not come to him and seemed like everything he said got away with her big time. To keep on arguing in your head nights with the one who showed you how to love. Now what was that? Was it still love? Was it miss? Habit? Seemed to Woodrow love was just as hard now that Sarah was dead and gone, and in some ways even harder, for who did he think he was fooling when he got up and pulled on his waders and packed himself some bologna biscuits and a can of syrupy peaches like he liked and boiled up last night's coffee and poured it in his thermos and took his flashlight out to search the weeds in front of the house for the stub of a Sweet he might have thought he'd finished one day when he was cigar flush? Sarah knew what he was up to. When she was alive she had been no easier to fool than God in heaven and now she was up there looking down on his every move and seeing right through the walls of his heart to whatever hurt he was hiding. Will it ever get any easier, Woodrow said to the sand fiddlers he'd sent sideways into their holes with the beam of his flashlight. Woodrow let the light play over the marsh, wishing he could follow the crabs down underneath the island, though there was no escaping Sarah.

"Y'all be around way after I'm gone," he said to the crabs. "Y'all wait, y'all still be here when this house is nothing but some rusty nails in the sand." He imagined his crabs crouched just below ground, ready to spring right back out once he switched his light off and gave up on trying to find something to smoke himself awake good, imagined their big pop eyes staring right at him now, maybe their ears poked up listening to this sad old man out talking to the island like it cared to listen.

Woodrow cranked his outboard and throttled slow through the inlet toward the sound. The night was still and big, white-hot stars and huge moon. Sarah I just can't sit up in that chair all night when there's enough moon for me to find my pots. Woodrow talked out loud to her to hide the thought he had and hated and could not let loose: that, had she lived, she'd have left him, gone on across without him, fed up with Whaley's mouth and Maggie's stumbling across the creek in her dirty shirt to interrupt her radio with a whole bunch of Where's Woodrow at? Worse than her leaving, that he'd have let her go, would have stayed on just like he was doing, providing for the sisters, getting hurt over not much of nothing, wasting his last days waiting on that wind, the big one that would take the three of them off island.

Checking on the first of his pots, Woodrow let the rope slide slowly through his hands, lowered the empty pot into the deep, cut the engine. What was his hurry? He had a good four hours until it heated up out, and if the sisters needed him for something, well, hadn't they proven when he was down island lying back bird-watching that they could get on by themselves? If he went first, like they claimed likely for men, the sisters would have to leave. They might have managed those couple weeks while Woodrow sulked and cussed their cold hearts and tried to catch a ride with every wave-skittering bird, but if he up and left now, for good, wasn't any way the sisters could stay.

Peering back toward the island, Woodrow saw only a low dark line on the horizon, but when he lay back in the boat and lit a Sweet he saw sudden movement behind the smudgy glass of the window boxes in the old post office. Was it his big secret come to him after all these years? Would it let him know how come certain things would not aggravate most men in the least got away with him big-time and would it tell him what made him stay on the island tending to his white women sisters and why was it that love was harder now that Sarah was gone? Woodrow thought about how the Tape Recorders had wasted yards and yards of tape on the wrong questions, and he thought about making a list of those he would give a straight answer to, having finally figured out himself which questions were the ones to ask. He fiddled with the locks on the little glass post office boxes, opened one right up, stuck his hand in. Wiggling his fingers around in that secret inside felt familiar, warm, toes in wet sand, the slick of bait as he hooked a line. Woodrow smiled and puffed on his Sweet. He closed his eyes knowing he would not leave the sisters on the island because here he was taking the island with him, right across the sound, him and the wind.

VII

Theo Whaley
Morehead City, North Carolina

WAITING IN HER ROOM for little Liz to show up with her tape recorder, Whaley sat in her wingback under the portrait of her great-great-great-grandmother, thinking over what she was going to tell. This would be her last session with the Tape Recorders. There was a time she could not imagine not having another story to tell Dr. Levinson and little Liz, but now that she was stuck in what they were calling a nursing home (wasn't much nursing to it far as she could see, just uppity girls shoving people out into the halls or back into their rooms and a once a week doctor asking you rude questions about your bathroom habits and a whole lot of people a whole lot worse off than she'd *ever* be talking crazy talk and wetting themselves) across the sound from that island where she was born and planned on by God dying, she was all of a sudden tired of talking about it.

Life on the island, that is, which is what they were wanting to know. Dr. Levinson and his team loved interviewing her best because she alone kept the old ways alive, if not in practice, then in memory. She understood and appreciated the past. Maggie liked to say she lived in it. Maggie claimed she wouldn't know the here and now if it up and crawled in bed with her. Leave it to Maggie to go talking about something crawling into bed with her.

Whaley never set out to become the official island historian. Just that the others were not fit for the job. Somebody points a tape recorder in your face and asks you to just tell a story, nine times out of nine that story's going to be about you. Whaley kept herself out of it. She told how they got by back then, how they made do.

Whaley got up and rang the buzzer for a gal to come bring her another chair so she and Liz could set up by the window overlooking the sound. At first they'd stuck her on the highway side of the building and she raised Cain, said she'd take over the dayroom, which had three windows featuring the waterway and nobody even bothering to look outside in favor of that television they kept on all day and night even though half of them in there were too deaf to hear it. But within a week, somebody over on the sound side passed. Maggie accused her of foul play, but Maggie too wanted a water-side room so she could sit and watch the sailboats and yachts streaming by all day long, open the windows and listen to the water lap the shore when they had a little wind.

Here they were, still sisters, all that was left of the island, sent to spend their last days on the mainland. Woodrow gone, the island run by the Park Service, half the houses rented out to hippie-looking things, come to rough it for the summer. Back to the land, they declared. Most of them lasted a month or less. Mosquitoes got to them. She knew a dozen ways to ward off bugs but wasn't about to share them with any stranger trudging up the beach road pulling along a generator on a child's red wagon. She wouldn't even share her bug secrets with Liz or Dr. Levinson; do, they'd turn around and put it out there to the public, and the bugs were the only thing keeping people off the island now. Lack of electricity didn't seem to stop them, nor storms.

Little Liz would be wanting to talk about Woodrow and them, their so-called social dynamic. Whaley told her on the phone, Sure, honey, come on down, I'll tell you all about it, but when she mentioned to Maggie what Liz was after, Maggie turned sullen and cold and had kept it up for a full week now. Though they'd been known to go months coddling hurts, had even let some things fester for years without talking them over (Sarah's death, for one; Maggie's next-to-last trip off island, for another), lately they'd both been trying harder not to let things get away with them so bad. Part of it was just being so old, not having the energy to go around holding in hurt, real or imagined. Most of it, though, was that it was just the two of them now, and even though they were off island, across the water in a place she'd always said she'd as soon die as settle over here with all the others who turned tail and left over not much of nothing but a squall, they *were* the island, only bit of it left, two old sisters so far from their cottage on the briny deep, precious close to their time to die.

Whaley thought the only way to keep the island alive was to tell about it: how it was. Maggie disagreed—said she'd rather sit in the dayroom watching *Dialing for Dollars* with the droolers than hear her sister expound on the Social Dynamic of Yaupon Island in Its Very Last Days, Home Only to Two Old White Women and a Black Gentleman. She said she'd stick her head in and say hey to little Liz, who wasn't so little anymore—it'd been ten, fifteen years since she showed up on the island toting Dr. Levinson's fancy recording equipment around, a tiny thing studying for some degree or another up at Chapel Hill. She was married now and had two or three children, and her husband let her pick right up and drive by herself down to Morehead to spend a couple days tape-recording an old lady in a nursing home. Whaley couldn't say she understood it over here, the way people acted. She couldn't say she liked it either. Morehead was loud and dusty and ugly as sin, laid out like it was along a road so busy they split it into two halves and run train tracks down the middle. The town was built back up off the water so there wasn't any breeze and the houses lining the sound were built so close you couldn't park a skiff between them. Across the water lay Bogue Banks, overrun with tourists for whom they'd ruined the island with tall hotels and a trashy boardwalk and something called putt-putt, a game you played with golfing sticks and balls and two-story plastic alligators. Good God, the houses over there. People called them cottages, but wasn't any cottage to it. They looked like they'd sleep a third of Yaupon in its heyday, some of them. The doctor who came by to check on her claimed he owned one. Whaley asked did he stay over there all year long, doctor said, Tell you the truth Miss Whaley I don't get over there near as often as I'd like. Four or five times this summer is about it, he said. Rest of the time he stayed up in New Bern. Had him two houses not fifty miles apart.

Nights Whaley had to pull her curtains to block out all the twinkling lights of Atlantic Beach. Back home on the island she didn't even need any curtains.

Liz had asked her on the phone to write some things down, all she could remember. She best be buying the paper, Maggie said when she heard it. Maggie resented Whaley for her memory. Blamed her for paying attention. She was jealous, surely. She didn't have too much she wanted to remember.

That Boyd. Though Whaley assumed her sister was long over him, it occurred to her more than once since they'd arrived in Morehead that Maggie might try to look the boy up. Though he was hardly a boy now—over fifty he'd be. She never brought it up, for it was one of those things they never had talked about.

That was a story should never be heard: how Maggie threw herself at a near boy, shamed herself and her family name and eventually the whole island when she went across the water looking for him. Whaley stayed mad at Woodrow for years, him and

Sarah both, though it was easy now to forgive Sarah for everything, considering what happened to her, Whaley's hand in it.

Which was what she was wanting to tell Liz. Telling it might
make it easier to live with, though she realized she was a hypocrite
for claiming so, as every time her sister tried to talk about that
Boyd after he left her, Whaley'd cut her off. She felt bad for that.
But in a way she had no choice but to tell what happened to Sarah.
If little Liz really wanted to know about the social dynamic between the three of them, what happened when she sent Woodrow
over to Meherrituck that day changed everything. Plus, she'd
given Dr. Levinson and them everything else: the family trees, the
accent, the odd sayings, the recipes for making candles and soap,
how to cook loon and the correct way to string a net between
dunes to trap morning robins, the famous personages who visited
the island back in its heyday as a bird hunting paradise, including
Babe Ruth and Grover Cleveland. She'd given them everything she
had known about her great-great-great-grandmother Theodosia
Burr Alston and Theodosia's famous traitor father, Aaron Burr,
how the ship carrying Theodosia ran aground off Diamond
Shoals and how her life was spared by Thaddeus Daniels, black-
heartedest pirate of them all, because she appeared to be "touched
by God."

Once, with Dr. Levinson egging her on with his "fascinat-
ings" and "interestings," she'd even revealed how she'd sometimes
thought of herself as the reincarnation of Theodosia's spirit. After all, she was the only one who had been named after her in

several generations. More curse than blessing, actually: it was such a cumbersome and antiquated name that for years, after her parents died, she went by her middle name Linda, though changing your name after the age of six months in a place so small was a frustrating endeavor. You really need new people in your life to change your name, and for many years new people were as rare on the island as fresh fruit. Most people just called her Miss Whaley. Prematurely, in fact—they started calling her that when she wasn't yet thirty—but she knew there was something stiff and self-righteous in her demeanor that encouraged them to treat her like a spinster.

But it wasn't just the name. Whatever she'd gone by, she'd still have felt the vestiges of some former and indomitable greatness. Theo, as she referred to her in front of the Tape Recorders, had dined with George Washington, Thomas Jefferson, her father's enemy Hamilton; she'd entertained the highest social order in New York and Charleston, had served as official hostess for her husband, governor of South Carolina. She spoke French, played piano, and had been unique among the women of her time for studying Latin and Greek and reading ancient history. Whaley did not in general give a damn about high society or excess schooling— she was way more concerned with putting away enough beans and squash to get her and her dreamy sister through the winter—but there was this other part of her who had lived it all, balls and visits to the White House and fine dresses and expensive wines. As she told it all to Dr. Levinson she was slightly aware that she was presenting as handed-down fact and lore things she had read in books special-ordered from off island, but this hardly seemed an infraction, as Dr. Levinson and little Liz responded so passionately to her confession that she decided in the moment to take them over to the house to see the portrait of Theo that hung over the mantel, which hung now over her bed in the nursing home. As she led them from church to house she told how Theo and her great-great-great-grandfather Claxton Whaley had broken into Thaddeus Daniels's compound near Nag's Head while the crook was out thieving and had stolen the portrait that hung over his mantel (according to local gossip, Daniels actually prayed to it, confessed his sins to it, was rumored to be driven mad by it), loaded the portrait into a skiff, and paddled south down to Yaupon, how after Theodosia's death of a stroke while she was hanging out the wash, her children found the painting hidden in their mother's bedroom, how it hung in Aunt Mandy's parlor, which was where Whaley first remembered seeing it as a young girl playing with Mandy's fat tabby cats.

Maggie was in the kitchen that day she brought over the Tape Recorders to see the portrait. Apparently she overheard Whaley carrying on about Theo. Later that night Maggie came into her room and sat on the bed. Whaley was working her word puzzle but not really—more dragging her eyes across the page waiting to fall asleep.

Maggie said: "I heard you talking about Theo."

Whaley put down her puzzle book and waited. She felt foolish for going on about such in earshot of her sister, who did not need encouragement in the fantasy department.

She said, "Well, you know, Mag, Dr. Levinson and them love a good story. You tend to talk a little out of your head around them, just giving them what they want and all."

"I've never heard you talk out of your head around them before," said Maggie. "Or around anyone. Anyway, you don't need to defend yourself, I'm not criticizing. I just wanted to tell you, see, I feel the same way."

"Feel which way?" Whaley did not want to talk about this with her sister. She made no attempt to hide the irritation in her voice.

"Like a part of her—Theo—is inside of me too. I don't know near as much about her as you, you read all those books about her father, I mean, I only know the basic story. But the part of her I feel wasn't in any of those books."

"What part would that be?" Usually Whaley was able to shut her sister up with her tone. But Maggie wasn't listening, obviously, to her questions or the way they were pitched.

"Well, I'm not real sure, exactly. Not the Theodosia who grew up in New York and entertained presidents and spoke French and married a governor and all. I guess that's the part of her *you* feel . . ."

"And what's wrong with that?"

"Nothing. I told you I'm not criticizing. I'm just saying, for me, it's the part of her that all of a sudden turned up on the Banks having had this whole other life, all these things happen to her. And the way she nearly died but got spared, that especially."

Whaley nearly hyperventilated exhaling her dramatic sigh, not that her sister noticed.

"You know I'm not real big on religion. But her being, you know, spared because they thought she was touched by God, well, that too."

"What do you think God spared you from?"

"I know, it's not like some murderer was about to toss me overboard. But I'd have gone a whole lot crazier than I did whenever Boyd left me . . ."

"I cannot believe you even remember his name. It's been years since you even laid eyes on him."

Whaley thought this would shut her up for certain. In the past it was easy to shame her into silence by suggesting that she was willfully prolonging her hurt. But none of the old failsafe ways were working. Maggie seemed to be off in one of her foggy dream-states, and Whaley, it seemed, was the one who put her there.

"Whatever reason, and God knows what that reason was, I was spared. God or whatever's out there touched me too. People could see it, so they let me be. But that's not the most powerful part of her I carry around. The deepest part is, well, I don't even know how to begin to talk about it."

Maggie nodded toward the parlor, where the portrait hung in the deepening shadows of nightfall.

"Sometimes, I'll happen to look up at that picture of her, not often because we've had it all these years and you know how it is, you don't hardly see it after so long. But I'll be walking past her and I'll feel her eyes on me and I'll stop and look up and it's like her loneliness is whispering to mine, like she's saying, I know you don't belong here either but you too are touched, this island is all you have, don't you dare give up on it because let me tell you child, anywhere else you go you're going to feel a whole lot worse."

Maggie had half-turned to Whaley and spoke in her direction, but it appeared like she was well across the island, her eyes unfocused and watery.

"I guess that's how come I stayed. After Boyd left, I felt like there was nothing left of me. And then, whenever I went over to Morehead that time with Woodrow, I thought I'd surely have to leave the island after that. But I stayed because of her. She let me know somehow it wouldn't be any better anywhere else. Hell, it'd be a whole lot worse. I could look at her long enough and gain the strength I needed to stay here, even after the storm took Sarah, when there wasn't but you and me and Woodrow left."

Maggie looked at her—seemed to see her—for the first time. But Whaley turned away. It seemed her sister sought her sympathy, that she felt she'd opened herself up, but Whaley saw it as further proof of Maggie's self-absorption and could not keep from saying so.

"Well, I appreciate you telling me all this, Mag. Reason why is, it makes me accountable for what I told Dr. Levinson today.

Which was all lies. I got caught up in the story I reckon. Wanted to spice it up a little. Truth is I don't have one iota of that woman in me. She's—you reminded me of this and I thank you for it—she was a vain, selfish, foolish thing from all I've ever heard of her. Lived off in her head most all of the time, expected everybody else to take care of her. Wasn't for your great-great-great-grandfather she would have starved to death over at Nag's Head, or got herself killed stealing from that man who spared her life. She was touched all right—not right in the head."

Maggie just sat there going tighter around the eyes and mouth as Whaley laid it out, until she was looking somewhere to the left of Whaley with this what-did-I-expect-opening-up-to-her, she's-always-like-this kind of smirk on her face. She got up and left the room, didn't say word one.

But as far as Whaley could remember she'd never strayed with Dr. Levinson and them into an area she ought to have avoided. Until today. Maggie said she was going to stick her head in, say hello to Liz. Whaley was going to see to it that she did just that, stick her head in, keep the rest of herself out in the hallway, for she didn't want her sister to hear what all she had to tell Liz.

Which in her head went like this:

One day in late September, Whaley met Woodrow at the back door when he brought the mail. Usually Woodrow came and went, leaving whatever he'd brought—mail, vegetables from the garden he tended, fish or crab he'd caught, something she'd asked him to fetch for her over in Meherrituck—on the back stoop, rattling the back screen door on its hook once or twice to signal he'd come and was going. One of the things she liked most about Woodrow was that, unlike Maggie, he wasn't one to waste hours going on.

She figured she knew Woodrow as well as anyone except Sarah. They knew each other so well they scarcely needed words, could read each other in the shorthanded and invincible way each had learned to read the sky, the wind, the tide.

That day she asked Woodrow into the kitchen where she had money counted out and folded in an envelope. She told him she had something special-ordered coming in on the three o'clock ferry the next day and could he meet the mailman at the store in Meherrituck around four?

Woodrow looked at his shoes like he always did when he didn't want to do something she was wanting him to do. In so many ways Woodrow, like Maggie, was like a child.

"I got to take the boat out first thing in the morning," he said. She knew this already. She'd predicted he'd use this as his excuse. She knew when he fished, knew the tides, knew his hours. She knew where he was fishing now, up the ditch behind Blue Harbor, and she knew he would not want to go up there early, bring back his catch, head out again.

"Surely you can find something to do to amuse yourself for a few hours over there." She allowed herself a smile. He didn't seem to notice.

"Fish'll go bad."

She said, "They got ice. You got coolers."

He said, "I ain't lost nothing over to Meherrituck I got to waste three hours trying to find."

She said, "Take Sarah over, y'all go visit." Whaley knew of several colored families over there at that point, assumed that Woodrow and Sarah were friendly with them, that they'd rather be around their own kind any chance they got.

"Sarah ain't lost nothing over there either," he said. "She ain't about to break up her day across over there, you know that. Besides, it's fixing to blow."

"Woodrow Thornton!" said Whaley. "There isn't a cloud in that sky!" She summoned up a shocked tone, tried to shame him, but she'd read the almanac and it called for squalls or worse, though it was true what she said—wasn't cloud one in the sky that afternoon. Not that it could not change in a matter of hours, especially on the sound.

Truth was, she'd ordered a new dress. It had been well over a year since she'd bought anything for herself, some five or six since she'd ordered something instead of buying off the very limited rack over at Meherrituck. Like everyone else on the island used to, she made her own clothes. But Dr. Levinson and them were due and she wanted to look good for the camera and what was wrong with that? If she did inherit some part of her great-great-great-grandmother Theodosia, it was a love of fine, frilly things, unlike Maggie who went around for ten years in a T-shirt given her by that Boyd. She kept that shirt on her back until it was see-through as Saran wrap. It was stretched out and paint-stained and about as much protection from the elements as a couple of Band-Aids but she wore it right on until one day she was pulling it over her head and it ripped into threads. Just disintegrated. Thing had been ready for the rag bag for a good decade and still Maggie went moping around for weeks like she'd lost her best friend. Whaley wouldn't be at all surprised if one day some archaeologist unearthed it in a grave marked with clamshell and braided sea oat.

She wasn't about to go around looking like that herself, even when there wasn't anyone around to see them. But they were going to have visitors, which beside the tourists the O'Malleys ferried over, who were all the time asking them to pose for pictures and leaving their picnic trash on the island and tearing up the dunes and being general nuisances, was occasion to warrant a tiny indulgence.

Oh, there were a dozen ways to justify what she did.

Woodrow wasn't having any of her naive "not a cloud in the sky." He would not dignify such a remark with a serious response. He'd looked straight at her then, a rare meeting of her eyes, and it had made her feel, well, guilty, even though the next moment she was back to manipulating him any way she could to get that dress.

"If it *is* going to blow, you'll be back across by the time it gets bad."

"I don't want to get stuck over there, leave y'all by yourselves in a storm."

He said "y'all," but she knew he was talking about Sarah.

"We'll look after Sarah," she said.

Woodrow said, "Y'all check on her if it starts to blow?"

"Good Lord, Woodrow. Of course we will. What do you think?"

It was clear what he thought by the way his gaze shifted once again, finally, to his feet, the floor—anywhere else but to her eyes.

Next morning just past dawn she sneaked down to the inlet and watched him off. Sarah was down at the dock with him, which wasn't usual—Woodrow went about his business, Sarah went about hers, it was the way it was done on the island, black or white. Whaley stood a good ways up the lane and watched the two of them talking down on the dock, then hugging on each other, which made her feel guilty to witness. She felt a little bad to be out checking up on him anyway, though Woodrow didn't always do what he said he was going to do and she wanted that dress and if he had not arrived at his boat toting coolers she'd more than likely have marched down there and reminded him. Right in front of Sarah. Just in case he forgot and all. Or Sarah talked him out of it, said to him (Whaley could just about hear her), Why you wasting your time on old sour Whaley, she want whatever it is so bad she can ride over there with you, you can pick her up tomorrow, why not? Whaley always assumed that Sarah undermined her loudly and with vehemence every chance she got. With the respect given to an opponent whose strength and patience is formidable, Whaley cared what Sarah thought. But there were only four of them left on this island now and somebody had to take charge and even though Woodrow and Sarah were each more capable than her little sister, it would not do to let them run things.

Besides, Woodrow was more comfortable being told what to do. The times she'd asked his opinion about something of importance to the four of them—to the island—he'd seemed reluctant to take charge. Too much responsibility made him nervous. Some people had no interest in leading; they were made to work behind the scenes. She had no illusions about what her life might be like without Woodrow, but they were a team, clearly. They worked together in their own inimitable, mysterious way. She'd never be able to explain it to Dr. Levinson and them because she was sure they'd judge her if she were honest—they'd figure her for a card-carrying member of the Klan—and if she were dishonest, if she pretended everything was equal, well, what would be the point of that? For years she'd avoided talking about her relationship with Woodrow and Sarah. When they'd asked she'd just smiled and changed the subject, and they knew better than to push.

After watching Woodrow load coolers in the boat, Whaley made herself scarce before Sarah caught her spying. She picked across the old Pollock place to check on the stock, down by that point to a dozen sheep, three cows, two ornery ponies. On the way across the island she happened to notice the sky, which had darkened to the south, though the highest clouds were a milky yellow. She thought of climbing a dune to study the sea, but she convinced herself that if it was to blow, it wouldn't be anything they hadn't seen before and more of it.

But when she came up on the stock she heard the ponies neighing, saw in the scuttling of sheep and the odd manic movements of all the animals some proof undeniable that it would be more than just the routine battering of wind and water.

Her daddy and other old-timers used to claim that if you saw a pig with a straw in its mouth, a bad storm was on its way. Whaley avoided going anywhere near Woodrow and Sarah's where the only pigs on the island might be sucking on straws.

Back on the sound side of the island the day was calm, near windless. She put it out of her mind, tried to get some work done. But along about noon Maggie came in from God knows where and said, "It's curious out there."

Whaley, unable to resist, said, "How so?"

"No mosquitoes," said Maggie.

"Wind changed," said Whaley, her tone a shrug, a don't-you-know-anything edge to her words.

"It's fixing to blow," said Maggie. "Where's Woodrow?"

Whaley did not think it time to tell Maggie about the dress. She didn't think that time would come, in fact. She said Woodrow was where he was always this time of the morning, out on the water. But she went a little further, though she did try to stop herself from lying. She said, "He mentioned something about needing to go to the store this afternoon."

"He'll change his mind," said Maggie. "If anyone can sniff out some weather, it's Woodrow."

This got away with Whaley, Maggie's innocent yet wholly accurate statement. More the bit about Woodrow changing his mind, maybe. Whaley didn't want Woodrow to change his mind. She wanted the wind to shift, the storm to turn and head up the coast or stall out before it ever reached land, she wanted Woodrow to meet the ferry, she wanted her dress to wear when the Tape Recorders showed up with their cameras this time. One thing she did not want was her sister knowing the reason she'd sent Woodrow over there.

But now, years later, knowing what she knew, Whaley often wondered why Woodrow went. He could have said no. He wasn't her slave (though once Dr. Levinson had taken her aside and told her that Woodrow's great-great-great-grandfather Hezekiah Thornton had in fact been sold to her great-great-great-grandfather, a fact she saw no sense in ever repeating to Woodrow or Maggie either, as she surely would have told it). *No* was definitely a word in Woodrow's vocabulary, though she'd hardly ever heard him utter it outright. When he did not want to do something it did not get done. If it was something Whaley deemed doing, she'd ask him again. (Ask, not tell; she always asked, said Would you?, said Please.) If he did not do it, she'd ask-not-tell a third time. If he did not get round to it the third time, she'd leave off and either do it herself or find something else to stew about.

Woodrow must have known well before she did how bad it was

going to blow. Yet he went. Maybe he wanted some time off island himself. He'd spent years away, all because of Sarah. But knowing Woodrow like she did, she had to wonder why he allowed Sarah to take him off island for all those years. She knew he loved this island, hated being away from it, even for a night. Must have been love, though if that was what love did—make you court misery in order to make someone else happy—she did not want any part of it.

Whaley went about her business that morning, which was indoors. She scarcely looked out the window. What could she do about the weather? If it was going to blow, it was going to blow, only thing she could do was clean the yard and porch of anything the wind might pick up and, if it got bad enough and hit at high tide and there was a surge, head for the church, which not only crowned the highest point of the island but had a balcony built more with high water in mind than overflowing crowds come to worship a merciful God.

Midafternoon it started to rain. Lightly at first, an intermittent drizzle, but within an hour it was heavy and wind-sheeted. Maggie came in from wherever she'd been, wearing an ancient, peeling slicker the Life Saving station had issued their father, her hair soaked, her face wide with questions she did not let herself ask.

She did not say what they were both thinking. Their father's old ditty: Wind before rain, soon fine again. Other way around, get out of town.

There wasn't much talking during supper. The radio spoke to

them from a corner of the kitchen, Elizabeth City station with its reporting pitched to Knotts Island, Little River, and the Northern Banks. Morehead City station was only high whistling, as if the wind itself had taken over the studio and was broadcasting itself out to all those poor fools wanting the radio to tell them something they didn't already know. If Whaley thought at all about Woodrow it was to think, He's on his way home now, he and Sarah settling into their after-supper routine, whatever that was. All these years living just across the creek from the two of them and Whaley had no earthly idea what they did nights. She knew one thing, though, which comforted her: Sarah loved her radio, had it on from the time she got up in the morning, every time Whaley was by there she heard it blasting her gospel music, all the hand clapping and the Jesus shouting and the swelling organ chords. Sarah would have the radio on, in case Woodrow had not come back. She'd know anyway, with or without the radio, that a storm had hit. She'd know what to do.

Right out of the blue she said to no one—to herself, to the radio playing a song asking her did she know the way to San Jose— "What do Woodrow and Sarah do at night?"

The problem with her outburst was: Maggie in the room.

It took a minute for Maggie to get over the shock, visible in her wide eyes (actually she looked a little terrified), after which a smile took over her face, then gave just as quickly away to a familiar smirk.

"Must be the drop in pressure," she said.

"What?"

"Making you all of a sudden curious about other people for once in your life."

"I'm plenty curious, just not nosy. I'm not a gossip."

"To answer your question," said Maggie, uncharacteristically ignoring this jab, "seeing as how they are the only couple on this island, I'd wager that whatever they do, it's way more fun than reading aloud grocery store prices."

"You *would* be thinking that."

"And you *wouldn't*."

Whaley figured she'd ignore a jab as well, though it wasn't easy.

"Lord, they've got, what, ten or eleven children? Woodrow's every bit as old as we are. I don't think it's on their minds every night."

She wouldn't have been talking to Maggie at all—especially not about this—if she hadn't been feeling guilty about that dress. It was revolting, her speculating about Woodrow and Sarah's private business. But somehow it brought Sarah into the room with them, out of the rain and wind, safe, sheltered. Woodrow too. She thought of him every time the wind rushed up to drown out the radio, every time some debris tapped against the side of the clapboard.

Maggie crossed her arms beneath her chest and sat there studying her. "Well, we ought to go check on Sarah. She ought not to be down there by herself in all this."

She was half out of her chair when Whaley shot up and nearly shouted, "Stay here, I'll go, you wash up now."

Maggie lowered herself onto the chair. "You're acting strange, Theo," she said. She never called her sister by her given name. She never really called her anything at all, but if she had to get her attention she'd say Whaley first, or Linda.

Whaley was in the mudroom, pulling on their father's peeling oiler, still dripping from Maggie's earlier outing, and then she was out the door.

What she found first was a stillness so total her mind and body were put to rest: there would be no danger tonight. But as soon as she got out on the beach road, headed down the hill to Woodrow's, the gusts came. She staggered into them like a drunk. The yucca rustled in the breeze and Whaley thought of how adjustable to the elements was everything on this island. Even, maybe, her sister, who she'd always thought of as fragile, weak, lazy-willed. Yet she'd survived. She was here still. She'd been here nearly as long as Whaley. To remain, she had to be stronger than Whaley gave her credit for.

As she neared Woodrow's the rain was sideways, and down in the bottom, where Woodrow's great-great-great-grandfather had chosen to rebuild his house after a storm came through and blew away both Hezekiah's shed and Theodosia's home place, the water had begun to pool. She felt it lap her ankles. She sloshed right through it, for even though she had years of evidence to the contrary—quite a few deaths to boot—Whaley feared the wind more than the water. She could climb up to the balcony of the church, could climb even higher, up the steeple if the water rose that high. The water would not wash away the church, which had stood there now for over 120 years. But the wind could take it all away.

Even though she meant to fetch Sarah and bring her back to the house, where the three of them could weather the storm together, and Sarah could be closer to the church in case the water rose, Whaley stole up on the porch as lightly as a cat. She told herself she didn't want to scare Sarah, for who else besides her husband would come clomping up on her porch boards in the middle of a storm. She had never been down here to see Sarah. She'd always been here to see Woodrow and she always treaded lightly on the porch so as not to call attention to the fact that she was a white woman come to order around a black man.

She was about to knock when she heard that music. Loud as it'd be if the band were playing in her kitchen. Whaley figured the sound could not go any higher. She could have heard it up the hill to the house had not the wind been roaring and seething.

Sarah came into view. She stood on the threshold of that kitchen Woodrow'd tacked on to keep Sarah from having to tote everything up from the summer kitchen. She was holding her Bible and her lips were moving and she was swaying a little, to the music obviously, though when she came closer, into the lamplight,

Whaley saw the look on her face, pure fear, no sign of the comfort she ought to draw from songs praising his only Son our Lord, from the leather book she clutched hard to her breast.

Before she could even think, Whaley was tiptoeing off the porch. The wet wind nearly blew her back up on it, for she'd lost her wits, forgotten how to walk in a storm. You have to act drunk to negotiate a sixty-mile-an-hour gust. Forget your bones, flow loose in the hips, fluid, let the wind move through you. The rain, well, it hadn't bothered her on the way down but on the way back up the hill, every isolated drop stung like truth.

In the yard the island lit white with lightning, a quarter second's clarity: things were forever after changed. She heard a pop, the house went dark, thunder followed. By the time she managed to push open the door that fought her off as if the house knew what she'd done, Maggie had the candles lit, was fussing with their grandfather's old whale oil lamp, converted now to kerosene.

Maggie stopped her wick-twisting to ask with a look where in the world was Sarah.

"She didn't want to come. Said she was fine where she was."

Maggie said, "Whaley?"

"Oh, we're back to Whaley now? What, Mag? I went down there, I asked her, I can't order her, she doesn't belong to us. She's got her pride, that girl."

Maggie said, "It's just, Woodrow—"

"Woodrow obviously has nothing to do with whether she's got the sense to save herself."

But Woodrow, of course, had everything to do with why Whaley lied. The truth is she never let herself admit her reason for leaving Sarah alone. For years when she thought of why, she pushed why quickly out of her mind. She knew it had to do with Woodrow but it was only now that Woodrow was gone, that the island was abandoned, that she and Maggie had been sent across the sound to die, that Whaley could admit to little Liz and the readers of the Norfolk newspaper and the whole world what she only vaguely felt that night in the storm: Sarah, sooner or later, was going to take Woodrow away. If Woodrow left, they'd all have to leave.

"If anything happens to Sarah," said Maggie, "I'd say Woodrow's going to have something to do with it."

"Nothing's going to happen. She knows where to go if the water starts to rise."

"I ought to go down there and talk to her."

"Nonsense, you're not going anywhere."

"I'm just saying—"

"That she hates me and would rather drown than take my advice? I reckon it's you she loves."

"We get on all right."

"Oh yeah, Mag. She loved it when you spread sin all over her backyard, shacking up in her summer kitchen with your high school boy."

Maggie fell silent. She was like the storm outside—any lull was bound to be followed by fury.

"I guess I'll be having that incident thrown back in my face until I die, won't I?"

"No, Mag. Just happens to pertain to the subject of how Sarah hates me but loves you."

"Everything in your mind *per*tains," said Maggie.

"What in the world's that mean?"

Another four seconds of calm. Whaley held her breath.

"Just that it must be very comforting to have everything all tidy and settled. Knowing you're right, having all the evidence of everybody else's wrongness—it must be nice."

Whaley could not show it, but these words stung more than those gale-force-wind-driven raindrops. She did not want to talk anymore—in fact, she wanted very much to be alone—but she knew she needed to distract Maggie from the plight of poor all-alone Sarah. So she engaged her sister in a protracted and repetitive argument, the subject of which was the same subject they'd been arguing about for nearly sixty-odd years: who was right.

Sometimes, when Whaley sat listening to her sister tell her stories to the Tape Recorders, it occurred to her that there was more than one island. Three, actually—Woodrow's island, Maggie's, her own. The Tape Recorders never could get Sarah to talk to them, which Whaley secretly appreciated, for there was no telling what sort of fourth island might have emerged had Sarah got to tell her side of it. But the thought that there were three islands was not at all pleasing to Whaley. She tended not to recognize but the one, her own, for the others seemed to her soggy and vulnerable places, no more secure than driftwood tossed about by the waves.

The argument was not winnable or even decipherable after all, for it degenerated into a splinter argument about the way Maggie misbehaved thirty or so odd years ago. Even Whaley wasn't sure she had the facts so straight any more, though she did not say that to Maggie. Twice Maggie, insulted, got up to go leave the room, but she realized she would be alone in an increasingly threatening storm, and besides, fighting made the time pass. They argued. The radio, packed with batteries, had long since given over to whistling, and even if it had been working it would have told them things they'd *been* knowing, as by the time word of any storm got on the air on the mainland stations it had already hit the island and was likely out to sea by then.

Around five in the morning Whaley went to the back door to check on things. She saw the water then.

What she should have done was come right back inside. But instead she stood there, hesitating, trying to decide was it too late to run down there and fetch Sarah. Her being gone so long's what brought Maggie into it. Whaley heard her gasp when she saw the surge coming up past the clothesline, almost to the house.

"Good God Almighty," she said. "We've got to get Sarah."

"It's too late, Mag. We got to get to the church."

"If it's up in the yard here it's bad high down there in the bottom. We've got to get her."

"You go down there now, you'll get sucked right out in the sound."

Maggie went inside. In a second here she came again, the slicker half on, an arm in, one out.

Whaley had to grab her. Maggie fought back, the two of them struggling out in the rain then. "You will die if you go down there," Whaley said. "Sarah had her chance. Now you get your head on and come with me up to the church."

Whaley held her sister until she went limp. Let Whaley grab her hand and lead her like Woodrow's old mule, Pilothouse, back into the house where Whaley grabbed some food and then the portrait off the wall, which she wrapped in a blanket and carried with her right up the hill to the church, through the rising surge, alive with boards from buildings down island washed away already, the other crazy things a flood will float right by you: an ironing board, somebody's bait buckets, a crutch. It was just light out. Water lapped the church steps. In ten minutes it had risen to float the purple pew cushions. They made their way from the pulpit through the cold water up to the balcony steps. It would have been plenty safe there, the water had never risen that high, but Whaley wanted to see what the storm had done so she kept climbing up the ladder to the belfry. There, in the cramped space aside the bell, she wedged herself up toward the window and saw Woodrow's half-flattened house.

Not the water but the wind. That flimsy kitchen Woodrow had tacked on out of boards washed up on the beach, some rusty tin he traded the O'Malleys for—she'd told him from the start how it would not withstand even a moderate blow. Woodrow, stubborn Woodrow, well, no—he would not listen to any of that. Won't nothing wrong with that kitchen, he claimed. Just because material wasn't store-bought did not mean squat. In fact, it made it much better, for most of this mess had survived the sea, the sun, which made it even stronger, more likely to withstand all God sent to test it.

It's not the materials, Woodrow, she tried to tell him, it's that you're a waterman, no builder. His great-great-great-granddaddy Hezekiah was a skilled builder but most of his handiwork was long washed away, and after he passed, the Thornton men went back to the water. The houses on the island that had survived were all built by the same family—the Pender men, geniuses at construct-ing a dwelling uniquely suited to the limitations of sand, low water table, relentless wind, rising water. The rest of Woodrow's house had been constructed by Arthur Pender Jr. But when she told him this he said only, I don't know any not-dead Penders and besides I'm a little short to be hiring myself an arch-itect.

Now she had her proof that he ought to have listened to her, not strayed into areas where he had no expertise, but it did not make her feel any better. Soon as the water went down they'd go check on Sarah, but God help her she had the good sense to stay away from that kitchen.

Which God knows she did not. Which Maggie discovered herself because Whaley could not bring herself to go down there.

It was midmorning when the wind quit whipping at the stained glass and the quiet rose up into the balcony like something you're supposed to experience in church, a deep calm that entered you like breath, like air sweet and pure ushered down from heaven. Then the sunlight kaleidoscoping those windows, which she'd always found wasteful—she remembered when they were brought over in a crate from Norfolk, how the so-called stained-glass artisan who she figured for a crook took forever to assemble them in front of an audience of half the island who treated his show as if it was the Sistine Chapel getting a touch-up. Now the light slanted down through the glass and the colors collided in twirling prisms above the ruined pews and for a few seconds Whaley was taken away from the utter mess of the church and no doubt the entire island, which would likely not be the same as long as she lived there.

She struggled up from her slump against the back wall of the balcony where she'd been sort of sleeping. Maggie was gone. Whaley pulled herself up to the window, saw her sister picking her way down the hill, negotiating the ravished island. Detritus everywhere and most of it belonging to those who'd already given up, left for the mainland. What got away with Whaley was the notion that she was going to have to clean up after them.

There was no scream, no Maggie running back up the hill, but Whaley knew Sarah was dead because her sister did not seem any changed. She wore the same dazed expression on her face, took the same tentative gait, as if she'd spent the last twenty-four hours on rough seas and was struggling to get her land legs back. It was as if she had known already, before she went down there, what she'd find.

Plus, no Sarah in tow.

Whaley met her on the steps.

"Well?"

"She's in the kitchen. All I saw was her legs."

"Did you even check to see was she still breathing?"

"I felt of her leg. She's *been* dead. Go check yourself since you don't believe me."

"I believe you," said Whaley softly. She felt nauseated, but she couldn't say even then that she realized her hand in all this. More the shock of having a country of four dwindle down suddenly to three. She had a thought she wished she'd never had, but she had it: about how three is always a cumbersome number. Shifting alliances, two against one.

"I don't understand why she didn't just come with you. I mean, I never figured Sarah for outright wanting to die."

Whaley said, "Just because she stayed behind doesn't mean she chose to die. She might not of thought the storm would amount to anything."

Whaley remembered the look on Sarah's face, the Bible in her hands, her pacing up and down that hall. She remembered that awful loud praise-him-on-high music. She could hear it now in her head as if someone had put her inside the radio.

Whaley said, "I have to sit down now."

Maggie said, "What's wrong with you?"

Whaley said, "I don't have the right to feel bad?" She meant to say "sad." She flushed and a wash of nausea came over her and this time she really did feel bad, terribly bad.

"No love lost between y'all's all I'm saying."

It helped the nausea to have something to get indignant about. She was thankful to her sister just then for drawing her into an argument.

"Don't you go getting self-righteous about her dying," said Whaley. "We might not have got on so great but she's dead and poor Woodrow and poor Crawl and all them others to have lost their mama this way."

"This way? Seems like a good way to me. I'd just soon get clobbered in the head by something the wind shook loose as drown or, worse yet, waste away in some hospital."

"We don't get to choose, sister."

Maggie sat down beside her on the soggy pew.

"We hardly ever get to choose. Oh, they're plenty of choices. Just look at the paper, you'll see they got all kinds of choices. But none of them are the right ones."

Maggie said, "We need to get you to bed."

"Take me home, Mag. I want to go home."

Maggie tucked her sister in upstairs and trudged back up the hill to the church to fetch the portrait. But as soon as it was propped up on the sea chest at the foot of her bed like she asked, Whaley found she could not look at it. Something in the woman's eyes, something haughty and defiant, that she felt she shared. It shamed her to think about how she'd gone on once, and on tape too, about the kinship she felt with this woman, when what she ought to have been talking about was the first days she could remember on this island in the house so pretty painted white with all the green grass like a carpet and the white sand. Ducks would light on the water so many they looked like an island. Decorations for woman's hats out of the plumage. Babe Ruth came, asked to meet Al Louie. My little sister and I we loved so dearly those cats.

When she woke it was dark. Light rain falling on the tin roof. For a full blissful minute she forgot everything—the storm, her lie, Sarah, the church—and the darkness she mistook for predawn of a new day. But then it all came rushing home to her and the black shadows of her bedroom turned sinister.

There was no power, no light—in fact, the power and the light would never return, though she did not know until weeks of darkness that the storm had severed the cable. Fine by Whaley, really, that the island moved backward in time.

Maggie sat at the kitchen table, the kerosene lamp dicing a circle of wavering light from the gloom.

"You let me sleep too long."

Maggie got up and began to run water in a pail. There was mud on the floor, mudstains six inches up the cabinets, staining the legs of the table. The smell was rank and would only grow worse.

"I had things to do."

An iciness in her voice. She would not look Whaley's way, much less meet her eyes. As if Whaley had been off on a drunk, had done something to bring unfathomable shame to the house.

"You've not been to bed?"

"I had things to do," she said again. The water rose in the bucket. Maggie looked out the window as it began to spill over the lip, and Whaley just resisted the urge to tell her not to waste water, especially not now of all times.

"What things?"

Maggie sighed—or was it a gasp? A cynical snort?

"Sarah's body? I just couldn't leave it there for him to find."

"Where is it?"

"In the church, laid out on the altar. He's up there with her."

"He's back?"

"I said he's with her."

Whaley scooted her chair back in the mud. As she was rising Maggie turned on her. "Where are you going?"

"I've got to go to him."

"You leave him be. He wants to be alone with her."

"He'll need help preparing the body."

"I cleaned her up best I could with what I had. She bled to death? The roof collapsed and a piece of tin sliced her neck and she lay up under that rubble bleeding to death while we were safe and dry up in our white-people-only church?"

The way her sister turned statements of fact into questions terrified Whaley. As if these things were unbelievable, as if it would take forever to accept that they had a hand in these things, it would take amazing strength not to deny it all.

"She was certainly welcome in that church and you know it. Don't go changing what happened."

"I don't know what happened. All I know is she's dead and we're alive and we ought to have gone down there and dragged her black ass up the hill."

"What are you talking about? If you'd of gone down the hill when you wanted to, we would have lost two. I told you then and I will tell Woodrow to his face: ain't no sense in a person dying to save someone who didn't have sense enough to get out of the way of a storm like that one. You need to change what happened to feel better, fine. But you keep it to yourself."

When Whaley rose again the chair shot back onto the floor. But instead of the snap she expected there was only a thud, for everything was muffled with mud now.

"I'm telling you Whaley," said Maggie, "leave Woodrow alone with her."

Whaley thought: she has the power now. She knows something and she'll hold it over me just like I held Boyd over her only what I did is worse than her falling in love, however foolishly. Still, the idea that Maggie was going to make her pay, that she would dole out oblique accusations for the rest of their life together, made Whaley want to scream.

But instead she breathed big through her mouth to avoid the stench and said, "How did you get the body up the hill?"

"Put it in a tarp and dragged. Why?"

"Why didn't you just wake me up?"

"Seems like you had some things you were needing to sleep off."

Whaley thought of confronting her but did not have the energy. She would win this the way she'd won everything else: by being implacable.

But it was hard, harder than anything she'd ever done, especially when she laid eyes on Woodrow, saw how he was taking it. She waited, as Maggie suggested, for a few hours, left Woodrow alone with his bride. She even let Maggie go up there and help Woodrow clean the body up for burial. Woodrow claimed she wanted to be buried on the mainland, near Crawl; there wasn't any way to get word to the family save Woodrow taking the skiff back over to Meherrituck, getting on the phone, which he wasn't about to do and Whaley wasn't about to offer to do for him. He would just have to show up across the water with his dead wife. That was the way it used to be, before phones and all. Sometimes people went off island and died and you didn't hear about it for a year or so. Of course to Whaley's mind, once you went off island you were in a way already dead.

"I'm so sorry, Woodrow," she said to him that afternoon in the church. He wouldn't look at her, which wasn't anything new. He mumbled something she didn't catch, which Maggie obviously heard, for she looked to her sister for interpretation—sometimes Maggie understood Woodrow better because she followed him around like a toddler—and saw her sister wince. Later, when she asked what he'd said, Maggie had sighed and left the room. She never did get it out of her.

"It wasn't anything I could do," she said. "We would of lost another one, going down there to get her."

Woodrow turned to her then, finally. He said, "I know, Miss Whaley. Wind wants to take you, can't do nothing to stop it, can you?"

This made her feel worse, and though more words passed between them, and Woodrow went on to outright accuse her, when she said everybody's time is going to come, of helping Sarah's time come, she told herself that it was the wind.

And they did not speak of it again. Woodrow took Sarah across the water that very day, buried her in the churchyard where Crawl and them worshipped. He was back within a week. For a while they saw nothing of him. He spent his days off by himself, down south where the storm had chewed a new inlet in the island. She had no idea what he did down there. She spent a lot of time outdoors trying to catch sight of him, but if she saw him at all he was moving away quickly, over the dunes, in and out of hammocks, blurred by shimmering heat, an apparition.

Then one day he turned up with a sack of croaker he caught. First time since she'd known him he ever came to the front door. She hardly knew how to act. Her jaw muscles ached from smiling. They stood there for a long time without saying anything, Woodrow looking over her shoulder at what she finally figured out was the portrait of Theo. Before he left he allowed as how they favored some. She never did know what to make of that, though afterward she took to trying even harder never to look above the hearth.

The Tape Recorders came not long after Sarah's death, having read about it in the paper. They were all hot to talk about the New Dynamic. Maggie said to Whaley, "Don't go talking to them about all that. Have some dignity."

"You're going to lecture me about dignity?"

"Go ahead and throw it in my face if you want, every bad thing I ever done. But look: I'm not about to go telling them things that Woodrow wouldn't want them to know."

"How do you know what Woodrow wants anybody to know or don't?"

"I know he wouldn't appreciate it, you talking about Sarah to them. He's a private man. And listen: there's only three of us now. Ain't no black and white left as far as I'm concerned. We might be kin, but he's as much a part of the family as we are, you ask me. If he wants to talk about his wife dying in the storm, let him talk about it. But if he doesn't bring it up, that doesn't give you the right to tell it."

"You act like I'm going around gossiping. What these people are doing is important, Maggie. Without them the history of this island would be lost. No one else is going to tell it. And if we don't tell it the way it happened, they'll just make it up to suit them."

"So you're going to tell it the way it happened?"

Whaley reminded herself that her resolve *was* this island. Without it, even Woodrow would have given up long ago, followed Sarah to the mainland. All she had to do was *act right*.

Still, it was a victory for Maggie, for the Tape Recorders did ask, and she told them she'd rather not talk about Sarah's death, it was too soon, too raw still, and even Dr. Levinson, who had a way of needling you until you told him things you didn't even know you knew, left off then.

Slowly Woodrow came back to them. Nights when the breeze kept the mosquitoes away and some when it didn't they'd sit together on the steps of the church. Whaley would read out her prices from the paper and they would discuss the ways the world had gotten away with them.

One night they were out on the steps. It was early spring and so clear the stars popped out before the sun went down. They'd had an early supper, had met up at the church; Whaley had a fat stack of prices to get through. Some of them were fixed to items she had no iota what they were talking about. A Weed Eater? A microwave?

That night, Woodrow had a letter from Crawl. Maggie read it aloud for him. Crawl claimed Woodrow was about to turn eighty. Whaley knew Woodrow was older than her but she did not figure him for eighty.

When Maggie finished reading the letter, Woodrow said, "Crawl don't know nothing about how old I am."

Maggie said, "Old enough to know better."

Whaley said, "Too old to change."

She wasn't exactly joking, but she did not mean for him to take it so seriously. She saw immediately that what she'd said hurt him, for he made like a bug had bit his neck and slapped himself so hard she started. For the life of her she could not figure what got away with him so bad. They were all three too old to change, and what of it? What was the point in changing your life when it was nearly over and done with?

But Woodrow took it wrong. He sat there stewing. She could feel it coming off of him, a fog of resentment, even before he came out with it.

"Y'all ought not to have done me like y'all done me," he said before he got up and picked his way down the stairs and headed down the lane home.

Well, he just didn't understand her, that's all. It wasn't like she was criticizing him. The opposite: his ability to roll along with whatever the wind blew in was what she admired about him. It was what they shared, this unflappable bedrock strength. What had kept them together on this island all these years when everyone and everything—wind, water, bugs, sun, Army Corps of Engineers, Park Service, Other People—had conspired to push them off.

It was just the two of them left on the steps. Whaley said, "I believe I hurt Woodrow's feelings."

Maggie, characteristically taking any point of view but her sister's, said, "I'd say you did."

They spoke no more about it until they were back home, standing in the kitchen, getting ready for bed. Maggie had poured herself some milk. She had her hair down, and it was brown and gray and straggly and it looked a sight stringing all down the T-shirt she wore for a nightgown. Whaley kept hers up, had for years. It was unseemly, wearing your hair down at their age.

"Well, it was a compliment," said Whaley. "He just took it wrong."

Maggie put her milk down. She was facing the window over the sink and stared out it for a moment before she turned.

"A compliment?" she said. "How is that a compliment, being too old to change? You'd like to be told you're too old to do anything?"

"We are old, Mag. It's a fact."

She started to add, Wearing your hair all stringy long and sleeping in some ratty T-shirt won't change that. But she said nothing.

"Everybody likes to believe they can change."

"Not everybody."

"Okay," Maggie said. "Everybody else."

Whaley scooted a chair out from the kitchen table and sat. She said, "I really do not understand this, Maggie. I want to, though. I want you to explain it to me. What is it you want to change for? How do you want to change?"

"You're asking me? Don't ask me, it wasn't my feelings you

hurt. You didn't tell me I'm too old to change, though I'm sure you believe it."

"See, that's what I want to know. You're not listening. I'm seriously interested in how come y'all want everybody to think you can go around changing all the time."

She was serious, she was interested. But like most questions she asked of her sister, she felt like she had the answer already, and she knew that she wasn't going to change her mind. Still, she wanted to hear her sister's side of it. She was generally curious about this idea of changing, why it meant so much to people like her sister.

"Let me ask you a question, Whaley. You think people are born one way and they die that way? That there's never any chance they can become, I don't know, different?"

Whaley pretended to give it some thought. "Yes."

"So, just for instance let's take you and me. You think you were born to do the right thing and I was born to fail?"

"That's not fair and you know it," Whaley lied.

"What's not fair about it? When have you failed?"

"More times than I care to count."

"Name one."

Whaley thought about Sarah. It shocked her, this thought, for she never let herself entertain it. It was so buried, so wrapped up in justifications and rationalizations, the story so shifted, that she was nearly brought to tears by the way it so quickly surfaced.

"Okay," she said, swallowing. "I knew you were going across to see him that day. I did nothing to stop you."

"You knew? How?"

"Woodrow told me." This was true: Woodrow did tell her, he was worried about his role in the whole affair, he knew or at least suspected there would be trouble over there. She knew how much Maggie trusted Woodrow and she hated to endanger that trust, but it was a far preferable failure to admit than the one that had, seconds earlier, nearly caused her to cry.

Maggie sipped her milk. She tried and failed to look unfazed.

After a pause she said, her bottom lip quivering, "Well, that doesn't really count as much of a failure. I mean, it's not really your job to go around stopping me from making a fool out of myself."

Full-time job, Whaley thought. She said, "I should have done something."

"Why?"

"I hated to see you hurt like that. I could have done something to help."

"You can't stop me from hurting. You surely can't stop Woodrow from hurting. If you could, well, wouldn't you be using your power to try and get us to change how we are?"

Whaley was silent. She wished she'd never admitted to this failure, for it was a lie. It wasn't a failure, and she knew there was nothing she could do to stop her sister from hurting.

"There you are then," said Maggie. "If you believe *you* can change me—or Woodrow or whoever—you must believe in the notion of change."

Maggie drank off the rest of her milk, wiped her mouth with the back of her hand like a child, and sailed up to bed.

Whaley reached over, turned down the wick on the lamp, sat in the hard darkness. She felt exposed and a little maligned by what Maggie said, and it did not seem fair to her, for she wasn't the one who'd gone across and made a fool of herself. Why should she feel bad? She'd let Maggie turn her words around, she'd failed to express herself. That was her only failure. She did not explain that you couldn't get rid of the wrongest parts of you; you just had to say no to them. So no, you weren't really changing, you were just triumphing over weakness.

She thought that this was something Woodrow knew through and through, though he let himself hurt, she'd seen him do it. He wasn't fragile like Maggie, but things people said got away with him, like they had today. Simple innocent remark about his age. Well, she meant it, she wasn't going to take it back, but on the other hand she did not mean for it to hurt like it did. Maggie and Woodrow were both so sensitive. She'd never ever meant this word in the positive way some used it—to describe a person who felt and cared deeply, intelligently, like Theodosia. She meant it as a criticism, a sign of weakness.

None of this would have mattered had they been three people living anywhere else, but that night she felt it all on her shoulders, the weight of this island, its fate. She felt their survival depended not so much upon Woodrow and what he did for them—bringing in food, meeting the mail boat, slaughtering hogs, fixing broke

things—but in her ability not to go sulking when someone flung
a certain random combination of words her way. This island was
not words. It wasn't feelings, for Pete's sake. It was sand, wind, sea
oat, wax myrtle, water bush, red cedar, live oak, yaupon. It was peat,
marl, loam and slough, hammock, marsh, and dune after dune. It
was sound on one side and sea on the other and a ribbon of sand
between, running right out toward the Gulf Stream, the crust of a
continent defying the overwash and daring a wind to take it away.

What would happen to the island when they left? This question kept her sitting up in the dark until first light seeped in the
windows. None of them had all that much time left, and when
they left, well, wasn't as if any of those who'd fled were going to
return. Oh, there was no shortage of fools wanting their own island, even some willing to put up with the elements to say they
lived all alone in a ghost town fifty miles out in the ocean. But
they were fools—summer people, tourists, kids, hippies—and
they wouldn't last.

She thought of Theodosia, how she'd come to this island with a
man so far from the type she'd been brought up to love. He taught
her how to get by, how to love this island that in Theo's day was
at its grandest, though Theo lived long enough to see it start to
dwindle down to what it was now: just the three of them. Her great-
great-great-grandmother had spent all her life looking, trying to fill
some hole—just like Maggie—and in the end she found her happi-
ness right here on this island. She adapted, what it was. Made do.

Thoughts of Theo and Woodrow kept Whaley up and tossing

until, near dawn, she decided she'd go down to the dock and see Woodrow off. It would be a test, see if he was still mad. He needn't be mad at her—she meant no offense, found it silly the way words got away with Woodrow so when he'd withstood so much worse.

From the beach road, just south of the dunes they used to call the Widow Walk, where women of the island went to spy their men coming in off the water, Whaley saw the empty dock. Squinting, she could make out Woodrow's boat, a smudge on the horizon. She took some solace in the fact that he was up and out on the water so early, for whatever she'd said to him couldn't have gotten away with him that bad, but then she remembered that Woodrow was not the type to lie about sulking. Whatever happened he went to work. Perhaps work was how he dealt with it, the pain. She felt a kinship there, for this is how she'd managed the loneliness in her own life, though she'd never admit as much to her sister or, God forbid, the Tape Recorders. First of all, to admit to loneliness would send the wrong message to them all—that everything she needed in the world was not contained here on this island that, sooner now, not later, she was going to have to leave. It was one of the first questions little Liz had asked whenever she managed to get with Whaley away from Dr. Levinson, who back then would not let Liz do much more than hold the equipment, fetch him water or bug spray. "Don't you get lonesome over here?" she'd asked. Whaley would have likely acted ill had Dr. Levinson asked this question, but he never would have asked it, for it wasn't his type question. He was more interested in hearing lore about

Theodosia, or about how they celebrated First Christmas instead of Jesus' birthday. Little Liz, though, how could Whaley get mad at that girl who was just as ignorant as she could be about any-place not Washington, D.C., where she had been raised up.

No, honey, I don't ever get lonesome. Never have. Plenty to keep me busy. I don't need television or movie theaters to take my mind off my troubles because at the end of my day I am just not that troubled.

There were so many lies in that answer she didn't even want to untangle them all. Maybe not lies—only what Maggie called playing it up to the hilt, the primitive Banker role. Once you got going down that road it was hard to admit you liked to sit out on the church steps and read aloud grocery store prices of an eve-ning. Didn't fit with the image. She had the island to protect too. Wasn't anybody else going to protect it, since it wasn't but three of them left and she was the only one of them could tell the story the way Dr. Levinson and them needed it told.

That morning Whaley watched Woodrow's boat until it slid over the sunlit horizon and then she walked home feeling as hol-low low as she had in years. She told herself it was lack of sleep making her feel this way, for stormy nights excepting, she always slept like the dead, went to bed at dark and got up at first light, was out when her head hit the pillow and stark awake when she swung her legs off the mattress at the rooster crow. At home she went straight upstairs to her room and crawled in bed with her clothes on.

Maggie woke her around two o'clock that afternoon.

"You feeling poorly?" She shook her shoulder lightly, and Whaley stared at her and then at the room, the full blaze of afternoon sun through the windows.

"What time?"

"Well after lunch. Two almost."

"I didn't get to sleep till late."

"Woodrow didn't come back yet," said Maggie.

He was usually back by noon, especially in the summer heat. Whaley said, "Maybe something's wrong with his motor."

"I'm worried about him for some reason."

"You're worried because you're a worrier."

"Too old to change, I guess," said Maggie as she left the room.

Whaley got up and got herself some toast and tea and went about the day's chores but it didn't feel right, this day—things were off kilter, her rhythm was awry, she felt, well, bad, empty, for sleeping the day away, and her sister's worry had gotten away with her too. Especially when Woodrow didn't turn up by suppertime.

Or the next day.

They didn't have any way of getting ahold of him, of course. There were other boats on the island but they had not been afloat in some time. When Maggie suggested they drag one of them down to the water and set out looking, Whaley dismissed this as craziness, said someone would come to them if anything happened to Woodrow.

Out in the yard plucking a tern that afternoon, she decided

he'd taken such offense at her saying he was too old to change that he'd decided to show her, loaded up his boat, and kept on going right over to the mainland.

She stayed right mad at him for that. The anger helped her get through the hours of that day and, more important, the endless night. She would not let herself feel guilty because clearly Woodrow was just proving a point, showing her how they all could change, how the island itself would change if only one of them—well, the right one of them—went across.

Okay. She gave up. He had proved his point. They ate out of the cupboard, cans: Chef Boyardee, peaches, green beans that tasted of rust. No mail. No prices to read aloud of an evening.

And Maggie, good Lord—you'd of thought she was married to Woodrow the way all the wind went out of her. She had not been this bad since that Boyd. Thing was, they didn't talk about it. Three days he was gone and not one word passed between them on the subject of Woodrow—on any subject much—until one of those O'Malley boys came dragging his bulk up the beach road late afternoon of the third day.

Whaley was sitting on the porch. She never sat on the porch in the afternoon but she could not bear the thought of Maggie seeing Woodrow first when he came back across. It was white-hot and breezeless and one of the O'Malley boys came up in the yard sweating and huffing.

"Miss Whaley," he said.

"I knew your daddy," said Whaley.

O'Malley looked a little emotional. "I *am* the daddy."

"You're Marvin?"

"Hiram."

"Close," she said. She meant the sound of his name was close to Marvin. But he looked bothered, and real hot.

"Well," he said. "It's Mr. Woodrow."

"That's what y'all call him?"

"Always have."

"To his face or behind his back?"

O'Malley took a red kerchief out of his pocket and unfolded it.

"Where's he at?" she said. Because she was still hoping this was some sick point he was hellbound out to prove. Okay, Woodrow. I give up.

"They found his boat almost clear down to Lenoxville."

"Just his boat?"

"He could have had a stroke. Fell out."

She looked past him, up the island. The steeple of the church showed passing boats here is God's love, bountiful and all-forgiving. But she hid there in the belfry and let the wind take Sarah and she said something to Woodrow so hurtful he up and jumped off his boat. Where was God's love?

She said, "Woodrow has not fell out and he did not either have any stroke."

Hiram or Marvin O'Malley said, "Well."

A long time passed. Her great-great-great-grandmother Theo floated in the breakers. Somehow the portrait Theo was taking to present to her disgraced father turned up on her doorstep. People left in droves. The progging fell off. Most of what washed up on the beach was Japanese and plastic. The roof of the old hospital caved in. Mail stopped coming.

"They'll find him directly," said O'Malley.

Storms battered the island. One took the power, the light. It cut an inlet down southside. That was okay. They had each other. Sisters. She never did marry. Ducks and egrets would light on the water so many it looked like an island. Babe Ruth came. Decorations for women's hats out of the plumage.

Maggie came up on the porch. O'Malley the younger shifted his bulk and said, "Miss Maggie."

"We killed her," said Whaley to her sister. Only it wasn't Maggie she was talking to but little Liz kneeling beside her chair in the little sitting area she'd set up for the interview.

"We let that woman die."

Little Liz shook her head, her lips tight and trembling.

"No, not we," Whaley corrected. "It was me. I'm the one. I done it."

Whaley took Liz's hand in both hers and squeezed. She said, "Woodrow asked me to look after her, I went down there that night I looked through the window I seen she was okay I came on back up the hill to the house I made Maggie come with me up to the church I wouldn't let Maggie go after her because what it was, it wasn't the water took her it was the wind."

"I never told Woodrow what I done but that morning he left

the island I went down there to apologize to him about saying he was too old to change. He was already gone. Next time I saw him he was laid out on the altar."

The O'Malleys took them across for the service. They were the only white people up in that church. It was so hot the air-conditioning was sweating. They held hands and cried and hugged and Whaley said to her sister, "Maggie, I'm sorry all these years I never acted like I love you but I do," and her sister didn't say anything just made that hush sound with the *s*'s streaming out of her mouth like water lapping the beach at night. She made a noise like the surf at night and it did not comfort Whaley for she knew all the wrong she'd done but it calmed her a little. That noise Maggie made with her mouth took her back across to the island.

"I told myself it was for the best, I reckon." Liz nodded her earnest red head. She said, "Hold on, now Miss Whaley, I'll be right back, okay?"

But while she was gone Whaley kept talking.

"No hell that's a lie it won't for the best I didn't I did not tell myself a goddamn thing," she was saying when Liz returned with her sister in tow, and she heard Maggie laugh and say to little Liz, "That's the only time I ever heard that word out of her mouth."

Whaley said, "I just blamed it on the wind."

Maggie came over and sat in the chair she'd set out for Liz.

"What are you saying, sister?"

"About what happened," said Whaley. "I'm just telling her what she needs to know."

"Why don't you share some of your recipes?" said Maggie.

Whaley laughed. "She's the one asked," she said, pointing to little Liz. "Come sit," she said. "I'm not through."

But Maggie would not get out of the chair. She said she'd stick her head in. Maggie had a story to tell too. Woodrow had one. Whaley said to little Liz, "Y'all never did get Woodrow down. Whatever he told y'all, it wasn't exactly a lie . . ."

"Hush, now, Theo," said Maggie, the *s*'s streaming out of her mouth like water lapping the beach at night.

"I'm just saying," said Whaley.

"I've got an idea," said Maggie.

"They're the ones asked," said Whaley. "They're wanting to put it in the paper."

"How about—" her sister said.

"I just wish," said Whaley.

"You tell us a story from when we were little."

Whaley looked at her sister. Beyond her, white sails and the inlet asparkle. Ducks and egrets would light on the water, so many it looked like an island. Decorations for women's hats out of the plumage.

Whaley laid her head back in the chair. She opened her mouth to speak. Said to her sister, "Move so I can see across."

ACKNOWLEDGMENTS

Though some of the people and places mentioned in these pages are real, this is a work of fiction, dependent upon the necessary fabrications, hyperbole, and transmogrification. Distortions notwithstanding, books are made from other books, and in this case I owe much to Richard N. Côté's *Theodosia Burr Alston: Portrait of a Prodigy* and Nancy Isenberg's *Fallen Founder: The Life of Aaron Burr,* as well as a shelf or two of memoirs and natural histories about the Outer Banks of North Carolina.

I am indebted to everyone at Algonquin—Craig Popelars, Michael Taeckens, Brunson Hoole, Kelly Clark Policelli, and especially Megan Fishmann—for their help with this book. Deep thanks to Bland Simpson for sharing his knowledge of coastal North Carolina and patiently answering my queries.

THE WATERY PART *of the* WORLD

An Interview with Michael Parker

Questions for Discussion

An Interview with Michael Parker

The setting and backstory of *The Watery Part of the World* seem a long way in time from when your stories and novels usually occur, which is most often present day, or at least in the later twentieth century. Why did you make such a big leap, or rather, what compelled you to dive into a story about Theodosia Burr and pirates?

I came across the Theodosia story while reading to my daughter from a book about myths and legends of North Carolina, where we live. This was years ago, when she was in grade school—she's about to graduate from college now—so it's hard for me to remember why Theodosia's story stuck with me. But it did. Maybe because I lived near the Outer Banks for a couple of years, just across the sound in a house with a widow's walk and hallways the size of thoroughfares, and could smell the Albemarle Sound from my front porch. Or maybe because I've always been interested in Aaron Burr, who was as compelling a figure as you'll find in Colonial America, to my mind. I never thought about the fact that I was writing about a woman who lived in a time about which I knew next to nothing. Something about her life—her brilliant but, as we say today, *imbalanced* father, her supreme education, her marriage, and of course her disappearance and the cult that sprung up around her disappearance—kept needling me. I really hoped it might go away. I've never written a historical novel before, unless you count a novel set in the 1950s. My notion of research, prior to this novel, has been to depend on the copy editor to tell me if indeed there was chloride in the water in the midsixties in some hamlet or the other. So all this was new to me, and trying, and also thrilling—a challenge. It made me uncomfortable. The pirates, at first, sounded like Cap'n Crunch or Al Pacino. Writing about a different time, though, proves to be like writing about anything else: the trick is in the rhythm of the sentences, in the pitch of the prose. At least that is what makes historical fiction of interest to me. So I did my research, but I did not depend only upon that sort of veracity to convince the reader I knew what I was talking about. I wanted the reader to believe in Theodosia's soul more than her diet or her garments.

Part of this novel grew out of a wonderful story of yours, "Off Island," which went on to win a Pushcart Prize. But how and why did you think to weave these two disparate stories together?

Failure is my prime motivator. I tried to write a novel about Theodosia and got halfway through and pushed it away. Then I tried to expand "Off Island" into a novella, for I felt that the story, formally, did not quite cohere. That didn't work out either. I had written a novel set in Mexico and North Carolina, about the owner of furniture factory and the Mexican workers he employs, and that, too, fizzled. So I went for a run. For a month or so, I mean. A lot of long runs, which is what I do when I get terrifically stuck. And on one of these runs I realized I had two half-finished things that were set in the same place—the Outer Banks. When I got home I fished them out of drawers and went to work putting them together.

This is the case for me so often: one idea falters, and then another, and at some point, out of frustration usually, I put them together, and combustion occurs. If it's true that we're always writing the same story, or a similar one, if we're writing out of the same old wounds or desires, then it makes sense to collect the shreds on the cutting-room floor and try to splice them into something new and *re*newed.

The island functions here not just as setting, but also as metaphor for the ways in which change is (or is not) possible. And all of the characters speak to the notion of whether a person can or truly ever does change to the core. But the image of the island suggests that though the borders and shoreline might shift, and though the shape of the island may be altered by wind and waves, it will always be fundamentally what it is. Or were you seeing the island more as an image of the fundamental aloneness of every person, no matter who might be near or with them?

Your interpretation of the island and what it represents—especially the notion that it shifts but remains essentially the same land mass, in a slightly different place but still on the map—is a part of what I intended. It's hard to write about an island without coming up against a certain John Donne quote, though. I did not want this novel to be either an illustration of that quote or a repudiation of it. It is hugely important that the setting is an island, that it is cut off, that it is hard to get to and people have left and they have mostly stopped coming, but the loneliness of the characters is not solely dependent on their being island dwellers. If you tie your identity too deeply to a place, any place, you're liable to be left behind in some ways. I suppose I have always written about places and the way people identify, or don't, with the land beneath their feet, but place, to me, seems so inextricably a part of character—no matter where the story is set, even if it is set in an elevator or cyberspace or a shopping mall—that separating it is like separating the way a character moves through a novel from the syntax the writer chooses as its vehicle.

I don't think I could write novels if I did not believe that people, however imperceptibly, are capable of change. But characters who change are no less alone. We're alone, and we aren't alone. It's one thing we can have both ways, because we have no choice.

Among my favorite parts of this novel are the occasional appearances of the Tape Recorders, whom Woodrow resists: he "wouldn't answer the questions like they wanted him to because

seemed to Woodrow they had the answers already, that the questions were swole up with the answer, like a snake had swallowed a frog." I can't help but think about the parallels between the Tape Recorders and the perception of Southerners by those outside the region, not only in relation to their accents but in race relations, and, for that matter, how Southerners are expected to write about the South and their history.

Woodrow is smart enough to know when he's being patronized. Some people love an audience, and might appear to be imparting useful and authentic information about folkways, but in fact they just love to talk about themselves, a distinction the Tape Recorders might not be able to make. Woodrow loves to be on his skiff on a day when the blues are running. He'd as soon not be asked the sort of questions the anthropologists ask.

As to the region and misconceptions about it, I love it when reviewers from outside the South use terms like *dialect* and *local color* to describe what writers everywhere worth their salt attempt to do, which is to make poetry from the colloquial. There is a difference between idiom and Uncle Remus. Since the South has largely disappeared into a strip mall of nail salons and Paneras and Mattress Worlds, you'd think the received ideas might have trailed off a bit. But in terms of race relations, even though there is no denying our tragic and shameful past, we're still guilty until proven guilty.

But it's not only people from outside the region who are keeping alive misconceptions about the South. There are plenty of

Southerners who cherish the mythic South and either outright refuse or are slow to acknowledge the changes—for instance, the rise of the Hispanic south, the influx of other races and cultures. I suspect this is true everywhere. I imagine there are more than a few natives of certain parts of Brooklyn who would rather not acknowledge the neighborhood as the hipster enclave it has become.

It's not easy or even all that advisable for a white man to write about a black man on an island who is subservient to two white sisters, one of whom refuses to believe that this black man has an inner life. It's a lot easier for white people to write about white people and black people to write about black people and dear Lord leave the Texans to the native Texans. The only way I could write Woodrow was to make him flawed. To make him ideal, to make him without fault or mistake or vanity, would be dishonorable if not outright racist.

Everyone I've talked to about this novel has a different favorite character. Do you have a favorite, or is there perhaps one with whom you sympathize the most? (I confess that by the end, although I fully expected to continue to dislike Miss Whaley, her final section broke my heart.)

I sympathized with them all, and they all, at one point or another, broke my heart. Sometimes, though, the characters lurking in the shadows—in this case, Theodosia's lover, Whaley, and Woodrow's wife, Sarah, neither of whom are given points of view in the novel—

are the ones that haunt. Their stories were told through the filtered consciousnesses of the other characters. What the reader gets of Sarah is not Sarah but Woodrow's Sarah, Maggie's Sarah, Whaley's Sarah. Had I included her point of view, she would be far less mysterious, of course. But that doesn't mean she's not important, as she's crucial to the more contemporary side of the story.

It's not a good idea for me to play favorites. Sometimes, though, the characters who are hardest to get on the page are the ones who loom, because so much has been invested in their verisimilitude. I sweated most over Theodosia, for all the obvious reasons discussed above—her time and place—but it was Maggie's section that I think I rewrote the most. From what I have heard at book clubs and from readers generous enough to share their opinions with me, people either dismiss Maggie as an immature drunken loser or they are devoted to her despite her obvious failings. Who you love and who you dislike in a novel depends more upon the matters of *your* heart than it does mine.

Questions for Discussion

1. Woodrow seems to take particular offense when Whaley says he is "too old to change." Why?

2. Why do you think the author did not include Sarah's point of view? How would the novel be different if we did have Sarah's point of view?

3. We see, and hear about, Sarah's death from several different points of view. Why do you think Parker gives us various accounts of her death?

4. Why do you think Woodrow chooses to stay on the island after Sarah's death?

5. Old Whaley allows the dog to attack Theo on her second trip to Daniels's compound. Why does he not intervene if, immediately after, he saves her life and takes her to Yaupon Island?

6. In the novel, much attention is paid to weather—to wind, water, tide, storm. In what way does weather not only shape the lives of the characters but enter into their inner lives?

7. Theodosia Whaley was one of the most well-educated women in America, yet she forgoes her pursuit of knowledge and culture to such an extent that she does not emphasize learning and artistic pursuits in her children. How do you feel about her shift from a precocious and promising young woman to someone consumed with chores and childrearing?

8. The Tape Recorders are never given a full-fledged scene in the novel, yet their presence hovers over the more contemporary side of the book. What is their role in relation to the characters and their histories?

9. There are several "mirrorings" between the Theodosia sections and the more contemporary sections—characters and scenes that compliment each other without exactly repeating. Identify these scenes, discussing how they work in relation to each other and in the novel overall.

10. *The Watery Part of the World* has been described variously as a historical novel, a mystery, and a long poem. How would you categorize it?

TASHA THOMAS

Michael Parker is the author of four previous novels and two books of short stories. He teaches in the MFA Writing Program at the University of North Carolina at Greensboro.

Other Algonquin Readers Round Table Novels

Water for Elephants, a novel by Sara Gruen

As a young man, Jacob Jankowski is tossed by fate onto a rickety train, home to the Benzini Brothers Most Spectacular Show on Earth. Amid a world of freaks, grifters, and misfits, Jacob becomes involved with Marlena, the beautiful young equestrian star; her husband, a charismatic but twisted animal trainer; and Rosie, an untrainable elephant who is the great gray hope for this third-rate show. Now in his nineties, Jacob at long last reveals the story of their unlikely yet powerful bonds, ones that nearly shatter them all.

"[An] arresting new novel . . . With a showman's expert timing, [Gruen] saves a terrific revelation for the final pages, transforming a glimpse of Americana into an enchanting escapist fairy tale." —*The New York Times Book Review*

AN ALGONQUIN READERS ROUND TABLE EDITION WITH READING GROUP GUIDE AND OTHER SPECIAL FEATURES • FICTION • ISBN 978-1-56512-560-5

A Reliable Wife, a novel by Robert Goolrick

Rural Wisconsin, 1907. In the bitter cold, Ralph Truitt stands alone on a train platform anxiously awaiting the arrival of the woman who answered his newspaper ad for "a reliable wife." The woman who arrives is not the one he expects in this *New York Times* #1 bestseller about love and madness, longing and murder.

"[A] chillingly engrossing plot . . . Good to the riveting end." —*USA Today*

"Deliciously wicked and tense . . . Intoxicating." —*The Washington Post*

"A rousing historical potboiler." —*The Boston Globe*

AN ALGONQUIN READERS ROUND TABLE EDITION WITH READING GROUP GUIDE AND OTHER SPECIAL FEATURES • FICTION • ISBN 978-1-56512-977-1

Join us at **AlgonquinBooksBlog.com** for the latest news on all of our stellar titles, including weekly giveaways, behind-the-scenes snapshots, book and author updates, original videos, media praise, detailed tour information, and other exclusive material.

You'll also find information about the **Algonquin Book Club**, a selection of the perfect books—from award winners to international bestsellers—to stimulate engaging and lively discussion. Helpful book group materials are available, including

Book excerpts
Downloadable discussion guides
Author interviews
Original author essays
Live author chats and live-streaming interviews
Book club tips and ideas
Wine and recipe pairings